IN THE ATTIC

I looked around me in some amazement. I was in a small, low room, almost empty.

Walking through it, I came to another. To my right was a door that opened into yet another room and then through another. Following these doors I found myself turned around.

I no longer knew which way I faced. It was disturbing and a little frightening.

Even odder were the acoustics; my steps seemed to have echoes. Or did they?

I was suddenly chilled by panic at the thought that I might not be alone. Turning quickly in the direction from which I came, I tried to open the door—

It wouldn't budge, and I realized I was trapped!

Trelawny

Isabelle Holland

GOLDEN APPLE PUBLISHERS

TRELAWNY

*A Golden Apple Publication / published by arrangement with
Weybright and Talley, Inc.*

Golden Apple edition / January 1984

Golden Apple is a trademark of Golden Apple Publishers

ISBN 0-553-19758-4

Published simultaneously in the United States and Canada

PRINTED IN THE UNITED STATES OF AMERICA

1

"I'll take care of everything," Jeremy said, as we stood on the sidewalk beside my car. "I just wish I could go up there now instead of later." He looked so wistful that for a moment I forgot that I was, at his ardent request, letting him sublet my apartment for about a third of its rent, and started to feel guilty. Then I got hold of myself. Making adults feel guilty has been a specialty of Jeremy's since he was five.

"I thought you wanted to work with Elmendorff. When you wangled the bus fare from Wyoming to New York out of me, you told me that an opportunity to work with a painter like Elmendorff came once in a lifetime."

"Absolutely, Kit. For sure. That's why I'm going to pass up being in Maine with you. I mean, working at Elmendorff's studio makes the heat and smog and dirt and pollution of a summer in New York well worthwhile, don't you think?"

His look of eager innocence would have shamed an angel. Jeremy didn't drop out, that is, he didn't abandon the establishment. He simply approached it from another angle. If he had lived in another time and place—say, England during the first half of the century —he would have been the perfect roving professional houseguest. At twenty-one he was good-looking, well mannered and modestly gifted. His overwhelming talent was in making people—me included—support him. He was my second cousin on my mother's side, and he was going to live in my New York apartment for the five months that I would be in Maine to take over my inheritance and see if I could turn it into a mini MacDowell Colony for promising, struggling, impoverished artists of all kinds. It was still early June, but we'd already had a tentative heat spell, and this had obviously turned Jeremy's thoughts away from his golden opportunity with Elmendorff and onto his gold-

1

en opportunity to go with me up to the Maine coast and Trelawny's Fell. The huge dark eyes looked at me out of his frail face and I could feel the words of invitation forming in my mouth. And then he made a serious mistake.

"I could help you around the house," he said winningly.

This reminded me all too vividly of the times he had made such an offer before.

"Good-bye," I said. I handed over the extra set of keys, put Josephine's wiretop carrier into the passenger seat of the car, checked the trunk to make sure the luggage was stashed in properly, bent to give Jeremy a cousinly smack on the cheek and got in the car.

A slightly tight look settled itself around Jeremy's mouth. Automatically he straightened his shoulders and shook out the beautiful waving chestnut hair that fell to below his collar. Jeremy might wear the faded jeans and paint-stained shirt *de rigueur* in his artistic circles. But his vanity was enormous, and he didn't like to be reminded that even when I wore the flat-heeled jodhpur boots I had on now, I, a female, still topped his five foot eight inches by at least another inch and a half.

Knowing exactly what was going through his mind, I grinned at him. This made him say rather acidly, "It's a good thing you didn't get some eensy-teensy foreign car."

Privately I agreed, which was why I had bought one of the small domestic types. Driving in a jackknifed position for twelve hours or more was not my idea of travel. "Cheer up," I said tactlessly, "people have been known to grow after twenty-one." I fastened my seatbelt. "If you must have pot parties, try to have them somewhere else and please be sure to forward all mail."

"Cousin Kit," he said reproachfully, back to the small-boy image, "do you think I'd break the law in your apartment?"

"Certainly, if you thought you could get away with it. I must tell you, I've given the super leave to check on the apartment now and then."

"If you don't trust me, why did you let me have your pad?"

"Because of your formidable powers of persuasion, as I am sure you know."

I put the car in gear and glanced up at the brownstone I had lived in for the five years I had worked in New York. For a moment the insanity of leaving it and my satisfying job in publishing washed over me. As though in confirmation, there appeared suddenly in my mind the picture of the huge, decaying monstrosity for which I was abandoning all this pleasantness: Trelawny's Fell (more often, and quite justifiably known as Trelawny's Folly), perched high on a cliff above a rocky coast, its front to the winds that lashed the peninsula and its back to the woods and the hill and the village. A shiver went through me. I glanced at the brownstone again. A small, inner voice said, "It's not too late. The apartment is still yours. You can get the job back. Bob promised you that. Sell the monster. It's never been anything to a Trelawny but trouble." But, stronger and deeper than that voice, stirred an old anger. The Fell might well prove a boon to budding artists. That, after all, was the purpose of my plan for it. But equally satisfying to me was the knowledge that their presence would send the ghosts of proud Trelawnys shrieking into the night. Various members of the family had considered themselves patrons of the arts, rather in the grand Renaissance manner. But that was a far cry from having bohemian riffraff (as they would unquestionably have called my future guests, however talented) housed on the sacred premises. No, Nicholas and Giles and their mother, the dowager Mrs. Chrétien Trelawny IV, would not have liked that one bit.

"You're looking awfully pleased with yourself," Jeremy said. "May I share the goody, whatever it is?"

"Sorry. Private joke." I nosed the car into the street, amused at his frustrated expression. To Jeremy, climber *par excellence*, inside jokes and gossip were dearer than gold. *"Ciao!"* I called, and headed towards the East River Drive.

There was a raucous yell from Josephine. I looked

down at her. "You wanted to come. So don't give me any of that."

I had originally intended to leave Josephine in the New York apartment—that was part of the logic of having Jeremy live there dirt cheap. But the pattern of changed plans that was to repeat itself again and again throughout the strange events that followed had started this morning. Josephine, whose ESP was extraordinarily sharp, had been restless and cranky for several days. This morning, when I got out the last suitcase, she followed me around crying in the loud, anguished voice that she must have inherited from some Siamese ancestor along with her thin, agile body and her ingrained sense of aristocracy. From other, and more plebeian, sides of her family she had taken her silky black coat and the white blaze on her chest. From the streets where I found her nearly five years before, angry, bedraggled and starving, she had undoubtedly learned her claws-first approach to everything and everybody. I scarcely had a friend who hadn't discovered this the hard, painful way. Only with me was she affectionate. With others, she was barely civil. I had hated the idea of leaving her behind, but she had always loathed travel—visits to the vet were nightmares for us both. She screamed all the way there and all the way back, attracting a good deal of attention and a variety of dirty looks and comments about cruelty to animals. Also she was, as far as the vet and I could judge, about twelve years old. So I decided it would be kinder to leave her in a familiar place. Jeremy, whose assets as a householder were almost nil, had always been good with her. But I should have known better or perhaps consulted her.

As soon as I got out my big suitcase the night before I left she got in and sat on the tissue paper. When ejected, she got into the other bag and wouldn't move to let me put in my shoes. This morning she refused her breakfast and then, to make her point even clearer, threw up. After that she jumped on my shoulders and bellowed.

The next thing I knew I had taken out her carrier.

"I thought I was to take care of her," Jeremy said in a wounded voice. "Don't you trust me?"

4

"It's just that I can't resist all this aggressive propaganda."

"I thought you said she was too old and set in her ways to get used to the wilds."

I don't know why I looked up at him at that moment. There was nothing in his voice to set up my alert system. Yet I did glance quickly at his face and caught an odd, smug look. I had seen that look before and I decided to call his bluff.

I put down the carrier. "Well, if you really want me to leave her behind. . . ."

"I'd love it," he said, with shattering sincerity, "but I'd hate to think of her being so unhappy without you."

I gave it up. I didn't have time to try and win this encounter.

"That's very touching," I said drily, and proceeded to put Josephine, screaming and kicking, into the carrier. It was, I could see, going to be a pleasant trip.

It was all that I feared and more. After we reached the East River Drive and were clear of the worst traffic, I opened the carrier's top and let Josephine out to roam around the car, thinking that much freedom might soothe her anxiety. It was better, but not much. As we got into Connecticut I told myself that her voice would undoubtedly grow tired. Not even a trained opera singer, I told myself, could keep up the resonance, to say nothing of the decibel count, forever. As we were about to leave Connecticut some hours later, I knew I was wrong. I was still on the parkway when her voice, so far from being tired, rose to what I'd always thought of as "impending-catastrophe level." I pulled onto the edge of the drive, took a firm hold of the harness I had had the forethought to put around Josephine's scrawny girth, and started to get out. Nature must be calling, I thought. I was right. It was. But we didn't make it out of the car in time. Released from her anguish by the simple fact that we were no longer in motion, Josephine gave her all on the newspaper that I had mercifully put on the floor of the car both front and back. By the time the newspaper was rolled up and decently buried behind a bush I had attracted the attention of a state trooper who had stopped and

5

wanted to know what environmental damage I was doing to the carefully landscaped parkway. By the time that was settled and I gingerly opened the door of the car to get myself in without letting Josephine out, my temper was frayed.

Josephine, returned to her carrier, was yelling, her energy and voice unabated. "Would you like to have a black cat?" I asked the trooper.

He grinned. "Do you mean that?"

I glanced down. Josephine, her green eyes almost crossed with rage and concentration, was not a lovely sight. An unmistakable and unpleasant odor hung on the air. I was by now convinced she would yell all the way up to Maine. I slid my hand under the wire cover of the carrier and stroked her back. "No."

"Why don't you give her a tranquilizer?"

As this perfectly lovely thought stole over me I couldn't imagine why it hadn't occurred to me before. I looked at the trooper who by now seemed to have sprung wings and a halo.

"What a marvelous idea! What a bright man you are! Where can I get one?"

He simply pointed to the sign at the nearby turnoff. There in letters a foot high were the magic words: Animal Hospital.

I started the engine. "If you ever need a character reference, Officer, don't hesitate to ask me," and I shot towards deliverance, Josephine, still in excellent voice, baying beside me.

Half an hour later I was back on the parkway with Josephine, drowsy and quiet, curled up in her carrier. A small box of pills and careful instructions were in my handbag. The relief was unbelievable. As the miles passed and I headed up through Massachusetts my mind started its familiar trek through the events that had brought me on the road to a house I had once sworn I would never again enter. Because it was in that house, fifteen years before, that I had had an experience that had changed and distorted my life and, I have always believed, destroyed my mother.

Events do not really have beginnings or ends. Behind every event is the previous one, causing, or helping to cause, what follows. So to pick any one place in the long and often dark story of the Trelawnys—of which I was still a part and which I knew in some strange way, even then, was by no means ended—would be purely arbitrary. But, as the teller of the tale, and an actor in it in ways I couldn't even imagine that day, driving up with my sleeping cat beside me, I had to choose a starting point, so the logical place was with Nicholas Trelawny, a wild young Cornishman who came via Westmoreland to Boston shortly before the Revolution. Nicholas fought in the Revolutionary army, rose to be a captain of militia, and after the war showed a marked talent for business. He married Chrétienne DuVal, daughter of a French Huguenot family that had taken refuge in the colonies after the religious wars in France. They had twin sons whom they named Nicholas and Giles after Nicholas himself and his own twin brother whom he had left in Cornwall and from whom, during the war, he had not heard. And thereafter one or two or all of those three names, Nicholas, Giles and Chrétienne (or Chrétien, if it were a son, but never, curiously, Christian, the English version) have come down in every generation of Trelawnys.

Anyway, Nicholas did some trading, importing and exporting and prospered. He became such a pillar of the establishment that the youthful United States government sent him on some kind of business mission to London. The first thing Nicholas did was to start inquiries about his twin brother from whom he still had not heard. The second thing was to fulfill a promise to his wife to have his portrait painted by Copley, a former colonial now living in London. The portrait was finished and ready to be taken back to Boston before Nicholas succeeded in locating Giles. And he achieved this only because he read in the paper one day that one Giles Trelawny, having been tried and convicted of holding up a coach in highway robbery, was to be hanged the following day. In the few hours before this unhappy (and embarrassing) event, Nicholas used what influence he had with the American Ambassador and various influential English businessmen to try and get a reprieve for his brother. But

Giles, he discovered, had not only robbed the coach, he had killed the father of the traveling family, a Justice of the Peace. There would be no reprieve. But he got permission to see Giles, and he went to the King's Bench Prison where his feckless and unrepentant brother was awaiting death.

History does not relate what passed between the brothers. But when Nicholas returned to the United States he bore with him, not only the Copley portrait of himself, but Giles' small daughter, who was brought up with her twin cousins and eventually married one of them, Giles II.

It sounded like a happy ending. But it wasn't. Nicholas's horror at his brother's hanging grew rather than diminished. Having been, by all accounts, a friendly, if taciturn and occasionally sardonic man, he retreated further and further into himself, as though, his wife wrote in her diary, he were being eaten from within. Finally, he withdrew altogether, and took his family with him. The house he built, perched on a hill above the northern coast of what was still then Massachusetts, reflected both his pride and his growing isolation.

Instead of being of wood, like all New England homes, it was made, stone by stone, of the hard native rock. Ceiling upon tall ceiling it rose, three and a half stories high with two wings, one for the kitchen and servants' quarters, one that looked suspiciously as if it might have been designed as a ballroom. It was considered by such neighbors as were within a day's ride ostentatious, alien and almost certainly a sign that the Trelawnys had fallen into the hands of the Devil. Nicholas called it Trelawny's Fell, using the old English word for "hill." The rest of the countryside called it Trelawny's Pride, and, after the mode of Nicholas' death became bruited about, a few mordant wits dubbed it Trelawny's Fall. Ensconcing his family there, Nicholas made periodic business trips to Boston, and when his daughters were old enough to come out, took a house on Boston Common just long enough to get them launched and married.

But as the years passed, The Fell, as the family came to call the mansion, seemed to develop a character of its own. There were Trelawnys that loved it

8

with a passion considered by the others sinfully out of proportion. There were those who hated it with an equal fervor and looked upon it as a prison, as it sometimes was. Two Trelawnys added to it. At least three Trelawnys tried to sell it. But there were no buyers. Several generations produced twins—always boys and always named Nicholas and Giles. And there was in every generation this double streak—a talent for business and for making money combined with a wild, feckless recklessness. One Trelawny went into shipping and increased the family fortunes considerably; his brother became a gunman out west and died at a shootout in a bar. During the Civil War the fourth Giles became a colonel in the Union Army and died at Gettysburg. His twin brother also died at Gettysburg, charging the Union lines under General Pickett. Until he threw in his lot with the Confederate Army, that particular Nicholas was running an extremely successful gambling house just outside New Orleans.

There was another and darker strain. The first Nicholas, having retreated to the house he had built, retreated still further as the years passed. At first he never left the second floor. For the last few years of his life he never left his corner room on the second floor. When his son Giles, who had married his first cousin, tried to interest his father in business matters, old Nicholas would not reply, but sat staring at his son out of the strange, almost luminous gray eyes that all the Trelawnys seem to inherit. Giles, looking back at his father out of the same eyes, eventually gave up expecting a reply, although he visited him punctiliously once a day, when he wasn't busy making more money in Boston. Old Nicholas didn't speak even when news was brought to him that young Nicholas had died in a tavern brawl. He just got up and went to the window and stood, staring out. The next day when Giles went to visit him, there was consternation. He was eventually found swinging from a rope he had flung over one of the huge rafters in the attic, his feet only six inches off the floor, because the Trelawnys were a tall race. He was the first of three to die from that rafter. That was when the local wits started calling The Fell The Fall. His great niece, Chrétienne, deeply in love with a local

9

farmer's son that family pride forbade her to marry, put the rope around her neck the day the young man married someone else. Several generations later, another Nicholas, Nicholas IV, I believe, died from the same rafter a few hours ahead of the police who had come to arrest him for larceny, blackmail, and murder down in Boston Harbor.

And so it went. By the end of the nineteenth century the various branches of the family, for business and social reasons, had established more or less permanent residences in Boston and New York. Yet the huge stone mansion, inconvenient, remote and, even in summer, rather forbidding, remained the family headquarters to which all members of the family returned for holidays and summers, and at times of trouble.

I saw it first when I was twelve. By that time it was even larger, having been added to by two more than usually ambitious Trelawnys, so that it sprawled over an acre, a huge shapeless mass of gray stone, its wings and additions of different heights and styles—grotesque, hideous, yet, despite its polyglot ugliness, compelling in its own right, as though it breathed, part of, yet separate from the arrogant family that it housed.

I will never forget the sight when my mother and I arrived in our third-hand car and stared, overawed and a little frightened, at the monstrous house. With the setting sun pouring from behind us onto it, the great gray pile looked even larger than it was, set off, bathed in gold, magical, a fairy castle.

"Never mind," Mother said in the rather loud voice she used when she was nervous. "It said—the newspaper story said, it's home to any of the family. And we're family. Why, at the end of a week it'll be like home." I don't think even she believed that. Her voice was quite loud now, as though challenging the edifice fifty yards away.

"Let's go home," I said urgently, tugging at her arm.

For a minute I felt her arm yield, and I knew she felt the way I did. She half turned. Then, "Nonsense," she said briskly, snapping around again. "I've dreamed about this for you. There's nothing to be afraid of. They're your kin. And it's important for you to know them. 'Specially now. . . ." Her voice trailed off.

"Why 'specially now?"

She hesitated, then said rather lamely, "Well, you don't have no—any—father."

Somehow I knew that wasn't the real reason. But when I tried to press for a further explanation, she snapped, "I've told you the reason. Now stop bothering me!"

How can I describe that week and why the memory of it lay like a scar across my life? My father, Kit Trelawny—Kit for Chrétien, which he insisted on spelling correctly, accent and all, on whatever documents came his way as he went from ranch to ranch as a horse wrangler—was the grandson of the Trelawny who died in a shootout in a bar in Kansas. The spelling of the traditional name was about the only thing he did insist on. The feckless streak in the Trelawnys came in him to full flower. He married my mother, daughter of the small, rundown ranch on which he happened to be working, partly because I was on the way, and partly because he had no choice. "Dad would have emptied both barrels in him," Mother once explained simply. When I was six, he got into the pickup truck one afternoon to drive into Jackson. The truck was found that day parked in the square. My father had vanished. Seven years later he was pronounced dead, not that anyone really cared. All he left behind was a cardboard box. But out of the contents of that box my mother spun dreams of glory.

There was in it a battered family tree going back past the first Nicholas to come to America to his great-grandfather, the youngest son of a Cornish squire. Long afterwards, when I found the yellowed, stained and torn paper, I was amused to note that while every member of the family was dutifully entered with birth and death dates, only those who achieved distinction—the senators, the governors, the civil leaders and the one university chancellor—had small biographies attached. Those who made their reputations in the areas of scandal and suicide were merely noted by name—with no undignified or demeaning details. There was not one hint in that remarkable document that three Trelawnys had died by their own hand, and that two had died under a cloud of scandal. The box contained

11

letters from his Boston brother to my great-grand-father, reproving, pleading, giving family news. There was a faded daguerreotype of a Nicholas Trelawny, my grandfather's cousin, I think, and when I saw it first I thought it was some kind of freakishly aged photo of my father: there was the same thick black hair, light eyes and pronounced bone structure. There was also an old newspaper story about the family.

My mother pored over these links to the kind of past she yearned for. I had been given the feminine version of my father's name, Chrétienne, and my mother, taught by her husband, was always careful to pronounce it correctly. But no child could go to a public school in the wilds of Wyoming with a name like that and live in peace. After the first dreadful months in first grade I became, like my father, Kit, and my friends slowly and mercifully forgot my real name.

Then, when I was twelve, my mother, who had saved nickels and pennies from her poorly paid jobs on other people's ranches (her own had long since gone, of course), decided to make the pilgrimage to The Fell. She and I would meet my distinguished Eastern relatives, she said. We would be taken in. Become part of the family. Life would be different.

It didn't go like that. Naturally.

I can see now how we must have seemed, my mother and I, as we arrived at Trelawny's Fell—unannounced ("It will be a nice surprise for them, don't you think, Kit?"). She had written that we were on a trip east and might drop by. That was all. Out where we lived people just arrived and were offered the hospitality of the house, whether it was for an hour or for a week. Even in the days of television and space flights, customs were not too different from what they had always been. Formal invitations were seldom given, times of arrival rarely set. Besides, as I realized later, by leaving the moment her letter had been mailed and setting no time of arrival, Mother had neatly forestalled any refusal. Along with the rest of the world I consistently underrated my mother. I was also ashamed of her. And my guilt over that had a lot to do with the way I acted: my pride, my secret embarrassment, my overfierce loyalty.

By the time she was sixteen she was both married and a mother. Her greatest disappointment was that I resembled her, with her Scandinavian fair hair and blue eyes, rather than my father. From both I got my embarrassing height. At twelve I was five foot seven with tow-colored hair, big feet and a figure like an ironing board. My mother, also tall, was heavy. She was still young, but she had done manual labor since she was a child, and she looked it. Having left school at fifteen, she was literate, but no more, and therefore commensurately proud of my straight A's, my compulsive reading and my ability to put words together that, to her, amounted almost to witchcraft.

The week was, inevitably, a disaster.

Even now my mind veered away from the memory of the small stinging details: the raised eyebrows, the exchanged looks of amusement, the shrugs, the patronizing voices, the even more patronizing servants. At age twelve, for all my schoolbook cleverness, I didn't know what the word patronizing meant, but I knew in an instant what it felt like when I, or worse, my mother, was the target. The Trelawnys—and there were more than a dozen of the clan at the house at that time—were good-looking, well-bred, some of them brilliant, all of them sophisticated and knowledgeable. To me they seemed like another race of people. I was so dazzled by them that it took me quite awhile to realize something else about them: that for all their blazing attractiveness—perhaps because of it—they were not kind. And they shared the misapprehension of many well-educated, well-bred people that those who are neither are therefore automatically insensitive.

There were scenes I shall never forget: Mother staring dumbly at her treasured paper bearing the family tree where Mrs. Chrétien Trelawny, dowager of the family, had dropped it and then spilled tea on it as she went off into gales of laughter.

"My dear," she said, when she could stop laughing, her fine dark eyes alight with malicious amusement, "imagine keeping that ludicrous document! Cousin Hermione"—she addressed a rather grand English relative—"do look! It's hopelessly wrong, of course!"

She picked up the paper and handed it over to her cousin. Then she turned back to Mother, whose face had the wooden look it wore when she was hurt or humiliated. "Sometime before you go you must see the real one."

And who there, besides myself, reflected that the dowdy countrywoman in the cheap print addressed by the elegant Mrs. Chrétien Trelawny of Trelawny's Fell and Boston, was also Mrs. Chrétien Trelawny, for all she was of Two Forks, Wyoming.

My mother had been bullied by her father and deserted by her husband. Sticking up for herself was beyond her imagination. But in a way that I did not understand then, my future was involved, and my mother, weaponless, launched into battle.

"I want Kit to come and live with you," she said bluntly, the alabaster-thin teacup rattling in her hand so badly that, ignoring in her nervousness the end table beside her, she tried to put the cup and saucer down on the floor, spilling tea on the Aubusson carpet. "She's a Trelawny, and she should be raised up that way."

"But my dear, she has you," Mrs. Trelawny pointed out.

My mother looked at her helplessly. Then she turned to me. "Kit, go and find your cousins and get acquainted. They're fine young men."

But I was sick inside with a terrible amalgam of rage, humiliation, shame and guilt. "No, thanks, Ma. I'll stay here." I had no idea then what Mother was going to say to Mrs. Trelawny once they had got rid of me. But I sat, gripped by a stubborn loyalty, all the fiercer for knowing that in front of these splendid, polished people I was ashamed of her and of myself.

"Do as I tell you," Mother said, with a sharpness I seldom heard.

"If dear Kitty doesn't want to leave—"

I turned to Mrs. Trelawny. "My name's Kit, like Dad's."

Mother put in, "Her real name's Chrétienne, like her father's, only the girl's spelling."

How fine our hostess's nostrils were and how delicately they arched. It was some time later that I

14

realized she had a strong suspicion of what was to come when I had been got rid of, and wanted to prevent that as much as I.

"Do as I say, Kit. Go find your cousins."

I glanced at Mrs. Trelawny. The nostrils were not only arched, the lines beside her nose were suddenly quite pronounced. Most obviously she disliked any implication of cousinship with us.

But I got up. Mother had used powerful bait to send me out. Although I had never said a word to her, she knew how I had tumbled into love with Mrs. Trelawny's handsome twin sons named, naturally, Nicholas and Giles.

To fall hopelessly in love when you're twelve years old is a terrible and wonderful experience, and the fact that I fell in love with both twins made it no easier. In their late twenties, they were the most dazzling human beings I had ever seen, one in the uniform of an Army major, the other in that of a lieutenant in the Navy with a pair of gold wings over his breast pocket. They were on leave from Vietnam, having managed to come home together, and they embodied all of my most secret dreams. Probably the fact that they looked like a burnished and infinitely improved version of my father as I dimly remembered him added the seal to my enslavement. Like all true Trelawnys, they were tall, with thick black hair and gray eyes that showed in the portrait of Nicholas the founder hanging over the tall mantel in the drawing room. At first all I saw was the extraordinary likeness between them. But almost immediately after that the differences became apparent: the bones in Giles's face seemed more pronounced and his eyes, in certain lights, were more blue-green than gray. Nicholas had his mother's arched nostrils, his face was more expressive than Giles's, and his almost silvery eyes more mischievous.

Tactlessly, as it turned out, I said to Mrs. Trelawny, "I thought they'd be more alike."

"My dear Kit, you must have seen them in different lights. And of course their uniforms are different. They're identical." She stated it with finality. I knew that somehow I had made a *gaffe*.

It was Nicholas who teased me, who took one look at my feet and sang,

> *"Light she was and like a fairy*
> *"And her shoes were number nine. . . ."*

He inclined his handsome head, his eyes dancing. "Welcome, Cousin Clementine!"

It stung, of course, because I was sensitive about my feet. But I forgave him because just to look at him made my heart skip a beat. It was Nicholas, especially, to whom I gave my adoration. When he suggested that I go sailing with him and Giles and Giles's fiancée, Charlotte Manners (to whom I took an instant dislike), my cup threatened to run over. But when I landed in the water, it was Giles who fished me out.

It was while we were cruising up the coast that I unthinkingly made the admission that I couldn't swim.

"Are you serious? You can't swim?" Nicholas asked, dawning delight on his face.

"Don't be silly," Charlotte said. "Everybody can swim."

I lied, of course. "I just meant I can't swim . . . as well as . . . I mean, I'm not good at it."

"Well, there's a sure way of finding out. Come along, Charlotte, take her feet. A one and a two and a three. . . ."

And the next thing I knew I was swinging through the air and hitting the water, screaming as I did so.

As Mrs. Trelawny afterwards explained to my mother when I was brought sopping and shivering and crying back into the house, "I know it must sound silly, but you see, I don't think it dawned on any of them that actually Kitty—Kit—couldn't swim. They just took it for granted. . . . How stupid of them! But there's no reason to be upset. I can't tell you how often my children have fallen out of boats and trees. A little wet won't hurt her."

A little humiliation was something else. Of course all the people they knew could swim. They'd been taught in country-club pools and in expensive private schools, just as they had been taught tennis and proper dancing. I didn't grow up near water, so I didn't swim. It was as simple as that.

It was curt, aloof Giles who had jumped in and wrestled with me in the water where, in my panic to hold on, I tried to drown him. He got me back on deck and slapped me out of my rising hysteria.

"Poor lamb," Nicholas said. "But how could we know you really couldn't swim?"

This upset me. I had decided that my heart belonged to Nicholas. By comparison Giles seemed almost surly —totally lacking Nicholas's charm and radiance. When I shyly spoke to him, he seemed to bite out replies, and there was no question at all that he resented my going on the sail, just as he resented my going along with him and Charlotte and Nicholas the following day when we took some horses out of the stable for rides.

But on a horse I avenged my honor. I had ridden since before I could remember. Our own ranch may have gone, but I had been with Mother on other ranches all my life. I had even worked summers on a dude ranch, where a friendly Englishman had trained me to ride on his English saddle in the English way. And I could ride without any saddle at all as easily as I could with.

"Well, well, so you can ride," Nicholas said, as we slowed down after a gallop over the rolling pastures and hills behind the house.

"Your girth is working loose," Giles said in his abrupt fashion. "Tighten it. Charlotte, I want to talk to you. Come on!"

The pretty girl put her head on one side. "But maybe I don't want to talk to you in your present mood."

"Nevertheless you're going to." He leaned over and took her rein above the bit. Charlotte tugged on the rein. The horse reared. Charlotte came off. Nicholas almost fell off his saddle laughing. I saw the murderous look on Gile's face and a chill went up my back.

"Serves you right, for being such a dictator," Nicholas said, still laughing. "Come on, Charlotte. Put your foot in my stirrup and we'll be off."

Charlotte swung up behind him without a word.

Giles and I sat there as they rode off. Then Giles dismounted and examined Charlotte's horse.

"Is he all right?" I asked timidly.

"Yes. I ought to have known better." He gathered up the reins of Charlotte's horse and mounted his own. "We'll ride back," he said.

We rode for a while in silence, the horse's hooves muffled on the path covered with pine needles. Over our heads met huge trees, bigger, I thought, than the ones I had grown up with. Less than a mile to our left lay the sea. We had followed a path above the cliff there before, going through the woods to the fields beyond, and were on our way back to it. I was used to seeing the Tetons, soaring up without foothills from the valley floor and, further south, the endless rolling plains of Colorado. The further east we drove the more cramped I felt. New England seemed like the gardens I had read about. But I was not prepared for the enormous trees nor for the sea. And the sounds of both—the sea, lapping against the rocks and washing up on the sand of the tiny beach below the house, and the wind, rustling through the leaves and pine trees— have always been part of my memory of that week.

We were still between the trees when Giles said in his abrupt fashion, "How long are you and your mother intending to stay?"

"Just a few days," I parroted Mother's reply when I asked her the same question. The trouble was, she had said it at the beginning of the visit as well as that morning, almost a week later. I had asked her not only because I wanted to bring the tormenting episode to a close as soon as possible, but because I decided New England did not agree with Mother. She looked sallow and unwell, as she had, once or twice, in the recent past.

"You must be wanting to get back," Giles said.

It was true that Nicholas was the twin I loved, but it was Giles who had rescued me from the water, and his obvious desire to get rid of Mother and me was bitter.

We broke out of the trees and followed the path as it veered towards the cliff. There was a lump in my throat and tears in my eyes and a savage pain in my heart. "You'll be rid of us soon enough," I said. "It's not polite to be in such a hurry. Out west—" But at that point a combination of homesickness and lovesickness was

18

too much for me. I gave a loud sniff and started to rummage around for a handkerchief.

"I didn't mean to hurt your feelings. But I don't think either you or your mother is comfortable here. Are you?"

I swung around in my saddle to look at him. "I don't understand you folks. You think you're so much above Mother and me. And it's true you've been to different schools and you've got money and—" I had no words to describe the ineffable difference. . . . "But we'd be ashamed to treat people the way you do. You're . . . not kind."

He stared straight ahead as we followed the cliff path. "No," he said finally. "We're a lot of things, but kind is not one of them." It was somehow easier to be angry with Giles. I was too frightened of Mrs. Trelawny, and too much in love with Nicholas to give voice or word to the anger bubbling up inside me. "It's nothing to be proud of—being unkind."

"I never said it was."

"Then why are you that way?" I asked. "You've got so much. Why can't you let other people have a little? Why do you have to keep them out?"

He didn't answer that. Instead he asked, "What's the matter with your mother?"

With every good reason to, I misunderstood what he was saying and flared back, "There's *nothing* wrong with her. Nothing at all. She married early and—"

"I mean physically."

Until that moment it hadn't occurred to me to think that Mother might be seriously ill. Yet, the thought must have been there, because the moment he asked the question, I knew there was something wrong. I stared at him, remembering my vague sense that the Eastern climate did not agree with her, recalling other scenes: the day Mother sat down suddenly on a chair in the kitchen back home, her visits into Jackson when she wouldn't allow me to accompany her, the strange yellowish look to her skin that somehow showed up here worse than before because everybody was so beautiful and bloomingly healthy. And at that moment everything fell into place: Mother's determination to come here, her sending me out of the room when

she wanted to talk to Mrs. Trelawny, her uncharacter-
istic oblivion of all the slights, her equally unchar-
acteristic courage in sticking up for herself and not just
slinking out of sight, which she used to do with my
grandfather and, I've been told, with my father.

Without thinking I had stopped my horse and Giles
had halted his too. I looked into his face as the truth
dawned on me. "She's going to die, isn't she?" Fear,
grief, guilt, shame were rising in me, so mixed that I
didn't know what I felt, and then above the others fear
and guilt overwhelmed me. "Oh, no, no, no," I whispered. I don't remember touching my heel to the
horse's flank. The next thing I do remember was galloping over the hill, urging the horse faster and faster,
as though I could outrun the storm inside me. Dimly
I heard Giles behind me, calling. But I didn't stop. For
a while I just rode, letting the wind rip every thought
and feeling away from me. Then behind me I heard
the thunder of another horse gaining on me.

"Stop!" Giles yelled. "Kit, for God's sake, stop! The
cliff turns back just in front of you!" Scorn and anger
filled me that he thought he could play that trick on
me. Then I saw dead ahead, less than fifty yards away,
the curving edge of the cliff and remembered that it did
curve in here. It was now less than twenty-five yards.
I pulled on the rein, but the horse, infected perhaps by
my own panic, had taken the bit between his teeth: I
might have thought I was galloping him; he was now
running away with me.

I tugged with all my might. Yet, curiously, my panic
had gone. I felt detached. The high edge was only a
few yards now. I knew that the moment he got nearer,
the horse would know the danger and try to lunge
back. But would he be able to do it? I took one hand
off the taut rein and touched his neck. "Quiet, Rusty,
quiet!"

I shall never know whether he heard or not. I was
yanked off his back and thrown unceremoniously onto
the ground, and from there I watched Giles fight the
horse away from the edge. In the midst of everything
else I paused to admire his skill. I had grown up
among horse handlers. I'd been to the local rodeo al-

most every Saturday night of my life and had come to hate the cruelty to horse and steer that was an integral part of it, while admiring the courage and ability of the riders. But I had never watched such consummate skill in handling not one but two bucking animals—because by this time Giles's own mount, terrified of the edge and the drop beyond, was giving trouble.

Miraculously, he got the two horses back from the edge and quieted. Then, leading my horse, he came over to me. "Are you all right? I'm sorry, Kit. I should never have asked you that about your mother. I thought—but it doesn't matter. I was stupid."

I got up, shaking a little now that the crisis was over. "I'm okay. It's not your fault. I should have known."

I mounted my horse and we collected Charlotte's and rode back in silence. Then I went in to get my mother and to tell her that we were going home. She tried to fight me, of course. And finally broke down and told me the truth. She wanted to get me settled with the Trelawnys where I would go to good schools and learn how to act right before what the doctor had forewarned could come to pass.

But I had always been the stronger of the two. The next day we started back to Wyoming. Six months later Mother was dead.

Many things happened to me in the succeeding fifteen years. Applying for every scholarship I could get, I found myself in one of the elite Eastern universities when I was seventeen, aided by the changing times and the efforts of such institutions to broaden their entrance requirements. There I studied not only the academic subjects, but the manners and attitudes of those who could look at the Trelawnys eye to eye. Those were grueling years. My scholarships were only partial. I learned how to put every second to use, studying, holding down a job, making myself known. I was driven by two overpowering emotions: a determination to succeed and wipe out the past, and a loathing of the Trelawnys. I knew that generations of money had produced what they had become, but it was not money I was primarily after: it was the assurance that enabled them to be what they were. And when

21

things got difficult, when I was tired or discouraged, I would lie in bed at night and go over some of the scenes at Trelawny's Fell and relive the sense of humiliating inferiority that they were so talented in evoking. It was like magic. No matter how down I was, I would get up the next day and put one foot in front of the other.

Once, to a counselor who was being very kind, I confided this goal that kept me going.

"But couldn't you find a better, more constructive motive?" he asked me, obviously appalled.

I knew then I had made a serious mistake in telling him. "It works for me," I said, and changed the subject.

It did. When I was through college (Phi Beta Kappa), I won yet another scholarship—this time an exchange scholarship—and went to the Sorbonne for a year. Then I worked in Rome for the next year, then I came back to the States after that. Finding a job was no trouble at all. Those who interviewed me didn't know that I was my own finest creation: well-educated, urbane, sophisticated, cool. I was also, by that time, quite good-looking—no one would have called me Clementine. The progress of fashion had fallen in my favor: tall skinny women were the height of chic. My feet were no longer outsized. In their expensive quadruple-A shoes they looked in beautiful proportion. My hair had darkened to a honey color, and I wore it either straight down, falling thick and graceful to my shoulders, or in a twist. Unlike my shoes, my clothes were not expensive, but they suited me to perfection and they were very well made—I know, because I had made a lot of them myself. That was one of the skills Mother had taught me and that I perfected, along with my French and my drawing-room manner, in Paris.

I became an editor on a high-fashion magazine, then I was lured to one of the better publishing houses to put out craft books and produced over my share of best-sellers for the company. I had, in other words, arrived. I was invited to fashionable parties well attended by celebrities. My name became known in the brittle, interlocking world of the arts. I was sought by agents and hopeful authors. I was seen at most of the right places with the right people. And while I knew, somewhere deep inside me, just how much such tinfoil public recognition was worth, I didn't kid myself about how much satisfaction it gave me. When I looked in my mirror, I saw my mother—at least I saw her as she might have been—and every success I had I took as one up for our side, hers and mine. My bitterness against the Trelawnys had faded—or perhaps receded would have been a better word. I simply did not think of them, or so I told myself. But one strange thing happened: once, at a party, some social-register type asked, "Are you related to those crazy Trelawny's up in Maine?"

To my astonishment I heard my voice replying, "No. Who are they?" But the savage pleasure that followed my lie startled me and gave me a surprising notion of how totally I had rejected my distinguished cousins. Well, why not? I thought. No rejection of mine could repudiate them more than they had repudiated me. Now it was my turn. I smiled on my questioner, "Why do you ask?"

He put his head on one side. "Well, it's hard to see why, but you have the look of them."

"That's ridiculous," I spoke without thinking, furious at myself for having pursued the subject. Why hadn't I left well enough alone?

"What do you mean, ridiculous? I thought you didn't know who they were."

"I just don't like being related to crazies, whoever they are." I tried lightly to retrieve my misstep. "Anyway, you haven't told me who they are or why they're crazy."

He shrugged. "One of the New York Trelawnys was my roommate at school and I went up to that castle of theirs north of Kennebunkport." He shuddered theatrically. "What a place! It would give Boris Karloff the shivers!

I decided to probe further. But how could I elicit news about Nicholas and Giles—especially Nicholas—having denied all knowledge of them. "Was it a large family?" I asked for openers.

"A whole tribe, headed by a grim matriarch who seemed to think she outranked the British royal family."

"Did she have the children to prove it—Queen Victoria-wise?"

"She had twin sons, about ten or a dozen years older than I. But boy, did she get her comeuppance through them!"

Just barely I managed not to grab onto his jacket. "Oh? How so?"

And at that point, when I was dancing with anticipation, some hearty type, the better (or worse) for drink, came rollicking up, slapped his hand on my companion's shoulder, and started asking him questions about somebody I'd never heard of. At any other time I would have snatched the moment to get away. But I stayed, nibbling various hors d'oeuvres, trying to look detached, until the drunk lurched off.

My friend turned back. "I think I'll work my way to the bar and get another drink."

"You can't leave me without the ending to the enthralling plot you were just unfolding."

"What plot?" My informant too had had a fair amount to drink.

"About the Trelawny twins."

But again I misjudged. "I thought you weren't interested."

"It's the editor in me. I can't stand unfinished stories."

"Oh, well. It's just that there's a queer story going the rounds. You know, or maybe, since you say you never heard of them"—he leered at me—"you don't, that they both got it in Vietnam, one of them getting shot down in a plane, the other getting captured by the Viet Cong. But the story is that one of them—only I don't know which one, and neither does anyone else—went over to the other side. Did broadcasts from Hanoi and everything."

Suddenly they were before me: Nicholas, with his mischievous eyes, and Giles, abrupt and taciturn, fighting the terrified horse.

My drunken friend peered at me. "Why are you

24

looking so funny? You *do* know them! You *are* related! Why did you lie?"

I thought of denying it, of making up some story about having that reaction to anyone who turned his coat in time of war. But I knew I couldn't get away with it.

"It's a long and boring story," I said. "I see somebody I know." And I made my way to the other side of the room and out.

It was odd that that happened then. I had not spoken of the Trelawnys since my mother died. There had been no one with whom to speak of them. Then, within less than six months, came that conversation with a stranger at a cocktail party given by someone I hardly knew, and a letter from a Boston law firm, asking if I could go up there to see them.

I had to go there on business anyway, so I dropped by one afternoon before getting the shuttle back to New York. It seemed incredible to me then that I had no idea what they wanted to see me about: that after careful searching up and down collateral family trees to discover who, according to the family trust, was to inherit The Fell and what was left of the Trelawny money, they had come up with me!

My first reaction was almost more than that staid firm could endure: I laughed and laughed.

After listening to this for a moment, the Boston gentleman sitting behind the desk cleared his throat in a testy fashion and said, "Really, Miss Trelawny! I had no idea this would be the cause of so much amusement. I would think—but never mind!"

"You would think I would be grateful, awed, stunned, perhaps."

Not being stupid, he caught the sarcasm—and didn't appreciate it in the least. "Surely a more natural reaction?"

"Natural? To whom?"

We stared at one another for a moment. "What happened to all the other heirs?" I asked. "The ones who, I am sure, came before me?"

"The immediate heirs, Nicholas and Giles, were killed in the late war—the war in Veitnam."

"Yes. So I'd heard."

He said sharply, "I don't see how you could have missed seeing the notices in the papers. They were both mentioned in *The New York Times*."

"When did that happen?"

"Nicholas was shot down seven years ago. Giles, who was then in Army Intelligence, disappeared a little before, and was later reported killed.

"I was in Paris and Rome." Suddenly I remembered the strange story the drunk had told me. "I heard that one of the twins defected, made broadcasts from Hanoi. Is that true?"

It was as though a huge ice cube had been lowered into the room.

"I know nothing about it," Mr. Edgerton said.

"But you did hear those rumors?"

"Rumors of that kind always circulate in a war."

It was like trying to move a granite boulder.

"D'you hold to the old cliché about where there's smoke . . . ?"

"That would be a mere speculation and a waste of time. Shall we return to the matter at hand? You asked about the other heirs." He picked up the papers on his desk. "Julian was killed in a car accident ten years ago. Richard committed suicide—most unfortunate. Mary died in the same accident that killed her brother Julian. John was killed in Vietnam. Those were all the younger generation of Trelawnys—first and second cousins of the main branch. Needless to say, of course, the older generation has all gone."

"But"—I searched my memory—"wasn't one of the twins—Giles, I think—engaged? To Charlotte Something? She was there when I was. Didn't they marry?"

There was a tiny pause. Then the old lawyer said, "She died. A car accident. Didn't you hear about it?" He asked the question so sharply I jumped.

"No. Why should I? We didn't get social news from the Eastern Upper Crust out in Wyoming."

It seemed to me he bent a very penetrating look at me, which I returned.

"Very well," he said finally, as though something had been accepted.

I resisted an impulse to say, "Very well what?" In-

26

stead, I commented, not bothering to soften my sarcasm, "So after all that history and all that arrogance there's only me."

The lawyer's mouth thinned. He plainly didn't appreciate my attitude. "You are inheriting a great responsibility. I hope you will use it with judgment."

"As far as I am concerned, the best thing to do with it would be to sell it."

A spasm of something very like fear quivered over his face. He moistened his lips.

"It would," I said, tightening the screws just a little, "make a marvelous lunatic asylum."

Again I had the odd impression that I had said something that frightened him. But he cleared his throat and said in his driest lawyer's voice, "In view of the conditions of the Trust, that would be a long and complicated process. I am sure you will find a better use for it before then."

"Oh, in that case, I will." Fully blown, an idea had come to me with dazzling impact.

He smiled a little. "Have you already made up your mind what you're going to do, Miss Trelawny?"

I gathered up my bag and gloves. "I have." I paused, because I wanted to savor the moment. I was only sorry that there was no Trelawny—no *real* Trelawny —alive and present to hear me. "I'm going to use the house as a colony for artists."

The effect was all I could have wished, even though it was only on this stuffy lawyer. "Artists!" he said, his voice all but quivering with horror.

I gave a final turn to the screw. "And dropouts. You know, the kind who can't make it in society." I got up.

He rose. "You can't be serious," he said, almost pleadingly.

"I had thought of making it a home for unwed mothers. But I'm not sure that nowadays they need one. Marriage is going out of style. And then I thought of drug addicts. . . ." It was really mean of me, I thought, to vent my ancient grudge on this poor old man who was only, so to speak, the messenger. "But then I realized I didn't have sufficient technical knowledge for that. Artists, though, I can manage. I really think

27

that's a good idea. Good afternoon, Mr. Edgerton. You'll be forwarding me the necessary papers, won't you?"

And that was what, six months later, had brought me on the road with Josephine, headed as fast as I could go, to Trelawny's Fell.

I looked down at the cat now sleeping placidly. "If there are any ghosts," I said, tickling the edge of her ear, "the new inhabitants will be a nice change for them. Broadening."

I was to remember that airy statement.

2

I broke the journey at Hatfield, about fifty miles away from Perkins, the village nearest The Fell. The motel manager wasn't enthusiastic about Josephine, but he also had a great number of empty cabins.

The next morning, with Josephine only partially tranquilized, we started off. One reason I had decided to spend the night on the way was because I wanted to see again the coastline as I approached from the west. The memory of the green shore with the pines going down and the inlets filled with reeds and morning light and wild birds was one of the few recollections of my visit that had remained unspoiled.

It was strange, I thought, how much I had remembered. I found the road that left the highway with no trouble and without referring to the map, and took the fork bearing east yet again that brought me to the narrow, winding road—really just a path—beside the water. Another miracle was how little it had changed. For whatever reason—inaccessibility, inconvenience, bad roads—this particular part of the coast had remained untouched by human meddling.

Just short of the village I pulled up. Woods on my left concealed the village itself. To my right there was another inlet with the yellow-green reeds marching down to the blue-gray water, a wooden pier bridging the marsh, and a dozen gulls wheeling and screaming overhead. In front and to the right a belt of trees— deciduous as well as evergreen—led up to the cliff on top of which, its roof above the tier of trees, was Trelawny's Fell.

I don't know how long I sat there, staring at it. At that moment it seemed inconceivable that it should be mine. Yet it was left so that it passed automatically to the next of kin bearing the family name—myself. Or at least, that was my understanding from the lawyer's language that had been read to me and the even more intricate comments that Mr. Edgerton had offered between paragraphs. In his unintentionally funny phrase, "there was a shortage of younger generation." Hence my unexpected inheritance.

I grinned to myself. A loss to the family pride would be my gain.

My mind ran over the nucleus of artistic types that were due to arrive in a week:

There was Frank Morse, a painter friend of Jeremy's. Age twenty-three, contribution—he would do odd jobs around the house. Not being a foundation nor enjoying an endowment, I had to insist that guests contribute either in money or services—preferably both. I wasn't wild about Frank, though beyond a sullenness of manner there was nothing objectionable about him that I could put my finger on. On the plus side, he was Jeremy's friend, he needed the time to work on a one-man exhibit he was planning, and I had been told that he was extremely talented.

There was Tess Farranicci, twenty-two, also a painter friend of Jeremy's, who would help me with the housekeeping and cooking. I had met her once at a party given in a loft off Houston Street to which Jeremy had escorted me. She turned out to be a pretty child in a granny dress and a solemn expression. How good her work was I didn't know. But some of the food at that party had been cooked by her, and that was very good indeed. . . .

Then there was Mary Butler-Longman, whom I had not met but with whom I had corresponded. There were two reasons why I had accepted her. The first was that she had come recommended by Mr. Edgerton, and

I thought that after administering the initial shock of turning the family pride into a commune, the least I could do would be to take his offering. The other reason was financial. The Butler-Longman Steel Company was second in size, fame, and profits only to U.S. Steel. Miss Butler-Longman could pay. When Jeremy heard that I had accepted her above a dozen or so others, his lip curled. "To them that hath shall be given," he said rather bitterly. "What does she have besides money?"

"It's the money I'm interested in. We have to eat, you know."

"I thought the estate left something besides the house."

"So did I. But we were wrong. There isn't enough to feed us for a month. This has to be a self-supporting commune. That's why I'm happy to welcome an honest-to-God paying guest."

"Does she have any talent. Or does it matter?"

"It would be nice if she had talent, but I'm not going to be intransigent about it."

Two days later Jeremy, who had been putting out inquiries said, "That Butler-Longman woman—she pots."

I felt a qualm. "You don't suppose she's planning to bring her wheel?"

He grinned. "You could set it up in the ancestral living room. I gather she also illustrates children's books."

The fourth was Rod Moscovitch, whom I also hadn't met, but who won my heart by sending an advance payment, a list of references, and an offer to do anything except hunt or fish. He added that he was cheap to feed because he was a vegetarian and would be happy to supply his own vegetables in place of any meat I would be serving.

I asked Jeremy if he had ever heard of him. Jeremy shook his head. "Better check those references. He may turn out to be your friendly neighborhood mass murderer."

"Ha-ha. Very funny." But I did send out letters to all the names he submitted and received replies to the general effect that he was a man of good character who paid his bills and didn't knock over old ladies. Nobody said anything about talent. I hesitated about him. I didn't want The Fell to turn into some kind of playground for the rich amateur. But as the weeks passed and I didn't get any applications that appealed to me more, I wrote and told him he could come. He returned a terse note thanking me, sounding much more like a banker than an artist.

After that, I decided that four strangers, or near-strangers, would be enough to go on with. If they worked out, I could add to them, one or two at a time. I had written to each of the four, giving an arrival date of one week after my own arrival. I felt I needed that week alone to sort myself out and get reacquainted with the house, although "reacquainted" was not really the right word. There was another, more accurate—but less acceptable—way I could have put it to myself: I wanted that week to exorcise not only old memories, but the ghosts of all former Trelawnys. In my memory the house was so impregnated with their arrogance and everything else about them that I had detested that I felt as though The Fell wouldn't be truly mine till I had been there and taken possession.

I had originally planned to visit the house shortly after I had received the property deeds. But each time I tried to go up there either my job intervened or the road leading to the house was so blocked with snow that the lawyers, who kept in touch with the village, warned me not to try.

I was less nervous about the condition of the house than I might have been, however, because Mr. Edgerton had had it examined from roof to cellar and every smallest ornament itemized and listed. Edgerton, Edgerton, Edgerton, Blount & Edgerton (who sounded like a parody of a Boston Brahmin firm, which was exactly what they were) might be stuffy, but no one could fault their meticulous care. In addition, there was, apparently, a caretaker who lived on the property and who had looked after The Fell for some thirty years. He had been left a pension and earned a few extra dollars a week from Edgerton, etc., for keeping an eye on the house.

I had put the car in gear preparatory to moving on, when I saw a foreign and rather dashing car coming towards me. The road was so narrow I thought I'd wait until it passed. Idly I watched its approach. As it drew level I saw that the driver was a man who looked about in his late thirties. To my surprise, he stopped and opened his window. A square, blunt-featured face peered at me. "Need any help?"

I shook my head. "Just resting."

Instead of driving on, he stayed where he was. I am neither particularly trusting of strangers nor gregarious, and I was contemplating moving on when Josephine, who had had only half her tranquilizer and no breakfast, let out a subdued squawk. The top of the carrier was open and she sat up and stretched.

"Almost there, Josephine," I said. "Keep it cool."

"I take it Josephine is Siamese," the man in the car offered.

"More or less. Mostly less. But there's some there." I started to ease the car forward.

"By the way," he said, "I'm Bill Seaward. Dr. Seaward." He hesitated. "I take it you're Miss Trelawny."

I shouldn't have been surprised. The caretaker had, of course, been informed when I was due, and it was inconceivable that, in a small country place, he would keep the news to himself. Still, I remembered the careful look Dr. Seaward had bent on me. "How did you know? Were you expecting me today?"

"I knew that Simon—the caretaker—was looking for you today. But"—he smiled—"to anyone who has known the Trelawnys it was a fairly safe guess."

"And yet I don't resemble them in any way."

"The funny thing is, feature by feature, you don't. And of course they're dark. Yet—I recognized you as a Trelawny immediately."

Flattery? I wondered. Yet there was the man at the party saying the same thing. How pleased Mother would have been! The old anger stirred in me. "I think you must be mistaken," I said rather coldly.

He smiled. "Well, anyway, welcome! It will be nice to have The Fell occupied again."

"Thanks. How long has it lain empty?"

"About five years. Since old Mrs. Trelawny died."

Into my mind sprang the memory of those dark, wickedly amused eyes, the arched nostrils, her hand on the silver teapot, slender and long-fingered; on her left hand a narrow gold wedding ring and on top of that, a magnificent emerald set in gold and cut so that green light flashed and winked from every facet.

Without thinking, I looked down at my own hands, also long-fingered but square-palmed—useful hands, unadorned, for despite the fashion for a scattering of rings, I had never worn any. Mrs. Trelawny's jewelry had gone to a niece back in England. In fact, everything she could leave away from the Trust she had. When her sons died unmarried, she must have known that the property in Trust would have to come to me. Mr. Edgerton had not said so, but I couldn't imagine that clever, proud woman not finding out who stood next in line to inherit The Fell. That was the reason, I felt quite sure, for the scrutiny of every possible family connection and branch that Mr. Edgerton had been careful to tell me about. And when the cards kept throwing up my name, how she must have hated the thought that I, my mother's daughter, would sit in her place.

Just thinking about that made me feel better, just as it had given me great satisfaction, after Mother's death, to return the large check Mrs. Trelawny had sent. How she found out that Mother had died I don't know. Probably she had paid somebody to keep her informed. The letter that came with the check was overwhelmingly gracious. Any lady of the manor could have written it to any servant. I tore up both letter and check and put the pieces into an envelope, and sent it, without comment, back to Mrs. Trelawny. That check would have seen me through my first semester of college later on. But returning it in pieces did far more for me.

When I heard Dr. Seaward clear his throat I realized I had been sitting there, staring at my hands.

"Sorry," I said lightly. "Just daydreaming. I must go."

"I'll drop by later today, if I may, to see if there's anything I can do. Though I'm sure old Simon has everything in order."

33

"Simon? Oh, the caretaker."

"Okay?"

I really didn't want him coming by. On the other hand, to refuse would be ungracious and it would not do to alienate the neighbors in a remote place like this —especially not the local doctor. For a second I wondered how old Mrs. Trelawny would have responded. As I well knew she did not relish people dropping by. But then, the less I was like her, the better. I smiled.

"About five then?"

"Fine. See you then." Was there nervousness under that hearty manner, or was I imagining things? He revved up his car. "Don't let the house get you down!" And with a wave of his hand, he drove off.

I drove in the opposite direction, aware of a feeling of irritation and . . . foreboding?

"Don't be ridiculous," I said to myself as I approached the minute village that lay in a small hollow about two miles from the gates of The Fell. Feeling the car in motion, Josephine gave another, and louder, squawk. "Soon, now, Empress," I said soothingly, and ran my hand down her ridged back. "Country cream and fattened mice, for you, milady. Or are you such a city slicker you prefer your dinner out of cans?" Josephine replied with her loud rattling purr. "That's the girl," I said.

Everything that could possibly be sold in the village was contained in one all-purpose store—meat, dairy products, grain, vegetables, fruit, hardware, work-clothes, stationery, even books. And at one end was a tiny post office.

It had been nearly fifteen years since I had entered the store, but from the outside at least it looked exactly as I remembered. I parked the car, closed Josephine's carrier by pulling the wire top down, and went in.

Stashed in the trunk of the car were all kinds of staples and canned goods, because I wanted to start off as independently as I could. But I had to buy milk, butter, meat and fruit. There were several people in the store—a couple of men in lumber jackets and parkas, because it was still cold up here, and two or three women.

Fifteen years before I had come into this store once,

34

with the twins. I remembered the occasion very well, because the woman behind the counter was not at all friendly, a fact that Nicholas found highly entertaining. He treated her with elaborate courtesy and tried several conversational gambits. I remember the fierce hostility in her ice-blue eyes when she said, "The law says I have to serve everybody who comes into the store to buy something, Mr. Nicholas. I don't have to talk to 'em. Will that be all?"

Nicholas laughed. He started to lean over the counter. Giles got hold of his shoulder. "Let's go," he said abruptly and pulled him out. It was only when we got outside and I suddenly smelled his breath as he turned that I realized Nicholas had been drinking.

I looked now behind the counter and saw that it was still the same woman. Her hair was now quite gray. But she was still as thin as a bag of sticks and her eyes were still that penetrating light blue. As I went up to the counter, the other customers moved away. They continued talking to one another in low voices, but I had a strong feeling that I was being watched.

"Good morning," I said cheerfully. "I'd like two dozen eggs and a quart of milk." I looked around the store. "Also some cheese, some apples, and a roasting chicken, if you have one."

The woman—Mrs. Bradford, I now remembered—cut the huge cartwheel of cheese, trussed up a chicken, and started putting apples from a barrel into a bag.

"How many pounds?" she asked.

"About ten."

As she was totting up the amount, a door behind the counter opened and a girl of about fourteen came out.

The woman spoke sharply to her. "See what Mrs. Fisher wants, Priscilla."

"All right, Granny," and she went to the other end of the long counter.

I found myself turning to look at the girl, but she was partly hidden by sacks of grain, and about all I could see was her dark head.

"That'll be nine eighty," the woman said to me. "Will that be all?"

"Yes. For now. I'll probably be back tomorrow or the day after for more or because I've forgotten something." I smiled at her but received no answering smile in return. Was she just being very New England, or was she hostile? All my intuition pointed to the latter, but I decided to make allowance for an overactive imagination and give it another try.

"It's Mrs. Bradford, isn't it? I seem to remember you from the last time I was here. But that was quite a few years ago." Deliberately I left it vague.

"Yes, Miss Trelawny. I remember. You'll be taking over The Fell, won't you?" She looked then straight at me, and there wasn't the glimmer of a smile.

I picked up the bundles. "Yes, I will. Good day." And I left, aware as I walked past the people who stepped back for me and stood silent until I got out, of an unmistakable tension in that room. The door had glass panels, and I turned back to look inside. The people had drawn together again. Mrs. Bradford was leaning over the counter, talking to someone. Idly I glanced to the far end of the counter. The girl, Priscilla, was staring at me, her eyes fixed on me over the bent head of the old woman she was serving. But the moment our gazes crossed, she lowered her head. There was something about her face that nagged at me. But I couldn't pinpoint it, so I dismissed the matter as I rode out of the village and up towards the cliffs.

The big iron gate was closed, and a thick belt of trees behind the wall hid any view of the house. I got out and opened the gate and then, when I had driven through, got out again and closed it. Less than five minutes later I had gone through the belt of trees and was facing the house as Mother and I did fifteen years before. I pulled up and sat looking at it.

The Fell was shaped like an uneven capital E—the result of afterthoughts and additions. Old Nicholas's neat Georgian mansion, symmetrical and balanced, had sprouted columned porches both front and back and ill-matched extensions on either side. These extensions had been added to, so that the profile of the roof facing me was a series of ups and downs. At both ends the final additions extended back towards me to form the upper and lower arms of the E. The result was an impressive hodgepodge, rambling over that whole section of cliff front. There were two main doors: one faced the cliff, the other inland.

When I had seen it with my mother, the afternoon sun had warmed the gray almost to gold and had winked and sparkled off the old-fashioned window-panes set in neat white frames. Some of the windows were raised, with white curtains billowing out in the wind that blew across this exposed apron of land on even the quietest day. For all its stone dominance the house had been filled with the quality of human life.

Now, except for its curious up-and-down profile, it could almost have been a different place. The morning sun was behind the house, throwing it in shadow, so that it seemed to loom twice its size, black and menacing. The panes looked opaque, the blinds drawn. There was nothing about it whatsoever that hinted of human life inside. Perhaps it was that, its air of emptiness and abandonment or maybe it was the different position of the sun throwing the house in shadow, that made me so intensely aware at that moment of its isolation, as though it and I were alone on some island detached and remote from anything I'd ever known. Quite suddenly I shivered and felt the skin tingle and tighten on my arms.

"Maybe," I said to Josephine to break the silence, "the old boy was right. I should have come up before now at least to see it."

But when one plan after another to come up here had fallen through, I decided to go ahead with my projected commune anyway. "After all," I said to old Mr. Edgerton on the telephone, "you assure me it's in good repair. Every last ornament and end table and pillow-case is itemized. What could be the problem?"

"I do think, Miss Trelawny, you should make at least one visit before you go ahead."

"Why?"

"Prudence would indicate that you should see what you're—er—getting into before you give up your—er —career." His retreat into Brahmin stuffiness irritated me.

"But aside from prudence, you don't have any specific reason why I shouldn't go ahead with my plans? Something a little more definite?"

My tone, my implied italics, disposed of prudence—
a quality for which I've had small use in my life. No
great works of art nor empires nor renovated human
beings were made by prudence, I always told myself.
So perhaps it was the sneer at the edge of my voice that
produced his dry, "Nothing definite, Miss Trelawny."
If there was something else in his voice, I ignored it.

Now I wondered.

"It's mine, all mine," I said aloud, to exorcise the
curious, uneasy feeling I was struggling against.

But it didn't look or feel mine. The Fell looked very
much itself, its own possession, or at least, perhaps, the
possession of those who had once lived in it.

"Oh, no you don't," I said, putting the car in gear
again. "I'll show you who's boss!"

I should never have said that.

The road up was not paved; it was made of an
amalgam of stones and dirt, which affected the quality
of the setting. Such a house in Europe or Long Island
or the South would have had a carriage sweep. But I expect old Nicholas did not want The Fell to appear too
welcoming to the outside world. We bumped over the
path and drew up on the stony apron in front of the
house.

"Well, Empress. *Nous sommes arrivées!*"

I rolled open the window and sat there. Except for
the occasional screech of the gulls, the silence was total.
The air was sharp and tangy and smelled of salt water
and pine. Up close the windows still looked opaque,
like eyes turned inward. I started counting them. Including the dormer windows there were over forty on
this side alone. I tried then to remember the inside of
the house from my stay there of fifteen years before. I
tried—and almost nothing came. Had I blocked it out?
Or were the people so powerful that they overshad-
owed everything else?

What finally came into my mind were high ceilings,
portraits, upstairs rooms that were two steps up or
three down, funny little staircases leading up into attics
that I never got around to inspecting, and a quality that
I could not define then but that I have since come to
know as Old Wealth. The carpets may have been

threadbare, the furniture plain, the whole lacking ornament. But the quality was unmistakable and somehow
made everything I saw afterwards that could remotely
be called "decorated" look vulgar and overdone by
comparison.

I got out and walked over to the door with its fanlight and dull brass knocker. Taking out keys that
looked to me as though they might fit the Tower of
London, I found the one marked Front Door—Rear
and fitted it in the lock. It turned easily and I pushed
open the door.

I was about to step in when I remembered Josephine.
I might as well bring her in and open up the carrier
and trust she wouldn't get permanently lost. I went
back to the car, snapped the locks of the carrier shut,
picked it up, and was about to carry it back to the
house when, out of the corner of my eye, I thought I
saw a curtain move in an upstairs window to my left. I
swung around, evoking a wild protest from Josephine,
my heart suddenly beating wildly. But the whitish curtain
now hung perpendicular and still, like its companion.

"It's your imagination," I said to myself. But I didn't
believe it. I knew that curtain had moved, and I could
have sworn in court that I saw, magnified by one of the
uneven spots in the old glass, a hand around the edge
of the curtain. And then, as I stepped across the
threshold, the obvious explanation came: of course, it
was the caretaker, Simon. Idiot! I said to myself, an-
noyed and astonished at the relief I felt. I was even
more irritated when the doctor's words flashed in my
mind: *don't let the house get you down.* Well, it's not
going to! I'm not about to be brainwashed, I thought.
If the Dowager Trelawny and her arrogant sons could
not do it when I was a child, the hollow remains of
their house would not do it now.

I was standing in a wide hall between the two front
doors. Like his famous contemporary, Thomas Jeffer-
son, Nicholas Trelawny did not believe in wasting
space on elegant sweeping stairways. So the staircase on
my left that went up to the second floor was rather narrow and functional, though the balustrade and ban-
nister were, I could see even from where I stood,
beautifully molded. Wide wooden boards covered the

39

floor, rubbed to a fine sheen by polish and years. The morning sun, pouring itself through the fanlight of the rear door facing the eastern cliff, lay over the floor and the two small Persian rugs in prismatic splendor. Lining the wall to the left were a chest, a looking glass, and a narrow, covered loveseat. On the right were a table, a bookcase and two fine tapestried chairs.

I set the carrier down on the floor. I could hear Josephine, now almost wholly recovered from her tranquilizer, thrashing around. I listened to her squawks for a moment, then I went swiftly out to the car and got the package from the store. Against my will I glanced at the window. The curtain hung straight. There was no one there. Returning, I tore open the paper around the butter, smeared some on my fingers and then lifted the carrier top. Josephine was quick, but I was quicker. I had her thin body clamped under my arm before she knew what she was about. Fighting every inch of the way (and feeling rather foolish) I got her four paws buttered which, according to old English lore, would keep her from running away.

"Now," I said, "you're on your own." And put her on the floor.

There was a flash of black fur and she was halfway up the stairs, licking her paws and eyeing me angrily through the balustrade.

Making two trips to the car, I brought in the baggage and shut the big rear door. The words I had spoken to Josephine seemed now applicable to me. I was, in truth, on my own.

I stood there for a minute, letting the house soak in around me, half waiting for Simon to make his way through the far wing, where I had seen him move the curtain to the center hall. But the silence was total. Finally, I opened the double doors to my right and walked into the drawing room—and into my own bitter past. It was dust-sheeted now, the blinds drawn. But the memories it evoked had color and sound and life. It was in that chair to the right of the fireplace, now merely a hulk under a sheet, where the dowager had sat, her slender hand on the heavily chased silver teapot, her body erect, her eyes mocking the awkward country woman in her cheap, fussy print, not knowing

40

what to do with the teacup that had been handed to her. It was on that huge couch over by the now darkened window that the dowager's two sons had sprawled, Nicholas laughing, Giles scowling, but both sharing the mockery that filled the room and of which Mother and I, but especially Mother, were the target.

I drew in a breath. The years had covered the shriveling sense of humiliation, but the room had brought it back. For a moment I saw my mother's face, bewildered, like a child's, and a pain beyond that of the humiliation made me for a moment feel physically sick.

"This won't do," I muttered aloud, and going over to the windows, started pushing aside the curtains and yanking up the blinds. Sunlight streamed in, and I stood there for a few seconds, at the last window facing the sea beyond, below the cliff edge, staring at it, smooth and aquamarine reflecting the sky above it. Nearer was an expanse of green turf jutting out to the very edge of the cliff. There had never been any kind of gate or guard, I was told.

"But what about small children?" Mother had asked.

"They must learn not to go too near the edge," the dowager had replied.

"But babies don't know anything about obeying."

The dowager's arched brows had shot up. "In this house they do. Besides, that's what the children's governesses are for—to keep them in hand."

But Mother barely knew what a governess was. I knew, of course, because I had absorbed such knowledge with all the books I had read, and I waited in agony for her to display her ignorance. But Nicholas diverted her attention by saying, with his attractive grin, "Mother always ran a tight ship."

I pulled myself away from the window and went around the rest of the room, opening the blinds and pulling back the curtains. The room ran the width of the house and once had windows on three sides. But when the first wing had been added to the south side, one window was left at either end of the side but the rest were closed. In the center of that wall now was another set of double doors, giving onto the southern wing, and beyond that, to the extension that was added at the end of that. With the windows now all letting in

41

light, I went around and started removing the dust covers, folding them and putting them on the floor behind the big couch. Later they could be taken up to one of the attics. When the covers were gone, I stood in the middle of the room, looking at it. I had been in many larger and more stately rooms in some of the great houses in Europe, both as tourist and, on a few occasions, as guest. But with all its painful memories, this room had remained in my mind as unsurpassed in beauty. All the way up I had wondered if, because it was the first room of its kind I had ever seen, I had overglamorized its memory. Now I knew I had not. It's difficult to describe what makes a room beautiful. Space and proportion form, of course, the essential ingredients. I was not enough of an architect to know what the magic combination of numbers was, but whatever it was, this room had achieved it. Only once or twice before, in eighteenth-century houses in England, had I seen rooms that seemed as near perfect. Now I turned slowly around, looking at the ceiling, the white walls, the chimneypiece and, finally, over the mantel, the portrait of Nicholas, the founder, the one painted by Copley while Nicholas was in London.

"All Trelawnys look alike," the dowager had said, with a mischievous glance at me, rejecting any ridiculous claim my mother might put forward to my being a Trelawny. "Look at old Nicholas, and look at young Nicholas and Giles and all the others in between."

So I looked again on the dark, saturnine face of my ancestor. There was the black hair, the light gray eyes under the marked black brows, the aquiline nose and the wide cheekbones. But the mouth undid the arrogant, self-assured rest of the face. Wide and shapely, it revealed a man who had many self-doubts, a man who might and did hang himself. My eyes went to the other portraits hanging against the walls. There was Deborah, old Nicholas's niece and Giles's first cousin and wife. The salient Trelawny features repeated themselves to a greater or lesser degree in almost all of the paintings, and since the Trelawnys had a habit of marrying cousins, the family characteristics continued to dominate over any other strains that were brought in. When there were twins, the two heads appeared in the same painting. There were other paintings in other parts of the house, but I knew that all those containing twins had been put in here, so I went around the room identifying them. To the right of the mantel and the portrait of their father were Nicholas and Giles, their black hair brushed, Regency fashion, forward. They both wore the Navy uniforms of the War of 1812. Then, two generations later, in sidewhiskers, another Nicholas and Giles. Their twin sons sported mutton-chop whiskers looking like shrubbery around the lean cheeks. In World War I uniform, Nicholas and Chrétien had mustaches, but except for that and for the high collars of their uniforms, they could have been the young men I knew. I moved to the next painting. There were Nicholas and Giles as I saw them for the first time, Nicholas in the uniform of a Navy flier, Giles in Army khaki. Could the difference between them as I had come to detect it be seen in the portraits? Nicholas was the older so, in the custom of all the twin portraits, he stood slightly in front, therefore the fact that their heads were level would indicate that Giles was about half an inch taller, as indeed I remembered he was. His head in the painting was more shadowed, making his eyes less strikingly silver, his face thinner. Or was it my imagination? I moved a little closer.

"Alike, aren't they?" a voice said from the door leading into the wing.

I spun around. An elderly man, tall, rather cadaverous, was standing, his hat in his hand, a lumber jacket on. He must have seen my bafflement because he said, "I'm Simon, the caretaker. Mr. Edgerton said you'd be coming up this morning."

I let my breath out. I must, I thought, get hold of myself. "I'm sorry—you startled me. How do you do? I'm Kit Trelawny.

"Yes. I recognized you."

"Recognized me? Were you here when I was a child visiting here? I didn't remember."

He pulled the door shut behind him. "Oh no. I was on vacation when you were here. I meant I recognized you as a Trelawny."

That was the third person who had said that. Without thinking, my eyes went to a long gilt mirror hanging from the wall. "Our magic mirror," Mrs. Trelawny had described it. And in a sense it was, because it reflected the mirror opposite which in turn showed the reflection, and so on, back and forth.

"I don't see it myself," I said. "The resemblance."

"It's there. Anyone who had known a Trelawny would see it."

The words were innocuous enough, yet there was something in his tone that made it not a compliment. I wondered if I had encountered an ally in my dislike of the family. I decided to put it to the test. "That's not really a compliment to me, you know. I didn't like the family."

"Most people didn't," he said.

"Because of their arrogance?"

"That—and other things."

"What other things?"

It was odd—as though a curtain had come down over that tight New England face, with its long upper lip and expressionless eyes.

"Would you like to see the rest of the place?" he asked. "I turned up the heat today, and I'd like to show you how the furnace works."

I could, of course, insist that he answer my question. But I didn't think I'd get any further, and I would alienate him. So I took one last glance around the room. There, on a table between windows fronting on the sea, was the silver tea service that I remembered so well: the heavy tray, teapot, sugar bowl, cream jug, tongs, strainer and little bowl under it. "You must have also cleaned the silver," I said. "It's gleaming."

"There's a girl comes in once a week and does that."

"Oh." I turned. "Tell me, are you Simon something, or something Simon? I mean, is it your surname or your Christian name?"

I thought for a minute he wouldn't answer. But finally he said, "Simon is my first name."

"But what is your last?"

"You can call me Simon. Everyone does. Mr. Edgerton calls me that." And I could tell that by evoking such a name he was telling me that it was the official version.

"All right," I submitted, not very graciously, "let's go and look at the furnace." But as he was about to take me out of the same door he entered by, something that had been bothering me suddenly surfaced. "You came in through this door, didn't you?" I asked.

"Yes."

"But I saw you in the other wing."

"The other wing? When?"

"This morning. When I was standing out front. You must have crossed over before you came in here. Or is there another way of going from one wing to the other, besides going through this room? I mean, because I came into the house right away and have only been in the hall and here. If you had crossed indoors, I would have seen you. You must have walked over outside."

His face had started off blank. But as I talked it changed.

"Yes. That's what I did," he said. "I had to see something—on this side. So I decided to . . . see it before I came in here."

Since that was more or less what I had thought he had done, it was odd that I was convinced he was lying.

We stared at one another. "That's it," he said loudly. "I crossed over outside and then came in here. Shall we go into the cellar? I have something to do in the village and we'll have to hurry. I thought you'd be here sooner."

At the end of two hours Simon and I had examined the cellars, the furnace, and the pipes; we had gone over the entire downstairs, including both wings, and the second floor of the main building. We would have gone into the wings from there if Simon, to my relief, had not remembered his errand and hurried away. I appreciated his conscientious effort to show me over the place. But I preferred to see it by myself.

From the drawing-room window I had watched him disappear in the direction of his own house, which, he told me, was located on the grounds but behind a stretch of trees about a hundred yards away from the edge of the north wing. Certainly it was not visible from the house. "Mrs. Trelawny wanted it that way," he said simply.

"When did you build it?" I asked, just before he took himself off.

"Eight years ago."

"Three years before she died?"

"Yes." He jerked a large watch out of his pocket. "Do you want me to get you anything in the village?"

I accepted the abrupt change of subject. "No. I can't think of anything. I stocked up on my way here. How late does the store stay open?"

"Till about a quarter to six. And you can always phone. Mrs. Bradford has a nephew who'll bring the things up. I'll stop by this evening."

I watched him go out of the room, then wandered over to the window and followed his progress down a path that led round the trees. In about five minutes I heard the faint sounds of a car being started. A rather ancient model appeared between the two clumps of trees. But instead of coming towards the house and the path leading from it, it was obviously taking another path towards the gate I had come in by. Or perhaps there was another entrance to the grounds. I would have to ask Simon, or explore myself.

I turned away and stood in the middle of the drawing room, staring at the portrait over the mantelpiece and, to the left, the one of the late dowager's sons. Then I went upstairs to the big master bedroom on the southeast corner of the main house where Simon had taken my bags, and stood rooted at the sea view that filled all the windows of the room that had once been old Nicholas's self-imposed prison. The sea was now a deeper blue trimmed in white where the breeze had picked up strength. I raised the window and leaned out. From there I could see the coastline, rocky and treelined, curving far to the left and right, with tall spruce and fir and pine growing sometimes to the water's edge, elsewhere soaring upwards above great boulders. It was a breathtaking vista. Yet once again I had an overwhelming sense of our remoteness, as though The Fell were both cradled and cut off by both forest and ocean. The air, filled with salt and pine poured into the room, chilling it, yet making it more alive. After a minute or two, leaving the window open, I turned around.

There were two portraits in this room, one over the bureau, one over a table, and, walking over, I peered at the nameplates underneath: the first was Chrétien Trelawny, this time with red hair and a beard. Where did the red come in? The other was Sarah Trelawny, a frail-looking blond lady with a lace fichu and a cap. The rest of the pictures were watercolors—seascapes, a lighthouse, some rocks, most of them conventional and insipid. But one, directly across from the big bed and above a fine kneehole desk, captured the eye and held it. In charcoal and watercolor it portrayed a man in a torn uniform bending over a boat, with jungle green marching down to the water and wooden houses on stilts. There was power in the painting and urgency in the figure of the man. Not another human being showed in the painting, yet I was quite certain the man was being pursued. I went and stared at it, searching for a signature. At first I thought there wasn't one. Then, peering down into the lower edge of the frame, I saw a charcoal stroke that could be the top of a letter, and behind that, lower down, what could be the curve of another letter. Or it could be part of the drawing itself. In either case, the frame had been a little too small. Odd, I thought. Because it was by no means a cheap frame. I moved back, still looking at the painting. The rest of the room was of the past. But this picture, like the sharp, salty air coming through the window, brought in the present, aggressive and disturbing.

I decided to unpack and then look over the rest of the house. Hanging my clothes in the huge old-fashioned wardrobe, I put the bags on the shelves of a linen closet and wondered where Josephine might be. I hadn't seen her since she had glared at me from between the spokes of the balustrade. I decided to trust that when she was hungry she'd find me.

I started my exploration with the second floor of the south wing, which I reached through a door at the end of the hall in the center building. The rooms here were less stately, the ceilings lower. I examined endless brass beds, oak chests, rag carpets, and bad portraits of long-nosed Trelawnys staring rigidly out upon a world of which they had obviously disapproved. The up-and-down profile of the house repeated itself in the up-and-down rooms. As I went down three steps, stooping beneath an overhanging ceiling here, and ducked as I went up two more there, I wondered how many heads of the tall Trelawnys had been cracked getting around their sprawling, uneven mansion.

On the third floor, the ceilings were even lower. Instead of portraits there were engravings and prints, and bowls and pitchers, remnants of pre-plumbing days, abounded. I could house a whole school here, I thought. Heaven knew there were enough rooms and beds! Finally, by way of a steep, narrow staircase, opening into a door at the far end of the south wing, I came to the attics—long low rooms, lit by dormer windows and crossed and recrossed by huge rafters. Wending my way through the south wing attics, I passed by the connecting door into the huge attic over the center building.

When Mother and I were being shown over the house by an overwhelmingly gracious dowager, I had stared up at the great rafters of the attic in the original center building and, curiosity winning over the certainty of a snub, had asked Mrs. Trelawny which rafter had carried the rope that had hanged old Nicholas, a story regaled to me by the present-day Nicholas.

"My dear, how should I know?" And then, with her taunting smile, "We don't put up plaques, you know."

But Nicholas, hearing later of my question, had laughed and taken me upstairs and pointed out one of the beams. "There it is, Kit. The hanging beam. Take a good look at it and beware! They say that every fifty years or so a Trelawny will hang him or herself from this. And the time is about due for another!" Then he had laughed and run down the rickety stairs, slamming the door at the foot shut, leaving me up there in the dusk with the rafter, the ghosts, and my own imagination.

"What stuff!" I said aloud to myself now. I would turn loose my commune up there, to see what they could create out of the broken odds and ends. I would —what was the fashionable word?—demythologize these attics, deghost them, exorcise the spirits of all the Trelawnys, living and dead and perhaps—who knew? —start a school.

Talking to myself in loud cheerful tones, I made my way to the entrance of the north wing. There was more than just a touch of whistling in the dark to my noisy passage. When I had pushed open the dormer windows in the center attic, there was a rush of wings deep within the eaves of the roof. Obviously I had disturbed bats. I shut the window rather rapidly, fighting the temptation to run. When, a little later, I heard a scuffling among the boxes on the floor, I liked it even less. The prospect of rats was even more daunting than the bats. Never mind, I thought, forcing my mind to the only possible silver lining, what a stalking ground this would be for Josephine. Resolutely I pushed open the door into the attics of the north wing and promptly cracked my head as I stepped down under a lower roof into a smaller attic.

I stood for a minute, holding my head and seeing stars. Then I looked around me in some amazement. Plainly the attics of the north wing were quite different from those of the south and the center. I was in a small, low room, almost empty. Here the attic, instead of running the length of the building, was divided into small cubicle-like rooms, of which some had low ceilings, while others appeared to go up to the rafters. Walking through the first room, I came into another, also small, and with a dormer facing inland. To my right was another door that opened into yet another room and then through another. Following these doors I found myself turned around. Some of the rooms had no windows, being lit only by a light turned on by a switch near the door, so I no longer knew which way I faced. After walking in and out of what seemed like an extraordinary number of rooms half-filled with odd bits of furniture, I didn't know whether I had crossed the entire north wing into the far extension—the north arm of the E at right angles to the wing—or not. It was disturbing and a little frightening. Even odder were the acoustics; my steps sometimes seemed to have echoes.

There had to be another staircase down, I thought, standing still and trying to get my bearings. But somehow, as I again went in one door and out another, this time trying to backtrack, I couldn't even seem to find where I had originally stepped into the wing.

"This is ridiculous," I said aloud, and at that moment two things happened. I stumbled against an old, dust-covered footstool, and I heard a noise behind me. I whirled around, kicking the stool halfway across the small room and raising a fog of dust. But there was nothing behind me except yet another door. Had I come through that? A few feet from the first door was a second. Or was it the second door I had come through?

I stood quite still, trying to orient myself. Then I went over to a small opening—it could hardly be called even a dormer window—and peered out. There lay the sea. Far north the coast curved out again, ending in a pile of rocks and a lighthouse. I must have been tired, or perhaps it was the sight of the sea, but I sat there on the small windowseat, looking at the ocean and thinking about that noise. Acoustics, I reminded myself again, were strange things. My foot had struck the old stool. Couldn't the sound have ricocheted off the wall and returned to me as the noise from behind me? My mind, perhaps in deliberate contrast to my mother's, had always been pragmatic and analytical, and I set it to try to define what that sound was: a foot against a hard object? The crack of leather against wood? No, it was neither of those things. But further than that I could not go.

I got up. "This is all rubbish," I said, and promptly went over to both doors and, arbitrarily choosing the left, went through it. This led through a windowless room into another room with a tiny opening, this time facing inland into the woods. At the far side of that room was a second door. I went through that down three steps and into a short corridor. At one end to my right was a small window facing the sea. At the other, a door. Facing me across the narrow hall was more old furniture: a table, a chair with a broken leg and an old clothes press. The door must, I decided, lead down to the third floor and out of this attic that was beginning to seem oddly like a prison. I also felt that I had traversed the roof of Trelawny's Fell not once but many times, and I was exceedingly tired of it.

But when I went over and tried to open the door, it wouldn't budge. It was a much heavier door than I had thought, looking at it from across the hall, and it was firmly locked.

Irritated out of proportion, I shook the door handle, but I might well have saved my energy: it didn't even rattle. By this time I was aware of another feeling that I did not like at all: alarm. Anything was better than just standing there. So, resolving to find the key to that locked door before I did anything else when I got downstairs, I started to go back the way I came in. But it proved easier in plan than in execution.

Trying to remember which doors I had gone through, I went from room to room, up two steps, down three, up again one, down four. Doors I was quite sure I had opened, and left open, were now shut. Tiny windows that I was sure faced front, faced back. Finally I came to the door through which, I was quite sure, I had come from the center building. There were the low-ceiling edge and the three steps up. With a bound I went up the three steps and tried to wrench open the door. That, too, was locked.

I stood in the middle of the floor and put my hands to my head. "Think!" I told myself. "Don't panic—think!" But all I could think was that it was in the north wing—this wing—that I had seen the curtain with the hand around the edge of it, move.

If I allowed the thought that there might be somebody in the wing, or worse, up here in the attic with me now, locking the doors around me so that I would be captured in my own house, I would be in serious trouble. "The funny farm for you, my girl," I said and bent my mind to recall some kind of floor plan. I had got in: ergo, I could get out. "Think, you idiot, think!" I muttered. As though in answer came one of the most beautiful and normal sounds I had ever heard: the cough and mutter of a rather old car. Going to the tiny porthole of a window, I stooped down and looked out to see Simon emerge from his rather ancient vehicle drawn up in front of the rear entrance.

"Simon," I yelled as loudly as I could. He turned, looking around.

"Up here, Simon. Up here!"

Eventually his eyes found me. He looked startled. "What's the matter, Miss Trelawny?"

51

"I can't get out. Can you come and rescue me?"

A slow grin spread over his face. "All right. I'll be there."

I added, *sotto voce,* as he let himself in the rear door, "And it's not that funny!"

A few minutes later I was meekly following the caretaker as he led me back through what seemed like a labyrinth through a door and down some stairs to the third floor.

3

"The trouble is," Simon said as we came down the final staircase to the main entrance hall, "that you crossed over into the second north wing—the extension at the end of the first—without realizing it. It isn't really that complicated."

"But I didn't feel as if I had gone that far—just chased myself round in circles."

"Ah well, that's because you went around the corner, turned the angle of the extension."

"But then wouldn't I have seen something different out of one of the windows—the other extension, the south one, for example, or straight north into the woods?"

"Maybe you didn't notice. It's a large place," he added in a kindly voice that somehow made me want to kick him.

"Well, it's hardly Blenheim Palace," I pointed out rather sharply. The ease with which he had both found me and led me through a string of rooms, through a closed door down some narrow steps towards the north end of the first wing, did nothing for my *amour propre.* "And anyway, what about those locked doors? Those are what kept me from getting down."

"If you say two doors were locked, I guess they were." His tone was that of an adult humoring an hysterical child. He saw me opening my mouth again and said, "Come to think of it, one of those—the one at the end of the little hall which is in the end of the wing—is always locked. It's nothing but a broom closet. Trouble is, the key's lost and nobody's bothered about it for years."

"Well I'm going to bother about it. I don't like living with doors that I can't open. Is there a locksmith in the village?"

"There's Pete Bradford; he'll open it for you."

"Son of the grim female in the shop?"

Simon looked quickly at me. "Grim?"

"To put it politely. Hostile might have been more accurate."

"You're just not used to New Englanders' reserve."

"Is that what it is? Anyway, if he's related to her, I can't think he'd do anything to oblige me."

"Well, of course you'd have to pay him."

"I wasn't thinking of getting him up here as a personal favor. But you haven't answered my question. Is he that woman's son?"

"Grandson," he said finally.

"Oh." I remembered the girl who had come into the store and who had called Mrs. Bradford, "Granny."

"Brother to a pretty girl who works in the store?"

Simon started moving down the big hall to the rear door. "That's right. Call me if you need anything else."

Belatedly I remembered my manners. "Thank you for coming to my rescue. Can't I offer you some food or drink or something? I really am grateful."

A smile relaxed his rather severe face. "Another time. I have to get back to finish a couple of things before evening."

* * *

Dr. Seaward arrived promptly at five. By that time I had removed all the dust covers in the main rooms on the ground floor and had lit the fire laid in the fireplace in the sitting room. I had also found my way to the huge kitchen and made some tea and was sipping it in the sitting room when he rang the bell.

He eyed the huge silver teapot on the silver tray which, in a moment of defiance, I had decided to use.

"I haven't seen that in many years," he said pleasantly.

"Do you think it's audacious of me? I was feeling a little cowed, and I thought it might boost my morale."

"Cowed?" He sat down in the big winged chair opposite me. "I find that hard to imagine."

"You should have seen me a couple of hours ago." I hadn't meant to mention my getting lost in my own attic, but I found myself making a funny story of it to the sympathetic man on the other side of the fireplace. "I think the thing that gets me is that it was so *shaming,* having to call in Simon. Like a scared child. By the way, wouldn't you rather have a drink? There's Scotch over there, or the makings of a martini."

"I'll start with tea. As I told you, I find your sitting there behind that pot singularly reassuring." He paused. "It might even be old Mrs. Trelawny herself."

I handed him his cup and decided to let that comment go by. To me it was anything but a compliment, but he couldn't know that, and I had no desire to tell him why.

"She was quite a woman," the doctor continued, innocent of my disapproval. "A *grande dame* of the old school. A relative to be proud of."

I put the pot down. "I am not related to the—to old Mrs. Trelawny—in any way. As I am sure you know, since you knew the family, I am descended from a ne'er-do-well who went west, probably fleeing the police, more than a hundred years ago."

"But Mrs. Trelawny was, herself, a Trelawny. Didn't you know that?"

I stared at him blankly. "No."

He stirred his tea and took a swallow. "The Trelawnys had a way of marrying their cousins, which is why the strain of twins kept cropping up again and again. Anyway, she was the granddaughter of a New England Trelawny who had married an English Trelawny in Cornwall, where he had gone to look up family records. She was probably a remote cousin herself, the grandmother, I mean. They remained over there, and Chris—Chrétien Trelawny, the husband of the late Mrs. Trelawny, and father of the current twins—met her over there when he was studying as a Rhodes Scholar."

"That explains why her cousin—Hermione, I think she called her—was English. I took her accent—both their accents, I guess—to be super-Bostonian, but of course I had never been anywhere but Wyoming, and the New England way of talking was strange enough to account for any difference."

He smiled. "You know, despite your coloring, you remind me a little of her. There's a Trelawny look about you."

"I hope not. I really don't have the slightest desire to be like the late Mrs. Trelawny."

He held out his cup for more tea. "I take it you weren't her most fervent admirer? Why is that?"

As I pretended to concentrate on pouring his tea I acknowledged that he had succeeded in asking the question I didn't want to discuss. "Oh," I passed him the milk and sugar, "she was rather haughty for a child to feel at ease with. I was very much of a country mouse."

"You know," he said, smiling at me, "I find that hard to believe."

"Did you find her sympathetic?" In asking that, I had really just batted the ball back into his court. But when he didn't answer right away, I looked up.

"You must know," he said in an oddly formal way, "that when I was a boy I had a king-sized crush on her. She could be"—he hesitated—"charming isn't a strong enough word. Compelling isn't right either. But it's nearer. Perhaps you didn't see that side?"

"I knew it was there. But it was never turned in my direction." I decided to change the subject. "Tell me about yourself. Have you always lived around here?"

"Yes. Born and brought up. My father was doctor here before me, and I prefer the slower pace. I trained, you know, in New York, and had a kind of worm's-eye view of medical practice there. The more I saw of it, the more I decided that country living, however bucolic, held more charm for me than city practice. Besides—"

"Besides what?"

"Well, you have more time for other things—interests. Dad, for instance, wrote a couple of books."

"Oh? What about?"

"His hobby, genetics. Twins especially. His book's in the library here. Have you inspected it yet?"

"No, I'm afraid all I've done is get lost in the attics."

He laughed and got up. "I have an old and bed-ridden patient to see yet this afternoon, so I'd better be off. Thanks for the tea." He got up.

I saw him to the door.

"By the way," he said as he was going out, "is what I hear true? That you're going to make this into a kind of artists' colony? A commune?"

He was standing with his back to the evening light so I couldn't see his face, which I regretted. Because I had a strong feeling that that question was not as casual nor as much of an afterthought as it sounded.

"Yes, I plan to. I am expecting the first contingent this week. Does that horrify you?"

"A little, maybe. I wouldn't like to see this house ... but then I'm sure you wouldn't allow that."

"Allow what?" Deliberately I moved out of the door so that he would have to turn towards me and I could see his face. It was a good idea, especially if it had worked. But it didn't. He did indeed turn so that the light was on his face, but the only expression I could read there was wry self-mockery. "I guess I'm too much the unreconstructed establishmentarian. The idea of the counter-culture rampaging over The Fell frightens the pants off me."

"They're not Attila and his legions," I said dryly. "Although"—I eyed his short haircut, tweed jacket and subdued tie over a white shirt—"their style of dress and coiffure may make you think so." I added lightly, more as a joke than anything else, "The tide of revolution must come even to farthest Maine, you know."

There was a moment's silence. The doctor's face, looking even more stolid than usual, showed absolutely nothing. But I had the feeling that he was weighing something in the balance. Then he gave his cheerful smile. "You're undoubtedly right. It'll probably do us all a lot of good. May I drop by again?"

"Of course, Doctor. Who knows, we may need your services." I said it as a pleasantry, having (mercifully) no idea of what a queer twist fate would lend to that light-hearted rejoinder.

"Any time. By the way, please call me Bill. Practically everybody does except those under eight and over eighty."

"All right, Bill. If you put it like that. Nobody would take me for under eight. And I don't wish to be thought over eighty."

He laughed and got into his car.

After I had washed up the tea things and poked around the kitchen, I made a half-hearted attempt to find Josephine, calling her as I walked from room to room. But after going over the first two floors of the main building, and calling through the doors leading into both wings, I decided that she would have to make her own way back in her own good time. Going to the pile of miscellaneous junk that I had left in the main hall, for want of a better place, I got out the two pans I had brought for her and the sack of litter. One I filled and carried up to my own bathroom. The other I left, for tonight, in the hall itself, sitting on a thick layer of newspapers.

I was about to go back to the kitchen when I remembered Bill's mention of the library, which, I knew, lay on the opposite side of the hall from the sitting room. Like the sitting room, it ran the width of the house, with windows at either end and books lining the other two walls. I stared at the shelves going up to the ceiling and the little ladders that rested against each side. Below were armchairs and a big kneehole desk. My eyes went back to the books. I have never been adept at calculating numbers, and I had no idea how many there were. But several thousand was a safe guess and I wondered if there were a catalogue, as in many English private homes. Idly, I opened the drawers of the desk. In the shallow middle drawer was a booklet, *Catalogue of Library*. I flipped through: *Books by Title, Books by Author*. I turned the pages more slowly. There, under T, was a whole column of books about twins. As my eye went down the list of authors it was caught by the name William Brent Seaward, M.D. Following the name was a catalogue number.

57

Vaguely amused that the Trelawnys were so pre-occupied with their genetic eccentricity, I put the catalogue back. Sometime I would look at the book. But in my list of priorities it ranked rather low—considerably lower, for example, than dinner, my need for which was beginning to clamor. I left the library, turning out the light. Another time, I thought, and made my way to the kitchen.

Unlike all the heroines I have ever read about, I have never been one in whom stress, fatigue, nerves or any other form of duress that I had ever encountered (except, perhaps, Mother's death) had produced lack of appetite. I was hungry, and all the more so for having missed lunch.

Forty-five minutes later I was having broth, broiled chicken and salad and drinking a glass of milk. Josephine still hadn't put in an appearance. The thought that she might have battled a rat and lost kept occurring to me, with increasingly depressing effects. So, as far as possible, I kept my mind off of it. Instead, I thought a great deal about that baffling maze of attics, like Chinese boxes opening around and out of one another, and about those two locked doors. They led my mind, straight as an arrow's flight, to the curtain that had moved in the far window of the north wing. It could have been the light. I had seen the shift of shadows on the other windows as I stood there. I knew that my imagination, for all its pragmatic bent, could take unfounded leaps. I also remembered that the house itself had always had an effect on me, as though it were a presence, something more than the total of stone and wood and plaster that comprised its parts. "Romantic rubbish!" I said aloud, and poured myself some coffee.

It was at that moment, sitting there, sipping coffee, staring into the dark outside the uncurtained and unshaded window, that I suddenly felt uncomfortable. I glanced up to see if there were a shade I could pull down. But there wasn't. I knew that window faced the sea, so that all that was, or should be, out there was a dozen yards of turf and the cliff edge, and a hundred feet below that, the sea. I stared, my sense of discomfort growing. For a moment I felt trapped, powerless, as though I were on a lighted stage, to which something outside was an audience. It was a situation I did not like. Deliberately I got up. Walking across the kitchen at my usual pace, I hurried through the other rooms, not turning on lights, until I came to the main hall. Then, opening the door facing the sea as quietly as I could, I went out.

This was the first moment since I had arrived that I had been on this side of the house. Away from artificial light, the night didn't seem quite as black as it had when I stared at it from a lighted kitchen. There were stars and, low on the horizon, a moon. I had pulled the door behind me almost shut and I stood there, listening. All I could hear was the shushing and lapping of the sea far below. Far to my left the light from the kitchen, which I had deliberately left on, poured a yellow wash out onto the grass. Anyone standing in its path would have been extremely visible. As far as I could see there was no one. But, made all the blacker by that light, were shadows beyond it. Besides, in the time I had run through several rooms, someone . . . anyone . . . could have taken flight around the other end of the house. If there had been anyone.

I stood there a while longer, relishing the stars, the thin moon, the sound of the water, the delicious smell of fresh air. Then I went inside again, locking the door behind me.

Going back to the kitchen, I took my few dishes over to the sink and poured water over them, intensely aware of the naked window, yet not feeling the discomfort that I had before. Nevertheless, I would leave the washing up until tomorrow morning, and tomorrow I would find a shade or curtain for that window. In case Josephine's hunts had been unsuccessful, I put down some dry food and a little milk. Then I picked up my bag and left the kitchen, turning out the light behind me. Back in the hall I made sure that the west main door, as well as the east, was locked. Then I went upstairs to my room. What I needed, I decided, was a long, hot bath.

An hour later I was in bed with the lights out. Through the open window came the cool night air. I was drowsy, tired, and, after my bath, relaxed. But it was a while before I went to sleep. Around me, like the

59

sea outside, stretched the silence of the enormous house. I wondered if I would ever get used to it. I also wondered if the four people who were going to share it with me were strong enough to have an effect on its atmosphere. I was still thinking about that when I went to sleep.

I don't know how long I had been sleeping when I woke up suddenly, my heart pounding, certain I had heard a noise. Leaning up on my elbows, I listened. There was a creak, as of old boards. I was wondering whether it were that noise that had waked me when there was a low cushiony "Chrrrrrp" and a plop on the bed.

"Josephine!" I said joyfully.

She marched up the bed and came to rub her head against my cheek. Her purr was so loud she sounded like one of the more polluting types of sports car. She also had a distinct and unfamiliar aroma. As we snuggled down together I said to her, "Where have you been, Josephine, and with whom?"

Later, just before I went to sleep again I thought I recognized that ordor.

"Good Josephine," I murmured sleepily. "You got a mouse!"

I was having breakfast in the kitchen the next morning when I heard a knocking somewhere in the direction of the larder. Following the sound, I went into the larder and located a door behind a screen and some washtubs. There was no key or bolt and the door opened when I turned the knob. On the other side was a large young man with a friendly grin.

"Simon said you wanted me to unlock some broom closet," he said pleasantly.

"Then you must be Pete Bradford."

He gave his amiable grin. "That's me."

I stood back, holding the door open. "You know, I didn't realize there was a door here. I haven't really had a chance to become familiar with everything. But since you came to this door, you must have been here before. Are there any other doors that lead out of the house other than the two main doors and this?

"Sure." He looked down at me. "Does that bother you?"

I made a face. "Not only had I not noticed this door before, I did notice that I didn't have to unlock it to open it. Maybe I've lived too long in New York, but the idea that there are more doors leading to the outside, probably unlocked, doesn't do anything for my sense of security."

He laughed then. "Nobody around here locks their doors."

I thought of all the portable treasures in the house. "Not even in this house?"

"Well, I wouldn't know about that too much. Nobody's lived here for about five years."

"But you knew what door to come to."

"I've done work for Simon."

I led the way through the larder into the kitchen. "What kind of work? And, by the way, how did you know I was in the kitchen?"

He put down the big toolbox he was carrying. "Process of elimination. I'd already knocked on the front door. If you'd been in that part of the house you'd have heard me. So I tried here. And I do general handy work, carpentry, hardware. That kind of stuff."

"All right. Let's go." I started towards the front of the house.

"Why don't we go up the steps here?"

I turned. "What steps?"

He looked surprised for a minute. Then he grinned. "I guess it does take time to find out all the nooks and crannies, doesn't it."

"Indeed yes," I said grimly. "I take it Simon told you about my little adventure yesterday."

He had the grace to blush. "Well—yes."

"I daresay it will be the village joke for a while."

"Well, you won't be the first."

"The first to get lost?"

"That's right."

I was immediately curious. "Who else had that experience?"

"Oh, nobody I know," he said. "Why don't I go ahead, since I know the way." And without waiting for

61

me to comment, he went back into the larder, wound his way through washtubs and a couple of old wringers, ducking under a network of clotheslines, and finally opened a door that was partially hidden by the tattered screen. "This way. No wonder you didn't know it was here." By this time I was through the door into a small passage, from which opened two other doors. One of these revealed a steep, narrow staircase. I followed him up that for what felt like three flights.

"Doesn't this staircase come out on the second floor?"

"No. Some of the stairs were built onto the ends of the old walls before the extensions were built. At least, that's what I gather. Anyway, they go straight up." With that he opened a door and stepped into what was obviously an attic room. Overhead were rafters. Dormer windows looked up the coast on one side and straight over to the lower arm of the E on the other.

"I've never been up here," I said, staring around. "I'm positive I didn't see this yesterday."

"Well, you could easily have missed it." He marched towards a door at the end. "You can only get here by that stair we used. There's no way into the rest of the house."

"Why not?"

"Well . . ."—he sounded a little surprised at the question—"that's the way it's built."

And with that he went through the door and left me to follow. As far as I could make out we were going back towards the main part of the house, that is, the north wing. But before I could be sure, my guide opened another door and—I could hardly believe it— we plunged down another set of narrow stairs.

"This may seem a little confusing to you," he said over his shoulder.

" 'Confusing' hardly describes it. Why are we doing this?"

"To get to that door you described."

"Yes, but—why do we have to come down again? That was up in the attic floor."

"Yeah. But there's no way straight across there." He grinned at the look on my face. "You know this isn't that different from a lot of old New England houses—

62

just bigger. My grandmother has a house like this—you can't get to all the attics on the same floor. It's because people built without any real design—just added on pieces here and there when the notion took them."

By this time we were on the third floor in a hall I hadn't seen—I could have sworn—passing bedrooms that I also hadn't seen, although with their low ceilings and bowls and pitchers and narrow iron cots they looked similar to the ones I had examined the day before. Before I could ask any more questions, he opened a door at the end of the hall and passed into the floor that I *had* seen, went up yet another staircase into the attics that seemed familiar from yesterday, and without a trace of hesitation, went through the labyrinthine maze of cubicle-like rooms, opened a door, and there was the little hall with a window at one end and a door at the other and a table and broken chair along the wall opposite. "There's the door," he said unnecessarily and went over to it.

Putting his toolbox down, he opened it and took out the largest bunch of keys I have ever seen in my life.

"Are those keys for The Fell?"

"Some of them. Others are just keys I've picked up that don't fit anything, but there's no reason not to give them a try." And he proceeded to do just that.

I went over and stood beside him. "That door felt awfully heavy for just a closet door."

He didn't look up, but kept on fitting one key after another into the old-fashioned keyhole. "I guess they do to you, ma'am. But they built doors and walls to last in those days."

"In that case, all the doors we've come through would be heavy. But some of them are quite light."

"I guess those were added later, when they stopped building for eternity." About a dozen keys later he said, "Eureka! I knew I'd find it somewhere in this bunch." With that I heard the sound of a lock, stiff with rust, finally turn. He grasped the knob and pulled open the door.

Inside was exactly what Simon had said: a broom closet, filled with brooms, mops and rags of every age and generation. The closet couldn't have been more than five feet wide and three deep. With an irritation that I could hardly understand myself, I stepped inside and looked at the stained walls behind the broom handles, and cloths hanging from hooks and nails, and ran my hands over the walls themselves. I felt every portion of the three walls that were within my reach and stared up at the ceiling. "Is there a small ladder anywhere?"

"Sure. What do you want it for?"

"I want to examine that ceiling."

"What do you think you're going to find?"

Feeling foolish as well as irritated did nothing for the sweetness of my temper. "Please do as I ask, Mr. Bradford."

"Okay." And off he went, his large boots clumping through the attics and down the stairs. After that, the sound faded. While he was away I felt the walls again and thumped them with my fists. They were so solid I couldn't even get a *thunk* out of them. In a surprisingly short time Pete was back with an aluminum ladder. I stood on it and poked at the ceiling, first with the end of a broom handle, then, after climbing up another rung, with my hands.

"What's above there?" I asked.

"The roof."

"How can I get there?"

"Well, through some more stairs up another way."

"Is it a room?"

"No. Not really. Just a sort of crawlspace. Not even big enough for trunks."

I looked down into his face. "Have you been up there?"

"Sure. Simon had me go up there not long ago to put down rat poison."

Despite myself I shuddered. I really don't like rats. "I'd like to see it now," I said firmly.

"Okay. But you'll get pretty dirty."

"What I have on can get washed," I said rather curtly. I could just imagine what a story this would be for the delectation of the village. ". . . And after lookin' at that broom closet, closed since I don't know when and solid as a block of concrete, what does she have to do but go up into that crawlspace. You shoulda seen her when she came down! She sure didn't look much like city folks then. Whaddaya suppose she was looking for? Ghosts? . . ." followed by loud, raucous, bucolic laughter. . . .

Ha-ha, I thought. What I said was, "All right. Let's go."

Back through the maze, down onto the third floor of the north wing, up some more steps that I hadn't seen, opening from behind what I had thought was a cistern. These gave onto a small platform up which went a short ladder to a trapdoor. Pete went up the ladder and pushed open the door until the flap was entirely back. Then he pulled a large flashlight from his belt and peered into the dark. After that he came down.

"Okay. Be careful going up that ladder. Here's the flashlight. I'll follow." His face was so solemn I knew he was trying not to laugh. "Thanks," I said, all but snatching the light, and went up the stairs.

When my head rose above the floor level of the trapdoor I saw that, exactly as Pete had said, there was a long crawlspace. Even where the roof came to its peak I couldn't have stood. The flashlight was powerful and I shone it in every direction. Other than the beams and supports, all I could see were what were obviously rat traps.

"Caught any rats?" I asked.

"Some."

"I don't see any caught there now."

"I just put up fresh a few days ago. Besides the rats are getting smart."

"And this is above that broom closet?"

"Yes, and the other little rooms in that attic."

"Why on earth did they chop them up like that, and put a ceiling on top?"

"I don't know, miss. I guess they had a reason."

"I'm going up," I said, not because I thought there was anything there, but because I could imagine all too easily his grin when he finished his saga to an admiring audience by saying, "And guess what? She didn't go into the crawlspace after all that. I knew she wouldn't." Well, I'd show him.

It was very unpleasant crawling around up there with the flashlight showing me what was in front but hearing nothing in the back of me except scrabbling feet and an occasional squeak, speeding, no doubt, away from the intruder. I gritted my teeth and went on, passing several large and still baited traps, and one or two that had been sprung unsuccessfully. My overactive imagination produced the picture of all the rats, mother, father, the lot, their teeth bared, laughing at me. But beyond the traps and a lot of dirt there was absolutely nothing. Just as Pete said.

I crawled out and backed down the ladder, pulling the flap after me. When I got to the bottom, I examined my knees.

"Isn't it lucky that jeans wash?" I said.

"Yes'm."

I looked at him, and suddenly, we both burst out laughing.

"All right, Macduff. Lead on downstairs. I'm sure there are whole areas of those attics I know nothing about. And I don't like it one bit. But right now there's nothing I can do about it. Is there?"

"No. And I don't know about any attics that you haven't seen yet."

"But then, you don't know what I have seen, do you?"

"No," he said, as though I had produced a dazzling riposte, "I guess not."

When we got back to the kitchen, Josephine was on the table, happily licking the butter.

"Sorry, Empress," I said, picking her up and putting her on the floor.

Josephine gave me an angry stare, then walked, tail up, towards Pete. Her ears slightly back, she sniffed around both his legs. Then she looked up and spat.

"I guess she doesn't like me," Pete said. "Or maybe it's my dog."

"Don't feel unique. She doesn't like anybody. And her manners are terrible."

He moved towards the back door. "Do you want me for anything else, ma'am?"

"Yes. Please put a lock on every door that doesn't have one. And show me where the other doors are."

Twenty minutes later I had been shown no fewer than five doors leading outside, only two of which had any kind of lock.

"I'll have to go back and get the locks," Pete said.

"All right. But do you think you can put them on today?"

"You expecting unwelcome company?"

"You know how nervous we females are," I said, deadpan, expecting agreement.

A slow grin spread over his face. "If you say so."

"All right, Pete. Put it down to my city upbringing. But please put on the locks."

I spent the rest of the week before the first of my paying guests—Tess Farranicci and Frank Morse, who were coming together—were due to arrive, going over the house, deciding which rooms I would use and which I would close off, and moving some of the more obviously frail and valuable furniture and *objets d'art* out of the way of immediate and potentially destructive traffic.

A day early I looked out the window and there, coming up the stone path, staggering under sizable packs, were three figures: Frank, Tess, and, not altogether to my surprise, Jeremy.

"I thought I'd help them settle in," Jeremy said engagingly while he was still ten feet from the front door. "How's my apartment?"

"Super. Everything in order."

I wondered how near the truth that was and stepped back to let them enter. The largest of the three packs, I noticed, was carried by Tess. Somehow I did not think she had suddenly had a burst of femininity and acquired a wardrobe. Today she had on jeans and a T-shirt inside of which her childish breasts didn't look much larger than two mosquito bites. But if that mountainous pack contained more of Tess's clothes than a change of T-shirts and the granny dress, I would have been considerably surprised.

I waved towards the pack she was lowering carefully to the floor. "Your wardrobe?"

"Not exactly." Her huge brown eyes looked over to Frank.

"My painting gear's pretty bulky," he said importantly. "I didn't want to get started and then find I'd left something I needed in the Village."

"No, of course not. That would be disastrous. I am so glad Tess was able to bring it."

I waited to see if he'd take offense and leave, removing Tess with him, and reflected that if I wished to hang onto my colony, I'd better discipline my sarcasm. But I needn't have bothered. As I was to learn, Frank wore aural as well as visual blinders. Anything that did not immediately serve his comfort and convenience simply glanced off.

"Where's the studio?" he asked now.

"I'll take you up there."

I had decided that the big central attic would be the ideal studio. In addition to the large dormer windows, there was, I had discovered, a skylight.

Jeremy was looking around him. "Wow! Cousin Kit, this is really some house. It's super."

"Yes. It will be a pleasant place for you to visit from time to time." I knew that if Jeremy had made up his mind to stay up here, there was little, including forbidding him to do so, that would prevent him. No matter how much of a manipulator I knew him to be, I would find myself accepting the inevitable. But at least I would postpone it as long as I could.

He produced a particularly guileless smile. "That's what I was thinking."

Frank was slipping on his pack again as he looked around. "Yeah, it must have taken a couple dozen slaves to keep this place up."

I glanced over to him. "To my knowledge, Frank, Maine was not a slave state."

"Underpaid exploited labor. Same thing."

Tess, bent almost double, was sliding the big pack onto her back.

"Don't try to carry that upstairs, Tess," I said. "The boys can take it up later."

Tess said quickly, still struggling to balance it. "I don't mind taking it up."

"But I do. That's not a woman's job."

"That's the kind of attitude that has kept women enslaved," Frank said. "There's been a sexual revolution. Didn't you know? We believe in sexual equality."

"In that case, why is she carrying the heavier pack?"

Jeremy stepped forward hurriedly. "I'll take it," he

volunteered, and started pulling it off Tess. "Kit's right, Frank. It's a lot heavier than ours. I'm sorry I didn't notice."

Frank had wandered into the living room and was looking at the portraits. I braced myself for a brisk talk on the counterrevolutionary aspects of portraits of (undoubtedly) exploiters of the poor. But after looking very carefully at each, especially at those of the twins, he simply came back to where we were standing waiting for him at the foot of the stairs.

I couldn't resist asking, "How did you like them?"

"They're okay—if you like that sort of thing. Ancestorworship and all that." I saw his eyes move again to the portrait of the most recent twins, Giles and Nicholas, that hung straight across from the double doors and could be seen from where we were in the hall. "Jeremy told me they were killed in Vietnam, but that one of them saw the light before he died—defected to the North Vietnamese." He looked me straight in the eye. "That true?"

"I didn't say it that way," Jeremy protested.

Frank's eyes were so dark and so deep set it was hard to see any expression in them. He was not a bad-looking boy, or he wouldn't have been if he had cut off about a pound of hair and washed what was left. I wasn't against long hair per se. But I admitted to a strong prejudice in favor of clean hair over dirty.

I said, "I know no more than anyone else," and reflected that I sounded like Mr. Edgerton.

"That'd be a great end for a family like this, wouldn't it?"

"But it's not ended," I replied sweetly. "I'm here."

He shrugged and went past me to the stairs. At that moment I was regretting accepting Jeremy's recommendation of Frank. Jeremy, his ESP working on all cylinders, must have picked this up, because he said, "Come on, Frank. Cut the political crap. You're supposed to be here to paint."

"That's no reason why he shouldn't express his opinion," Tess flared up. Tess who, I was sure, would agree with every revolutionary word uttered by her exploiter, and who considered herself a dedicated radical, nevertheless exemplified the real saboteur of any women's liberation movement: she was a naturally docile female who found her identity through the man who dominated her.

"None at all," I said, leading the way upstairs. "Nevertheless, in the interests of communal peace, let's keep arguments to a minimum." I turned on the top stair and faced them. "Okay?"

"Okay," Jeremy said loudly.

Tess looked at Frank. Frank stared back at me. My feeling that I had made a mistake in accepting him increased.

I gave him back his stare. "Frank?"

"Okay," he said noncommittally.

"Tess?" The girl certainly did not seem bellicose. But I wanted the agreement to be general.

She was still looking at Frank. "Okay."

Before we went up to the studio I showed them their rooms. I put Frank and Tess opposite one another and braced myself for a fight. But somewhat to my surprise there was no objection. Jeremy I put opposite me. Then I led them all up to the big central attic.

"Here's your studio," I said.

They stood around under the skylight and the great rafter and stared.

"It's *huge*," Tess said.

"Good light," Jeremy added.

Frank said nothing for a while. He walked around looking through dormers, at the chests and furniture and paintings and carpets that I had pushed to opposite ends of the attic.

"What's through there and there?" he asked, pointing to the doors to the north and south wings. He went over and tried the door leading into the north wing. "It's locked," he said.

"That's right. The attics through there are lower. They have no skylight and they're chopped up into small rooms."

"You got the family treasures there?"

I sighed. "No, Frank. The family treasures—such as they are—are on display downstairs where anybody can see them. But the caretaker had to come and rescue me when I got lost in the attics, and I don't want to have to send out search parties for any of you."

70

Frank shrugged and moved back towards us. He pointed to the door to the south wing. "That locked, too?"

"Yes."

He poked around for a bit, staring up at the skylight.

"Everything okay?" I asked, trying not to sound too heavily ironic.

"Yeah. I guess so. I'll get my stuff."

I felt as though I had passed some kind of exam.

That afternoon Pete Bradford arrived with several more chickens and some groceries. Frank and Tess happened to be in the kitchen drinking coffee when he knocked on the larder door. I invited him in and introduced him to the others and watched their reactions to one another with some amusement. They were all in their twenties, with Pete probably about twenty-two and Frank about five to six years older and Tess coming somewhere in the middle. And there any commonality ended. Pete's hair was not a crewcut, but it was short, with no sideburns, and despite his stained and calloused workman's hands, he looked scrubbed. Frank, until one noticed he was somewhat older, looked like anyone's model of a radical student of the late sixties, which was indeed what he had been, and Tess his female counterpart. To Frank and Tess, Pete must have looked the total hardhat who happened, at that moment, not to be wearing a hardhat.

"Hi," Pete said awkwardly, and looking as though he were confronting strange mammals from an unknown continent. It suddenly struck me that he was seeing in the flesh what he had probably, until then, only watched on television.

"Hello," Tess said shyly.

Frank didn't say anything.

Pete put the box of groceries down on the table, fished out the list and handed it to me. "Granny said she'd send the potatoes up later. They're due to be coming in from the farm later today."

"Sorry you have to make two trips."

"That's all right. If it's okay with you, I thought I'd go and check on the traps in the crawlspace."

"What crawlspace?" Frank asked, taking a raw carrot out of the box and biting off a piece, dirt and all.

71

"An area between one of the attics and the roof," I replied, and then to Pete, "Yes, do. I don't want bodies decomposing up there."

Pete grinned. "No, that's what I thought."

Frank said, "I'll go with you."

There was an odd little pause. For some reason that I had no time to figure out, I didn't want Frank to go ranging over the house with Pete. My hesitation was only in the interests of the most tactful way of explaining this. But for a second a look of dismay flashed over Pete's face, changing it subtly. For a second he looked older and, in some indefinable way, different. But before I could pin down the expression, his face resumed its almost vacuous good nature as he turned to me questioningly. "Some of those rats are rabid. I know, because we've had others tested. That's one reason I'm anxious to get them out. It'd be a pity if somebody, one of your guests, got bitten while they're staying with you."

"Since I carry no insurance for that sort of thing, it would indeed," I agreed heartily. "Sorry, Frank."

"Look, I'm not scared of being bitten. I've been around rats before. The building my loft was in was full of them."

"That was your responsibility, Frank. As long as you're here it's mine." I didn't add that I wouldn't make a penny bet on Frank's not suing me if he did indeed get bitten. Somehow I felt sure five minutes would not have passed before he got on the telephone with his attorney. I was about to add that the attics in the wing were out of bounds when, luckily, it came to me that there was no surer way of ensuring that Frank would be exploring every nook and cranny before dusk.

Tess suddenly spoke up. "I hate the idea of traps for animals. I think it's cruel." Her velvety dark eyes, taking up what seemed at least half of her face, glowed with indignation.

I saw Pete look at her as though he were seeing her for the first time. She was an extremely pretty girl. Red crept up into his fresh face.

"I agree," I said. "But it's either them or Josephine, my cat, who can—and will—go anywhere she thinks there's a rat."

"They'd bite her to pieces," Pete said. "And if people are going to live in this house again, the rats have to go."

Tess stared at him and then let out a sigh. "I guess so. But I still hate traps. Isn't there any other way?"

"I don't like traps, either, for any other creature. But these traps don't maim or just injure. Either the rat gets away or he's dead, instantly."

"I'll take you upstairs," I said.

One of the questions implicit in Pete's discouragement of Frank was now preoccupying me as we went up two flights of stairs. "How come you didn't tell me about the rabies before, Pete? Didn't you care whether I got bitten or not?"

"Sure I did. But it was your house, and I didn't think you'd be suing yourself."

"I wouldn't," I admitted. "Still, I might have gotten bitten while I was crawling around up there."

By this time we were on the third floor heading towards the steps up to the platform and the ladder beneath the crawlspace.

"You wouldn't have been," Pete said. "The rats were more afraid of you than you of them. Anyway, that's why I went up there first, to make sure they weren't up there holding a meeting."

"Then why wouldn't that be true of Frank—that they'd be more afraid of him than he of them?"

Pete paused under the ladder. "Did you want him to come up here?"

"No."

Again the grin. "That's what I thought."

"So you were deliberately discouraging him?"

"Sure. I thought you wanted me to."

That was entirely true. But I was somehow surprised that Pete picked it up. I liked Pete. There was a rock-like reliability about him. But I wouldn't have graded him high on perception.

I was still thinking about this when he went up the ladder, pushed open the trapdoor, and went through. Feeling superfluous, I hung around. In a few minutes his face appeared.

"The traps are full. I've got to rebait them and find out if there are any bodies that got away."

I stared up into his face. "I thought you said they were either dead or free and clear."

It seemed to me that those apple cheeks above me got redder. "I didn't want Miss Farranicci worrying."

Pete, I reflected, would not have given Tess the bigger pack to carry.

"Okay. I'll leave you to it."

It was an hour later that he came back downstairs into the kitchen, holding a canvas bag.

I looked at the bag. "Bodies?"

He nodded. "I'm going to take these off to the lab at the vet's. I'll be back tomorrow."

I had had that hour to think about the full implications of rabid rats around the house. "Look, I'm not at all happy about this situation. I don't want Josephine, who can go anywhere a rat can, getting bitten and going mad and biting everybody and they dying of hydrophobia, poor little thing. What are the odds about the wretched rats being able to turn up somewhere else?"

"Yeah. I was thinking about that. If it's okay with you I'd like to go over the house to make sure there aren't any holes they can come through. I did this about six months ago. But they can chew through stuff you wouldn't believe. I'll come every morning early so I won't be in the way. I don't think you're in danger on the first two floors. There are no holes there. I checked. Like I said, the rats are more afraid of you than you are of them. I'm pretty sure there aren't any new holes. Just want to make sure. Don't worry about Josephine. I'm sure she'll be okay."

"That's not what you said to Frank."

He smiled. "Yeah, well, maybe I played it up a little."

The trouble was, I couldn't be sure what game he was playing, or why, and I was worried about Josephine. But there was absolutely nothing I could do about it.

Frank and Tess settled in with less fuss than I had feared. That evening, without being asked, Tess turned up in the kitchen, and the meal that resulted on the table was an improvement over what I alone would have produced.

"Where did you learn to cook like this?" I asked

74

Tess, tasting a dish consisting of cucumbers and mushrooms with cheese.

Tess mumbled something.

"From your mother?" I persisted.

"It's time to take the bread out of the oven," Tess said. "Will you make the salad or shall I?"

I decided that she must be ashamed of her background and not to pursue the matter further. Silly child, I thought.

Two mornings later there was a sound like an approaching helicopter. I put down my shopping list, went to the rear hall door and saw a bright red MG snorting and muttering to itself at one side of the cobblestone apron. Rod Moscovitch, I thought, and sensed, rather than heard, windows opening far above me. Stepping out I looked up. One dormer window in the central attic was filled with Jeremy, another with both Frank and Tess.

But I was wrong. The little car door flew open and out poked a pair of immensely long legs that seemed to come in sections like those of a centipede. The legs were followed by a raincoat topped by a head wearing an enormous pair of glasses and straight mouse-colored hair.

"I'm terribly sorry," said an overwhelmingly well-bred voice. "Is it the right day? I couldn't quite be sure. Have I come at the wrong time?"

I moved forward. "Miss Butler-Longman?"

"Yes. Only everybody calls me Pogs."

I tried to ignore the fact that my stomach seemed to be sinking down into my intestinal system. I will kill Mr. Edgerton, I thought, and smiled. "No, not at all. I'm delighted to see you. Your room is ready. Let me help you with your bags."

It was the wrong thing to say. Distress swept the plain, bony face several inches above me (Ye gods, I thought, she is tall). "No, no, you mustn't," she almost wailed. And she rushed to the trunk, flung it open, and started hauling out bags, suitcases and what I took to be potting impedimenta. "I always carry everything myself."

As I watched, transfixed, she managed to load up

with two suitcases, three traveling bags and an easel. "Just show me where and I'll take these straight up. I don't want to be *any* trouble."

Left on the cobblestones were two small overnight bags. "I'll take these," I said firmly, ignoring the look of anguish on her face, "Just go ahead into the hall."

Viewed from behind she was like a stooped crane festooned with bags and suitcases of various sizes and with oddly shaped packages clamped under her arms.

Almost tripping over the shallow step up to the door, she blundered into the hall and stood there, looking like some huge bewildered bird. Then she saw the staircase. "Shall I go upstairs? I might as well, now I've got everything." Giving everything a hitch, she poked her head in the direction of the stairs and was about to follow it when there was an interruption. "Watch out!"

Frank, Tess and Jeremy, running along the second floor were bounding down the stairs. It was Frank who yelled, stopping halfway down the last flight and only a foot or so from the projecting end of the easel.

Miss Butler-Longman glanced up. "Oh, I'm frightfully sorry. How *stupid* of me. Blundering along like that without looking. Half a sec and I'll get right down and let you past."

"Jesus! Locust Valley lockjaw is with us!" It was Frank, of course, muttering but audible.

"How about you backing and letting her up with her things," I suggested. And then instantly regretted it, because it brought on a paroxysm of apology form the retreating Pogs.

"No, no, of *course* not. I wouldn't hear of it. I'll just get down—"

"Careful," I cried. But it was too late. Pogs, two suitcases, three canvas bags and the easel crashed to the bottom of the stairs.

"I'm absolutely all right," Pogs asserted, emerging from the wreck as Frank and Jeremy gathered up the suitcases and bags and Tess and I attempted to disentangle the long thin easel from her long thin legs.

"Need any help?"

We all turned and stared. Blocking the rear hall entrance was an enormous young man with blond hair and a curly blond beard. Behind him a second car was parked on the cobblestones. "I'm Rod Moscovitch," he said in a deep, chesty voice.

"How do you do?" I felt, somehow, that my hostess's responses were being strained to their capacity.

"I do very well," he replied, coming in. "But that's more than I can say for everyone. Pogs, you seem to have made a grand entrance."

I looked from one to the other. "You seem to know one another."

"Oh yes," Rod Moscovitch said easily. I turned to look at Mary. She was struggling to her feet, the exertion of which may have accounted for her very red face.

"It's quite all right. I don't need any help. Thank you very much." This was to Tess and Jeremy, who were handing her various packages.

I looked towards Rod Moscovitch. "I'm Kit Trelawny. Here, with the square package, is Tess Farranicci." I indicated the others. "Jeremy Andersen and Frank Morse."

"Hi," Jeremy said. Tess murmured "Hello." Frank gave him a sour look.

"Why don't we all help Mary up to her room with her things," I said.

"*Please* call me Pogs."

"All right. But what's wrong with Mary?"

"Well, it's what people—my friends—have always called me, and I *hate* Mary."

By this time the cavalcade was up on the second floor. Rod seemed to have acquired most of the suitcases, Jeremy was carrying the canvas bags, and Tess the packages. Frank had the easel.

I had originally planned to give the *soi-disant* Pogs the corner room on the north sea front, companion to my own corner room on the south sea front. Not, I assured myself, because she was a Butler-Longman of the blue blook, but simply because she was an unattached female. I was fairly sure by now that this would cause an uproar on more than one front, but I couldn't resist giving it a whirl.

"Pogs," I said, leading the way down the hall, "I've allotted you this room on the corner here," and I flung open the door and marched in. The others came in after me.

It was indeed a beautiful room. Originally it had had a whole side of windows looking north as well as those facing east. Attaching the wing had closed two of those windows, but one still remained, near the corner itself. Next to that now was a closet. Opposite the closet, as in my room, there was a fireplace and mantel. Over the mantel was a portrait of the dowager Mrs. Trelawny very much as I remembered her. Perhaps this was the reason I had chosen the southern rather than northern front room. I remembered too well those dark eyes sparkling with intelligence and malice to want to see them first thing in the morning. Instead of watercolors, there were more portraits, four of them, two on each side of the mantel.

"Wow!" Jeremy said.

"What is this?" Frank growled. "The master bedroom? I guess this comes under the heading of 'rank has its privileges.'"

I grinned. One of my predictions had come through. The other rapidly followed.

"Oh *no*," Pogs cried. "I'm sure this is somebody else's room. Please give me something less grand."

Jeremy was over looking at the portraits. "These are really good Early American, Cousin Kit. Who are they?"

"One is Giles Trelawny, circa 1820, and his wife. The other, on the right of the fireplace, is Chrétien Trelawny, circa 1845, and *his* wife."

"Chrétien. How *interesting*," Pogs said. "But not Christian?"

"No. For some reason the family never anglicized it."

"That's your name, isn't it, Cousin Kit? Chrétien?" Jeremy asked.

"Well—Chrétienne. Are you sure you don't want this room, Ma—Pogs?"

Tess, who was wearing a granny dress today and looking not unlike Mrs. Giles Trelawny, circa 1820, was poking into the closet. "These are some really cool clothes. Who do they belong to?"

"I don't know," I said. "I haven't investigated that closet yet. I've only been here a week and there's a lot

78

of unexamined stuff. Does it look like a man's or woman's clothes?"

"Both, I think."

I was about to go over when Pogs, who had left the room a few minutes before, stuck her head back inside. "I've found the dearest little room up some wee stairs at the end of the hall. Just right for me. May I have it?"

It was a third-floor room, of course, a former servant's room. I had toyed with the idea of putting all my commune up there and discarded it instantly as the kind of thing the dowager would have thought of, if she had allowed the thought of an artists' colony to enter her mind at all.

"Of course, if you prefer it. Are you sure?"

"Oh yes," she breathed. "So right!"

I went up the stairs behind her, expecting to turn left at the top into the narrow hallways from which opened off the third-floor rooms of the central building. But to my surprise, she turned right, going through the door that led to the third floor of the north wing, a door I had forgotten to lock.

"But that's—" I started to say, and saved my breath. She was already out of sight and sound. Feeling irritated and mildly dismayed, I followed her. It would have been hard to give a rational explanation for my reaction. I told myself that it was because I wanted to keep the occupied rooms in the central building, but even as the words formed themselves in my mind, I knew that it would be nearer to say I had developed a dislike of the north wing, and wanted it shut off and isolated.

"See!" Pogs said dramatically, standing in the door of a low-ceilinged room.

I went up to her and passed into the room. To me it seemed no different from any of the third-floor rooms except that it was barer and looked less comfortable. Most of the rooms had a bed, a washstand, chest of drawers, and easy chair. This had a cot, a rickety portable closet and a straight chair. That was all. Straight ahead, through the rather low windows, was the sea. It was a magnificent sight. But any third-floor room facing east would have shown the same. Plainly it was the austerity that appealed to her. And who was I to stand between her and the spartan discomfort she craved?

"If you want it, it's yours. But you'll have a long trek to the nearest bathroom. Either down to the second floor in this wing, or through to the central building third floor."

Her face screwed up again. "Will that be inconvenient? Oh I'm *so* sorry! Of *course*—"

"No!" I almost yelled. Then I walked over to her and put a hand on her shoulder. She jumped. I took my hand away.

"Listen," I said firmly. "Stop apologizing for living. If something you want or want to do is inconvenient, don't worry. I'll tell you."

"Am I making you nervous? I'm *terribly* sor—"

I fled down the hall, frightened for a moment that I would pick up the single chair and lower it over her head.

"Dear God," I breathed, my hand on the knob of the door leading out of the wing, "help me to have patience."

It was then, while I was standing there, trying to reassemble my nervous system, that I heard the footsteps over my head. They were firm but uneven and were going away from the central attic, not towards it. Then, suddenly, they stopped.

I had carefully locked every entrance to the north wing attics that I knew about, which did not mean that either Frank or Jeremy or both had not found a way to get in. It was the kind of thing they—or certainly Frank—would consider a challenge.

"Damn them!" I said to myself, and started down the stairs.

But I didn't get far. Just turning the corner from the second floor were Frank, Tess, Jeremy and Rod.

My heart gave a funny lurch and I stopped.

"What's the matter, Cousin Kit?" Jeremy said. "We're on our way to see Pogs's room."

"Nothing," I lied, my mind grappling with a suddenly very important question: who belonged to those footsteps?

4

I lay awake that night, thinking about those footsteps.

Most obviously they did not belong to any of my guests. This left either Simon, the caretaker, or Pete, both of whom had keys and both of whom had demonstrated that they could find their way through the north attics, an accomplishment that had so far proved beyond me.

Unfortunately, I had discovered it was neither of them by the simple act of telephoning as soon as I got downstairs. Simon had answered his own phone, and when he said, "Yes, Miss Trelawny, what may I do for you?" in that reserved New England way that I admire but that always leaves me feeling slightly snubbed, I hadn't any reasonable excuse at hand.

So I blurted out the truth, aware, after the fiasco of losing my own way in my own attic, that he would consider me an hysterical female. Which, of course, he did.

"Well now, Miss Trelawny, there's nothing strange about that. You've got a lot of people staying there."

"All of them were in the hall below me. I saw them not one minute after I heard the footsteps."

"Well, old houses have funny acoustics. You could have heard the echo of steps from somewhere else."

"Do you really believe that, Simon?"

"I wouldn't be saying it if I didn't." And I knew, by the huffy note in his voice, that I had offended him.

"I'm sorry, Simon. I didn't mean that the way it sounded. It's just, well—"

"I know, Miss Trelawny. Moving in so recently and with all those . . . those guests. . . ." (I could just imagine his careful choice of word for my benefit. I wondered what he would have used if he hadn't been watching his tongue. Had he seen them arriving from his house? Could he have seen them from his house?)

". . . and you have to keep an eye out with artistic types like that. . . ."

"Yes. Well, I will, Simon. Thank you anyway. I'm sorry if I sounded distracted."

"That's all right, Miss Kit."

Ah-ha! I thought, sounding bewildered and feminine had worked. Today's woman might despise my approach, but pragmatically speaking, it was a success. I had been promoted from Miss Trelawny to Miss Kit.

Then I called Pete. After he had been put on the telephone I told him bluntly about the footsteps.

"Yeah, I've heard those too, but after a while I discovered they came right after my own steps and were some kind of an echo. Had you been walking along the hall below?"

I had, of course, and admitted it.

"And did they stop suddenly?"

"Yes."

"Well, didn't you stop suddenly?"

"Yes."

"These old houses," Pete began, and got the full vial of my wrath.

"If anyone else talks to me about the whimsicalities of old houses, I'll have hysterics," I said. "Just as you all think I have, anyway."

"No, no," Pete said soothingly. "It's happened to me. Anybody could make that mistake."

I hung up rather abruptly.

"I guess I was rather rude to him," I said aloud up to the ceiling that night, as I lay in bed. And at that moment it struck me that I hadn't seen Josephine since early that morning, because it is usually Josephine I am addressing in those solitary soliloquies. Further, I remembered now, both her breakfast and her dinner had remained uneaten. I sat up in bed.

Moonlight poured into the room. It was not likely that Josephine was there without my knowing it, as she invariably announced herself with a "Chrrrrrrp" before she jumped on the bed, but I could see beyond any doubt that she wasn't.

Naturally, what I thought of next were Pete's rabid rats.

"Damn, blast and hell!" I said, getting out of bed. Maine nights, even in summer, are chilly. My nightgown, which was like a shirt that kept on going to my knees, felt like gauze. I put on my full-length robe and some soft-soled slippers. Then I plunged around in my drawers, looking for my flashlight. Next to the flashlight was a ring of keys that looked large enough for San Quentin. I put those in the pocket of my robe, carefully not thinking of the various doors they might open. Then I proceeded out of my room.

I walked the length of the hall calling softly and flashing the light into all empty rooms. Of course it was possible that Josephine had got trapped in a room that was occupied by one of my guests, but it was unlikely. A closed door to Josephine was a challenge, and she made such a clatter of complaint, and scratched at it so vigorously, that no one could, or would, keep her inside without her consent.

From the second floor I went to the third floor and looked in all the rooms. No Josephine. That left the third floor of the north wing, where Pogs might have incarcerated Josephine without knowing it—and the attic. I averted my mind from the latter and opened the door into the north wing corridor. Moonlight poured in from the ocean side, washing over the old uneven floorboards. Calling Josephine in a low voice I went from room to room, feeling rather like a ghost of myself. It was plain she wasn't anywhere on that floor. The rooms were bare, and if she had been there she would have been highly visible. I marveled again that Pogs should have chosen the room she did. Any of the others on that floor of the north wing would have been better. One even had a proper closet, which surprised me a little as I saw it. I went over and closed it, flashing my light behind the door that had stood half open.

Pogs herself, whom I saw through her open door, lay curled up like a woodlouse, whether for deep psychological reasons or, more practically, because the bed wasn't long enough. I reminded myself to ask her the next morning, and finally left that wing, shutting the door behind me. There remained the central attic.

I stood at the bottom of the stairs leading up there for a few minutes. But then I discovered that the longer I stood there the more reluctant I was to go up. "This won't do," I said to myself, and marching up the stairs, thrust open the attic door.

I had forgotten about the skylight, and so was unprepared for the moonlight that poured through it. I think I understood in that moment how the term "moon madness" came about and why the word "lunatic" derived from the moon. Standing there, an old nursery rhyme sprang into my mind:

> *Boys and girls come out to play,*
> *the moon doth shine as bright as day.*
> *Leave your supper, and leave your sleep,*
> *and join your playfellows in the street.*

But what playfellows? Nicholas and Chrétienne Trelawny, who had hanged themselves from that rafter? Who knew how many other Trelawnys had come up here to stand beneath the rafter and ponder about life and death?

It is hard to give any rational explanation for the feeling that was so powerful in me at that moment. But it was as though I were an intruder, had strayed by some clumsy accident out of my own time pattern into another.

The temptation simply to retreat through the door and go away was overwhelming. I was not afraid of the rats anymore, but I was afraid. I stood there, clutching the switched-off flashlight, looking at familiar objects, one by one, bathed in that fantastic light. Finally my eyes rested on Frank's easel, and in some way that broke the spell. It stood, angular and bleached, its shadow like an immense black arrow on the floor. It occured to me that though Jeremy had spoken of Frank's work with awe, and I had come across mention of his name here and there as a coming painter, I had never actually seen any of his work. Defiantly, I switched on the center light and went over.

I don't know what I expected—something vaguely fashionable and obscure and without definition. It was none of those things. As I looked, the strange lights and shadows assembled themselves into a portrait that grew and took shape, as though I were watching the painter in the act of putting them together. There were they eyes, the mouth, the face, the hands. But as I looked

84

they were gone—just an odd distribution of light and dark. I moved slightly, and they quivered and appeared and then disappeared.

My skin prickled. I whirled around. There was no sound, no movement of air. Yet for a moment I had felt quite sure that I was not alone in that room. My heart pounding, I turned back to the painting, now once again simply an unusual collection of colors and patterns. Finally I turned away. I knew now that Frank was indeed talented, but I was no happier about his being there. There was something about that painting —and I told myself that it *was* the painting and not anything else—that made my flesh crawl.

But a moment later I was not so sure.

Before leaving the attic something made me go over and try the handle of the door leading into the north attics, a door that I had securely locked.

The door opened quite easily. Tail up, giving her loud "Chrrrrrp," Josephine walked through and started to show her delight at our reunion by sharpening her claws on my wool robe.

The days passed with amazing speed. My mini-colony sorted itself out and settled down. Being regrettably (I felt) methodical, I had planned to go over the rooms one by one to check the contents and decide what, if anything, I wanted to get rid of, and also and incidentally, to keep the rooms clean. All too easily I could imagine the rot that would set in if this were neglected. And, despite Mr. Edgerton's off-putting techniques, I clung fast to the thought that I might want to sell The Fell at some time in the future. I say clung fast because it was getting increasingly difficult to remember that intention. In some strange way the house was beginning to draw me in, to make its claim on me—as though, I sometimes caught myself thinking, it had inherited me, not I it.

More cheerfully, I also made plans for the garden— a rather scraggy quarter of an acre back of the house and enclosed by shrubs, where flowers, plants and rather exhausted-looking vegetables had obviously fought and lost their battle with massed legions of weeds. Most afternoons, when it wasn't raining, I took refuge there, returning to the house refreshed for the various problems that lay in wait to pounce on me.

One of these was the big central attic. I had intended it for anybody who wanted to paint, but it soon became obvious that Frank had marked it for his own. I worried about this and spoke to Frank at breakfast one day.

"You know the attic's not your exclusive property. It's big enough for all of you."

Frank lifted his head from the three eggs and six pieces of bacon that Tess had cooked for him. "So?"

"So why don't you move your things to one corner?"

"I'm not stopping anybody."

"Maybe you are. Maybe they're too polite to ask you to move over."

Frank snorted. Bits of egg flew back onto the plate. He put up a dirty nail and started picking his teeth. "That's their problem."

It was, of course. And I knew that, although I had intended to find out if anyone else wanted to use the attic, that was not the reason for my brusqueness. I looked up and saw Frank watching me, a mocking glint in his eye, as though he knew exactly what was going on in my mind.

I turned to Rod Moscovitch, who was slowly and methodically consuming an enormous bowl of porridge, which he had made himself and to which he had added a large number of raisins.

"Rod, don't you want to use the attic?"

The blond head lifted. Absentmindedly he scratched his short, curly beard. It came to me that his head looked like the head of Zeus in some piece of classic sculpture I had seen somewhere. "No," he said, without equivocation. "I'd rather use my room. Or, if you can spare it, the room next door to me. I can put up my desk there."

"Sure. Go ahead. I'm not expecting any more colonists for the time being." I turned to the place next to him at the big round kitchen table, being certain, though, of the answer I would get.

"Pogs, what about you?"

She dropped her knife with which she had been peeling an orange. Rod picked it up.

"Oh, no, no, no," Pogs said. "My own little room is so *exactly* what I want. *Just* right!" The long, wide sleeves of her smock swept two pieces of orange peel onto the floor. Rod started to pick them up.

"Oh please. . . ." she cried on a rising note and plunged after the peel. Their heads bumped.

"And so they got married," Frank crooned in a falsetto. He pantomimed wiping tears from his eyes. "*So* sweet," he murmured.

It was funny. It was also cruel. Pogs's not very attractive face came up in red blotches. Rod looked across at Frank. "Cut the comedy, Buster. Stick to your painting."

"Please," whispered Pogs, on the verge of tears. "Not over me. I'm not that important."

Irrationally, my mounting irritation veered towards her. I took a firm grip on myself. "Pogs," I said as gently as I could, "you mustn't say that. If you don't feel what you're doing is important, then who else will?" I saw her mouth beginning to open and hurried on. "You—er—pot, don't you? Did you bring your wheel? Do you want to put it up in the attic?"

"Not near me," Frank said. "If it shakes the floor, I can't work."

"Oh, *no*," Pogs said. "I *do* pot"—why did that word make me want to giggle?—"but I'm not doing that up here, *most* unfortunately. I also illustrate children's books." She sighed. "So commercial. But I have an assignment I brought up."

"And you need the money so badly," Frank added.

Pog's red blotches reappeared.

"What's it to you?" Rod said. "It's no concern of yours."

"No, Frank," I agreed. "It isn't."

Pogs's long, rather beautiful fingers quivered around the mangled orange. "As a matter of fact. . . ."

Perhaps I should have let them go on and arrive at some kind of tribal peace by themselves. Maybe if I had allowed events, temperaments and personalities to take their natural course I might have saved at least one person at that table a good deal of anguish. But, in what I thought of as the best interests of group peace, I didn't.

"I am not running an encounter group," I said.

"Each person's financial status is his own business. Or hers."

"Don't you believe in participatory democracy?" Frank asked.

"Not here. This is an autocracy. And I'm the autocrat. *Ça va?*"

Pogs smiled, changing her whole face. *"Ça va bien,"* she said in an extremely good French accent.

"Well, well, the Jet Set is among us." Frank got up and slouched out of the kitchen.

Rod tipped his chair back. "Is his presence essential to our happiness?"

Tess, who had been looking unhappy throughout the entire interchange, rounded on him. "He's a marvelous painter," she said furiously. "The best there is among the younger artists. How arrogant can you be?"

Not entirely unexpectedly, Pogs took up with her. "Tess is right. Frank is much the best painter of the younger Loft Group. You shouldn't have said that."

Rod gave a massive shrug and stood up. Picking up his empty plate, he started to take Pogs's.

"I'm not finished," she said without looking up.

Rod stood for a second looking down at her. I was sorry I couldn't see his eyes. Then he went to the sink, washed his dish and spoon, and left the room.

Two things were obvious to me. One, that she and Rod had known each other before. Two, that she didn't want to talk about it.

It was several days later that I went up to Pogs's room to deliver some mail that had come and that I thought I might as well take to her since I was going up there anyway. At least that was the excuse I gave myself, knowing perfectly well that I was consumed with curiosity to see her work. Despite my more or less constant irritation with her chronic self-deprecation, I rather liked her. But I could not help but feel that Frank, boor that he was, was probably right in his general implication about her lack of ability, just as he was, unquestionably, right about her lack of the poverty suitable to a struggling artist.

Her door was open. Her cot had been jammed against the wall and the remaining space taken up with an artist's desk that had been put up by the window.

Hunched over it, lost to the world and my presence, was Pogs. But it was not she who held my horrified gaze.

Around the room on portable shelves and on the floor were Pogs's ceramics. My heart plummeted. They were dreadful: pseudo-primitive, fake Grandma Moses. I looked up to see her watching me anxiously, and my tongue clove to the roof of my mouth. I have broken most of the ten commandments, but lying is something I really prefer not to do. Then I found myself babbling, "The whole process is so fascinating. I know absolutely nothing about—er—potting."

"Oh, I love it. I feel that it's really me. I mean, what I am inside comes out then. Do you know what I mean?"

I did, and felt worse than ever. "But you're doing your illustrations now," I said, all but clawing the air for something innocuous and inoffensive to say.

"Oh yes." She studied the tip of the small sable brush in her hand, then absentmindedly ran it over the back of her hand, leaving a stripe of bright green. I paused, because she seemed on the verge of saying something. But after a minute, she dipped her brush in a little water jar, and ran it around the lid of her metal box.

"May I see?" I asked, hating myself for doing so, and thus subjecting myself to further frantic search for ways out of the truth.

"If you wish." She sounded, for a change, totally indifferent.

I went over and looked at the sheet she was working on and stared at it unbelievingly. Then I picked up the other sheets that were lying on the windowsill, tissue paper between them. They were as delicate and beautiful as the ceramics were clumsy and ugly. I have no idea what the story she was illustrating was about, but what came through the paintings were a sense of sunlight and spring, of children, not quite real, not quite fantasy, of mystery and joy. Yet they were neither sentimental nor fuzzy.

"These are marvelous," I said, "Why on earth don't you appreciate them?"

"They're so conventional."

"But they're not!" Just barely did I manage not to add, it's your dreadful pottery that's conventional in its artsy-craftsy horror. I said, "They're unusual . . . different."

She looked surprised, and not sure whether she was pleased or not. "I suppose," she said doubtfully, "it's because I think of them as commercial."

Thus the daughter of a long line of robber-baron business geniuses. Perhaps this was her atonement.

The steps I had heard continued to bother me, although for a while I did not hear them again. Then, about two weeks after the first time, I heard the same firm but oddly irregular stride, quite different from the way anyone in the house walked. This time it was late at night. Everyone had gone to bed—or so I thought. I had gone up to the third floor of the north wing looking (again) for Josephine who had been missing for two days, her food left untouched. Although I was reasonably sure by now that my little Reigning Empress was quite up to any challenge the house might offer. I was beginning to be puzzled by her long absences, particularly in view of the fact that when she did turn up she frequently looked, if anything, fatter and sleeker than before. Not only had her usually concave sides filled out, her black fur all but glistened. Was a solid diet of mouse that beneficial? Should it be bottled? Did it have commercial possibilities? Should I write an article?

All of these thoughts, ranging from the anxious to the frivolous, were playing around in my head as I walked along the third floor of the north wing and then, as I paused outside one of the bedrooms, glancing around the floor and turning my flashlight under the bed, I heard those steps: five of them, directly over my head. Then silence.

And this time, I thought, with a prickling at the back of my neck, I was standing still. So much for the echo theory.

But then, I reminded myself, I was not necessarily the only person in the house walking about, not even among those I knew about.

I glanced at my watch with the flashlight. It was one thirty a.m. It had been at least two hours since the others had gone to bed—or said they were going to bed.

I could, of course, go to each room and knock or simply walk in, but not only did I dislike the idea of doing that—feeling strongly about my own privacy, I had to feel as strongly about others'—but it wouldn't solve anything. I couldn't go thrusting into other people's rooms every time I heard steps. And with this thought I realized I had crossed over from merely speculating about the origin of the steps to some kind of an acceptance that they existed quite objectively. My skin prickled again and, at that moment, having myself still not moved, I heard them again.

I had not been into the north attics since the day I got marooned up there. I had meant to go up when Pete was there some morning, so that he could lead me by the hand through the labyrinth of rooms, all of which seemed to double back on one another. I had even considered going by myself, armed with a large ball of twine to unroll as I walked. But I had never found enough twine, and had consistently forgotten to order it from the store.

At that moment I had neither Pete nor the twine, but I knew I was going to have to go up into those attics. That there was something or somebody up there I now didn't doubt. That, if I waited until morning to go with Pete or someone else, whatever it was would be gone or hidden, I also knew. It wasn't until much later that I recalled how strange it was that I didn't even consider going to wake one of my guests to go with me. But as I stood there, shivering slightly in the third-floor hall of the north attic, it didn't occur to me.

Coward, I said silently to myself. Then I turned and went back through the dividing door into the central building and turned into the small hall leading to the stairs up into the central attic. Once there, I knew I could, easily enough, get into the north attic.

My slippers were soft-soled and I had turned off my flashlight, preferring to grope my way by the thin moonlight that filtered through the small window at the foot of the stairs. The stairs did not creak and the door at the top was slightly ajar, so I entered the lighted attic as silently as a thought, and came upon him as he stood, looking at Frank's painting. Behind him the door into the north attic stood open. Beside the door sat my errant Josephine, washing her paws.

It was Josephine who gave me away. Seeing me, she gave her welcoming "Chrrrrrp" and came over, tail in the air. Stooping down so I could touch her, but not taking my eyes off the man beside the easel who had abruptly turned, I said, "Well, Empress, have you dined?"

His voice echoed back through the years. "She has. Regally. Filet of freshly caught mouse *au gratin*. The *au gratin* was an accident. It was part of my dinner."

I stood up. My knees were quivering and I found it hard to get my breath. I was shaken, but in some strange way, not surprised. I stared at the tall man with the arrogant nose and black hair streaked now with gray.

"Are you Nicholas or Giles?" I asked, although I thought I knew.

"Does it matter?"

I took a deep breath, trying to slow the pounding of my heart. "Not really. Since in either case your—skulking—up here must mean you're in so much trouble that you can't even claim your inheritance. I don't imagine you'd let me think the house had come to me otherwise."

"I wouldn't."

His face was partly in shadow and I couldn't really see it, but for the moment all I could think about was that—once again—I had been well and truly had by the Trelawnys; again their lordly manipulation had reached into my life. I should have been astonished and bewildered. I wasn't. I was angry. "Your mother would really enjoy this denouement! How she would laugh, wouldn't she? Just as she laughed so hilariously at my mother and me."

He stood still as a monument, watching me, and his silence, his lack of reaction, was like a spray of gasoline to the fire inside me. "Well," I pushed on, "you can have your house back. Right now. I'll get myself and my guests out."

He moved then, as though with that childish sentence some danger had been averted. "And what would that accomplish, other than to satisfy your pride and expose me?"

"I have no desire to live in any house belonging to you or any other Trelawny."

"Including yourself? Aren't you being a little absurd? Particularly in view of the fact that you and your mother came some two thousand miles to inform us just how much of a Trelawny you were—with letters to prove it. Besides, you could have refused the house."

"And then what would have happened to it?"

He shrugged. "It would have reverted to the state. Torn down, perhaps. Turned into some kind of state museum. Feeling as you say you do, what difference would it make?"

"I preferred to disinfect it by putting in the kind of people I like and respect."

It was that piece of infantile rudeness that made me realize how little the old humiliation had healed.

"Including the perpetrator of this, I suppose." He indicated the painting. It was an awkward gesture, done with the wrong arm while the other hung at his side.

I forced myself to say, "I apologize for my rudeness." I added, more humanly, "What's wrong with your arm?"

"It's not very mobile."

"I can see that." By this time I had recovered myself enough to go towards him. As I did his face came into the light and I paused. To borrow from the great Gertrude, a Trelawny was a Trelawny was a Trelawny. He had the characteristic features: the gray eyes, the aquiline nose, the square chin. But everything else seemed to have changed. His face was thin, almost hollow, with vertical lines searing the cheeks and a scar that dug into the outer corner of one eye and ran into his upper lip. There was another scar going from the jaw into the hairline. But it wasn't the scars that pulled me up. Nor was it the fact that he had markedly aged. Certainly the attractive young man I had met fifteen years before was long gone. Yet it wasn't that.

"What's the matter?" he asked harshly. "Don't you recognize me?"

"Of course. It's just that you look—different." It sounded lame, even to me.

"That's hardly surprising. I was wounded and a prisoner of war."

That still told me nothing. Both Giles and Nicholas had been captured. It became very important for me to know which twin this was. "Let's stop playing games. Are you Nicholas or Giles?"

"If it matters, Nicholas. Come, cousin. You used to be able to tell us apart."

And then, obliterating the scars and the lines and the years, came the smile that I did indeed recognize. It was that smile, swift and mischievous, that had captured my twelve-year-old heart and blinded my eyes and, I suspected, the eyes of a great many others. For it I forgave the teasing and petty cruelty and insufferable arrogance and being dunked in the water and locked in the same attic after having the hanging rafter pointed out to me. Involuntarily, and with a strange constriction of the heart, my eyes went up to the beam.

His voice mocked. "Don't you know yet which is the hanging rafter?"

I looked again at his face. The laughing Nicholas who had appeared so briefly—and in that face, so incredibly —had gone. Perhaps it was the scar running into his upper lip, but what I heard and saw now was a sneer.

"I'm not twelve years old any more," I said sharply.

"I'm aware of that. Although, having watched you for the past few weeks, I can't see that you've changed that much."

It could have been his mother talking. But it wasn't that that was flooding anger through my system. It was my own reaction, a kind of inner shriveling that the Trelawnys had always been skilled at producing and that was happening within me again. I stood there staring at him, seeing how ludicrous it all was. I was whole, free and in possession of The Fell. Nicholas was maimed, disgraced and an outlaw (why else would he be hiding?), at my mercy, and obviously unable to dispute my ownership of the house. Yet I had to fight the old feeling of inferiority and powerlessness, to struggle against the overwhelming sense that Nicholas was the master of the house and of me and the outlandish situation.

"What is it," I asked bitterly, "that you Trelawnys

have? Why should I stand here, feeling like some usurping servant? What did they feed you in your nursery porridge to convince you you were lords of the earth?"

"If you think that in my present condition I feel like the lord of the earth or anything else, then you have less discernment than I gave you credit for. As for the way *you* feel, that is your problem." He indicated a couple of rather tattered armchairs that Frank had pulled out from the hodgepodge of abandoned furniture piled high at either end of the attic. "Shall we sit down?"

"Thanks. I'd rather stand."

"As you wish."

"Was it you who made those broadcasts from Hanoi?"

I was watching him carefully, expecting him to deny it, and saw his eyes flicker. "No, it was Giles."

I borrowed Frank's caustic words. "A noble end for the noble Trelawnys."

If the shaft hit he didn't show it. He said unexpectedly, indicating the canvas, "Tell me about him."

The cool of it took my breath away. "Let's have our discussion of art some other time. If it was Giles who defected or deserted or turned his coat or whatever, why are you hiding?" I picked my insult as carefully as his mother might have done. "Whom did *you* cheat?"

He came towards me and I knew then why the steps had sounded so irregular, because he half-dragged one leg. I was so preoccupied that I didn't realize what was happening until he had hold of my arm in his good hand and was staring down at me. "Careful, little cousin! Don't push your power too much."

I stared up into the scarred, sneering face. "Why not? You—and your mother—pushed yours on me and on my mother when we were guests in your house. Short of actually spitting on us, you did everything in your power to make us feel stupid, ill bred, unwanted. I'll say this for Giles. He may have turned his coat, but he didn't enjoy taunting us the way you and Mrs. Trelawny did."

He stared down at me for a moment. Then he dropped my arm and moved away. "I'm hiding, Kit, because if I didn't the police—either civilian or military or both—would pick me up within five minutes of learning I am here."

"What do the civilian police want you for?"

"Murder." He said it so calmly.

I tried to match his *sang froid*. "Oh really? How interesting! Of whom?"

"Charlotte. Charlotte Manners. Giles's fiancée. Don't you remember?"

"Yes. I remember her." I also remembered and now understood Mr. Edgerton's penetrating look. So that was what the old man was so carefully not talking about. "Why did you murder her?" I asked it as though I were asking, Why didn't you stay for lunch?

"Not I," he said gently. "Giles. The oldest reason in the world, jealousy. Charlotte was in the process of deciding she had chosen the wrong twin."

I remembered then Giles's anger that day when we were riding, as Nicholas and Charlotte galloped off. "How did it happen?"

"At the time it looked like a car accident. You remember my car?"

Indeed I did. Low, noisy, foreign, and expensive, it was the epitome of everything I thought of as sophisticated. I nodded.

"Well, Giles—er—borrowed it to take Charlotte for a ride. He was drunk, took a turn too fast and skidded off into some trees and down an embankment. The car turned over. Giles was just bruised, but Charlotte was dead—strangled, *à la* Isadora Duncan, in her own scarf and strings of beads and chains that got mixed up with the dashboard and gear. It was all very sad and we went to the funeral before returning to Southeast Asia. But somebody must have been suspicious. Instead of burying Charlotte, they performed an autopsy and discovered that she was dead before the car crashed. Had been dead for an hour or so."

In a strange way I knew what was coming, but I had to ask.

"So how did she die?"

His eyes flickered to the rafter. "Need you ask? According to family tradition."

"So if it was all Giles's doing, why are you hiding?"

"Because I, Nicholas, am officially dead. Declared so by at least six people. Therefore I must be Giles, who did the broadcasts and who killed Charlotte, and it would be a photo finish between the police and the military as to who would arrest me first."

"But Giles is dead, too."

"True. But not with witnesses."

I tried to sort this out. "So if they found you, they would assume you're Giles."

"Yes. Especially since Giles is rumored to have escaped and found his way back to the States."

"While Nicholas is dead, with witnesses to prove it."

"Exactly."

"Then if you're dead, with witnesses to prove it, how come you're here?"

He said exasperatedly, "I should think that would be obvious—even to you. It was Giles who died before witnesses, who did the broadcasts, who disposed of Charlotte—"

"Well, why did all those witnesses think it was you, Nicholas? And who were they? And where were they? Who was kidding whom? And why?"

"Those details can wait. I won't bore you with them now."

"How nice of you! In other words, I'm to take your word for it."

"Precisely."

"Well that's too bad! I'm sorry, but I don't!"

He shrugged. "Suit yourself."

I stared at him, at the scars, and again that intangible quality—that difference—hit me. "Oh, I believe you were wounded and captured." In some way I knew that to be true.

"Then what is it you don't believe?"

"I don't know. All that you said may be so. But it's not the truth. There's something missing or different. And I want to know what it is."

"I've told you all I'm going to." That was the old arrogance, ringing loud and clear.

"Very well. Perhaps you'll tell me what you hope to accomplish by being up here."

"Security, first of all. Security from being captured."

"And you expect to spend the rest of your life up here?"

"I do not." He paused, and then said carefully, "Not up here. Downstairs."

"Laird Trelawny of The Fell. Just as always."

Again the smile. "As you say, cousin."

"Curious, Nicholas. I have the oddest feeling that I'm being given an eviction notice."

"That was more or less the purpose. No use letting you get too comfortable."

In a detached way I admired his effrontery. With two hostile police forces and an equally hostile cousin blocking every exit, he was threatening me! I started to laugh.

"Something amuses you?"

"You do, cousin. You have the military and the police after you and you have me in full legal possession of a house you can't hope to get back, and you give me orders. Your *chutzpah* is staggering!"

He limped back towards me. I stood firm, forcing myself not to retreat because there was, suddenly visible in his face, that look of power and cruelty that I not only remembered from the past—it was the reverse side of the charming, teasing cavalier—but that I had seen to a lesser or greater extent in most of the portraits. Whatever their other differences, that look was common to all Trelawnys whether male or female. Certainly the dowager, Nicholas's mother, had it in marked degree.

He gripped my arm. "I not only hope to get it back, little cousin, I will get it back. Be quite sure of that."

"Let me go."

He released me. I rubbed my arm where his fingers had, I was sure, left bruises. "And what if I hand you over to the police?" Vaguely I noted that, up close, his scars looked more red and raw than they had across the room.

"But you won't, Kit."

"What makes you so sure?"

"You do. You're as much a Trelawny as the rest of us. We don't wash our linen in public."

"Before the hoi-polloi, the *canaille,*" I said silkily.

"Those, or anybody else. I told you before, you're free to call the authorities. But you won't."

"But aren't you forgetting? We belonged to the hoi-polloi, the *canaille,* my mother and I. We didn't know it, of course, until we came here. We were not, as your mother so often said or implied, of the *real* Trelawnys, emphasis hers, we—"

I stopped because either his scars were suddenly growing redder or his face was getting gray. I noticed then the sweat around his forehead and his upper lip, and that with one hand he was holding the back of the armchair beside him. I glanced down. There were white circles around his knuckles.

"You'd better sit down before you fall," I said.

He lowered himself, one leg held stiffly out. He was now a terrible color, and the scars looked like welts.

"In the next room, the north attic—some whisky," he managed to say.

I remembered that little room with its three steps down, low ceiling edge and its emptiness. How there could be whisky—or anything else—in there, I didn't know. But I went anyway. And then at the door I stood, amazed.

Behind the door itself the panel that had formed one side of the little three-level staircase down had disappeared. Instead there was a tall, rectangular opening and a narrow stair, almost a gangway, going up. At the top, I could see even from there, was the real north attic. As my nose rose above the floor I noticed on my left a chest, on top of which was a half-full pint bottle of whisky and a glass. I snatched them and went down and poured a stiff shot.

"Here," I said.

Nicholas drank it off in one swallow. I poured another one and he took that. The frightening gray receded as his normal color flowed back. He stood up.

"You'd better stay where you are," I said, less out of humanity than from the conviction that, lean as he was, if he fell I would never be able to move him.

"Don't worry, Cousin Kit. You're not going to have a corpse on your hands."

"Too bad," I said, and meant it.

At that he laughed, and it was hard to remember that he could look as he had minutes before.

I am tall. With most men I look eye to eye. With many, I look down. But Nicholas was more than half a head taller.

"Cheer up," he said. "The state may yet relieve you of my presence."

But as I stood there I knew that would never happen. That huge beam, the hanging rafter, was too near. Perhaps I glanced towards it. I don't know. But I almost jumped when Nicholas said, "Don't worry, Kit. I'm not going to take the family way out—yet."

I looked at him steadily. "That's a vicious thing to hold over my head. And I refuse to accept it. If you opt for suicide, it will be your act, not mine. You can't put that on me."

"So I see," he said lightly.

"There's more to your hiding up here than just security. What is it?"

He took a step and paused. "As you can see, I've not fully recovered. Until I do, I have to lie low."

"Recovered from what?"

"From the details I'm not going to bore you with."

He started to move around with his awkward gait. "Aren't you afraid someone might hear you?" I asked.

"Who, for instance? You're up here."

"I have four guests downstairs."

"You could always say I was your lover. However, I take your point." He put his hands on the high back of the chair and faced me. "In answer to your question, yes, there is a purpose to my being here, other than lying low. Somewhere in this house is something I can use as proof of my identity and, therefore, my innocence."

"Where is it?"

"If I knew that," he said impatiently, "I'd have located it long ago."

"All right. What is it?"

"I don't know that either."

"So you're lingering around here, hoping to stumble on something—although you don't know what—hidden in the house, although you don't know where."

"That's about it."

"That could take a lifetime."

"It could indeed. Although I was making quite good progress until you came."

"I'm so sorry."

"Yes. I'm sure you are."

"I don't have to do a damn thing to help you. Why should I? As long as you're stuck up here, a fugitive, the house is mine."

"And I will be your permanent tenant. How delightful!"

I resisted an impulse to slap that sneering face.

"In other words," he went on, "we have an impasse."

We stood staring at each other. I knew then that the war, the old war between the Trelawnys and me, was not over. On the contrary, it had been redeclared, with this difference: the combatants now confronted one another where the wounds inflicted would be far more deadly, perhaps—who knew?—fatal. As though pulled by an outside force my eyes went to the rafter. Charlotte died there by Giles's hand. Why shouldn't I by Nicholas's? A chill went through me. I dragged my gaze away and looked at Nicholas.

"So it's war to the finish?" I said.

That lopsided smile appeared on his face. "With the rafter hanging the loser? Agreed. And," he went on, watching me carefully, "in case you decide that the police are really the best solution, I will be dead before they get here. No one can get to the house without my knowing it, and that includes nighttime and when I'm asleep. I won't go into the means, but the army was very detailed in its training. The house may be nominally and temporarily yours. But it's mine, Kit, and I guard it. Don't ever forget that."

The trouble was, I believed him. I believed him with every bone and nerve end. But I would fight that Judas living within me as I would fight Nicholas himself. It made the odds two to one against me, but I had always been a fighter and I would fight to the end, even if that end was a rope around my neck and Nicholas's hand pulling it over the rafter.

I took a breath. "As I said, your suicide would be your doing. And it would settle my problems, wouldn't it?"

His laugh was one of genuine amusement. "If you really think that—then don't hesitate. Call the cops. What have you to lose?"

Clever Nicholas, clever bastard, I thought, and was groping around for some way out of the crafty trap, when I heard sounds from the floor below. I looked at Nicholas, who had stiffened.

He whispered, "Go down at once and talk to whoever it is while I get upstairs. And make plenty of noise to cover me."

I wanted to open my mouth and ask who the blazes he thought he was ordering me around, when I heard the soft sound of rubber-soled shoes on the floor below coming nearer.

"Why, Josephine," I said loudly, glaring at Nicholas, "what do you mean, hiding like this? Bad cat! Naughty Empress! . . ." and on I jabbered like any foolish woman talking pidgin babytalk to her pet, an insult, had anyone known or cared, that I had never offered to my fierce Reigning Empress and that she was now rejecting with her haughtiest stare.

By this time Nicholas had moved as lightly as his stiff leg allowed him to the opening behind the door. As he stepped in, I handed him the whisky and the glass and just barely saved my hand from being crushed as the panel slid shut.

"Come along, Josephine. We're going downstairs to bed, and I won't have any more of this nonsense, you understand?" I yammered on, raking the room with my eyes to make sure there was no evidence left of Nicholas and his visit. Then I picked up Josephine, who let out a squawk—her entire view of interpersonal relationships was that the options remained solely with her —and went over to the attic door, switching off the light when I got there. One arm was around Josephine, who was still emitting angry squawks. With the other hand I fumbled in the pocket of my robe for my flashlight. But there, at the head of the little staircase leading down to the north wing's third floor, I paused for a second before switching the flashlight on, quite why, I wasn't sure. Perhaps some sixth or seventh sense was working in the dark. Whatever the reason, I stood there. Josephine, perhaps resigning herself to the inevitable, had stopped yowling. There was, perhaps, a quarter of a minute of total silence. Then I heard it, audible, quite close and a little below me: breathing.

I was pressing down on the button of my flashlight when it was knocked out of my hand and fell with a crash and the sound of splintering glass to the bottom of the stairs. Worse, the blow had unbalanced me.

"Who's there?" I yelled, making a wild grab for the narrow rail of the banister.

Feeling my grasp loosen, Josephine leapt away and down. I fell, but, managing to grasp the rail, not too far. I pushed myself up, shaking.

There was no further sound, no breathing, no steps. Whoever it was had gotten away. I was alone.

5

I felt my way to the foot of the stairs and groped around for the flashlight. From the pieces my fingers encountered I could tell the plastic case had cracked open, and the glass was shattered. Picking my way over the debris to the doorway leading to the hall, I turned on the light, partly so that I could see to clean up the mess, more to find out if my assailant had left any kind of clue in his or her flight. But the light revealed nothing except bits of glass and plastic.

There was a broom closet on every floor, so a pan and brush were not far away. I was busy sweeping up the last remnants when I heard a *slap-slap* down the hall and a startled, "Oh my goodness!"

"Hello, Pogs," I said rather sourly, without looking up. Who else could it be?

"Oh dear! What happened? Can I help? Tell me what to do."

"I'm doing what has to be done," I said grumpily, then relented a little. "Thanks, anyway." As I stood up I looked at her thoughtfully. It was in her hall that I had heard the feet. There was nowhere else they could have come from. Therefore was all this stammering, apologetic gaucherie so much brilliant camouflage? And if it were, camouflage for what?

I said, feeling my way, "Sorry I woke you. I suppose it was the crash when I dropped my flashlight."

"Oh, no! You didn't wake me up. I thought I heard voices a while ago, and then I heard somebody come along the hall. That was before the crash. Perhaps I startled you. Is it my fault? I'm terribly sorry. . . ."

There was no excuse for my rudeness that followed, but something in me went snap. "If you think it's your fault, it probably is." And I stalked out of the stair closet, through the connecting door to the central building, dumped the contents of the pan into a handy wastebasket, shoved the pan and brush into the nearest broom cupboard, and went downstairs to my room.

Josephine was sitting in the middle of my bed, conducting a detailed, leisurely grooming. I took off my robe, slid into bed and turned out the light.

For a while I just lay there, letting my eyes get used to the dark, and then seeing the silvery wash of moonlight coming through the windows, along with the fresh, salty air. Beside me was the rasp of Josephine's tongue as she went over her coat, patch by patch, as careful as any furrier.

I thought unhappily about how rude I had been to Pogs and remembered a story I had heard when I was a student in Paris. It concerned a good-hearted Englishwoman who had gone to see some Armenian refugees who had been commended to her by friends. The refugees were living in impoverished circumstances eking out a meager living. Unfortunately, after she had been with them about an hour, their patient manner and sorrowful gaze had a disastrous effect on her and she left abruptly, lest she give in to an overwhelming desire to persecute them. I had always found the story wryly amusing. Now I knew it to be true. Furthermore and worse, I had not fled but had given in to my brutish desire to persecute Pogs. She was neither impoverished nor a refugee, but her everlasting apologizing had evoked the bully in me, and I didn't like it.

Then there was Nicholas. . . .

Why, oh why, didn't I let whoever was at the stairs, listening, come up? Nicholas would have been discovered and the matter would have been taken out of my hands.

But even as I thought that I knew it was no solution. The war between Nicholas and me could not be resolved by default. And the anger and fury I had felt upstairs took hold of me again. This time, rather to my astonishment, I burst into tears. After a minute Josephine stopped washing and padded up to my pillow and pushed a paw into my face, making periodic "Chrrrrrp" noises. I put one arm around her. She curled into a ball somewhere in the general region of my middle. Thus comforted, I felt somewhat better. But I still cried myself to sleep.

The next morning at breakfast I awaited Pogs's arrival. She was down last and seemed rather subdued when she showed up, and I braced myself for another apology. But she didn't say anything. After Frank, Rod and Tess had eaten and gotten up and she was about to go, I said, "Wait, Pogs. There's something I want to talk to you about."

Everybody turned around. "Just Pogs," I said firmly. They looked disappointed, but left. When they had gone I said, "It's my turn to apologize. I'm sorry."

I expected a deluge of reassurances. To my shock, she said in a sensible way. "Don't start now, Kit. It's pure nerves. I reverted to some subadolescence when I was six feet tall and for miles around at school and dancing class and everywhere else there wasn't a soul over four foot ten."

I looked at her sympathetically. "I suppose it shows how narrow-minded and what a snob in reverse I really am. It never occurred to me that anyone with wealth and social position should be eaten away with an inferiority complex."

"No," she said wryly, stirring her coffee, "nobody ever thinks that. That's what Rod—" She stopped.

I waited. Then I said, "I don't mean to pry, but it certainly looks as though you had known each other before."

Pogs's hand promptly knocked her cup onto the floor. "Oh dear! I'm—"

"No!" I almost screamed. "You're going to break that habit!"

She emerged from under the table with the cup and put it back in the saucer. Then she got a piece of paper towel from above the sink and mopped up the floor.

"We were married," she said flatly.

"Good heavens! But how awful for you. If I had known, I wouldn't have had him here."

"It's okay. But that's why I have attacks of nerves." She threw the soaked paper into the garbage can. "Just so you'll be straight on everything, he left me, not the other way around." She slewed around and for the first time I noticed her eyes behind the enormous glasses. They were a wide clear gray and did not go with the rest of her face, which was heart-shaped and was responsible for the frightened-fawn, waiflike look that seemed so ludicrous on top of her long, gangling body. But her eyes were neither frightened nor doelike. They had intelligence and some quality that vaguely disturbed me, but that I couldn't define. As she turned and left I found myself wondering again how long she'd been awake the previous night, and how much she'd heard.

I had decided to pay a visit to the nearest town that boasted a good-sized public library, and was about to leave through the rear door with my shopping list, when Jeremy, backpack on, came down the main stairs.

"Good morning, Cousin Kit," he said with that air of overpowering innocence that always puts me on the alert.

"Good morning, Jeremy." I eyed the pack. "Whither away?"

"I thought I should return to New York," he said virtuously. "I don't want Elmendorff to think I'm not interested in working with him."

"Are you?" I asked.

He came around the corner of the staircase. "Am I what?"

"Interested in working with Elmendorff, or anyone else, for that matter?"

His face took on that hurt, wounded look that in some way reminded me of my mother and produced in me both irritation and guilt. "You don't take my work seriously, Cousin Kit."

"I would if I thought you did," I replied brutally. "Anyway, I'm going into Merton. They undoubtedly have a bus service there to New York. I'll give you a lift."

"I planned to hitch," he said.

"All right, I'll take you to the highway."

We went out and got into the car while Jeremy preserved a dignified silence. I wondered how long it would take him to say he wanted to give me the privilege of buying his bus ticket to Manhattan. I had every intention of doing it, but there was a certain artistry in the way he went about conning me and I didn't want to miss it.

We drove in silence for a bit. Then, as we turned into the road that led past the village and onto the highway he said, as though continuing a dialogue, "Of course, I'd get back a lot quicker if I went by bus, and I'd be able to help Elmendorff with his exhibit."

"Yes," I said thoughtfully. "What a pity you didn't think of that earlier so you could have left sooner."

"Yes. But I wanted to make sure that Frank and Tess and the others were settling in all right. You know, in case there was any problem. So that you could have a man in the family around."

I looked quickly at him in the rearview mirror. His face registered nothing but an earnest desire to please. "Did you hear the crash last night?" I asked.

The fine dark eyes gave me a quick sidelong glance. "What crash?"

"Come on, Jeremy. They must have heard it down in the village." I glanced at his feet. He was wearing sneakers, as he nearly always did. But why would he have knocked the flashlight out of my hands—if it had been he?

"I did hear something. Maybe it was that. I wondered what it was, but went back to sleep before I could get up and investigate."

"I thought I heard something in the attic," I said, experimentally, "so I went up to investigate. Then when I was up there I heard footsteps on the floor below, wearing either slippers or sneakers, and went to the stairs to investigate. But"—I glanced quickly at him again: his eyes were on me intently—"like an idiot, I dropped my flashlight down the stairs."

Did his face relax, or was I imagining things? "Find

107

anything up there?" he asked, and that intent watching look was back in his eyes.

"Yes. Josephine. With mouse."

"Oh," he laughed (in relief?). "I bet she's a great mouser!"

"She is." I pulled the car up just as we reached the main road. "Here you are," I said. "Cars come along here all the time. You won't have any trouble."

He didn't move. "Did you know that Mar—Pogs and Rod were married once?" he asked.

"Yes. I learned that this morning. How long have you known?"

"Oh, a couple of days. Rod told me."

"Thanks for passing it along."

"Well, I was going to, only I forgot."

Slowly he got out. I leaned across and said through the window, "Any other fascinating tidbits of news?"

He shook his head. "No."

"Are you sure?"

He hesitated. Then, "Yes. I'm sure."

"All right," I said admiring his strategy, despite myself. "Get in and I'll take you to the bus station." I knew that I would be buying what he was holding back, but I was willing to pay the price. If there were anything to know, the chances were one hundred percent that Jeremy would know it.

But then he surprised me. "No. It's okay, Cousin Kit. I'd just as soon hitch—really. Bye!" and with that he ran along the highway, waving his thumb at a car that was coming along at a crisp speed. It stopped. Jeremy got in and waved at me again as the car passed.

As I crossed the main highway and drove into the town I didn't know whether I was irritated at Jeremy for playing games or getting a ride so rapidly. It was almost indecent, I thought indignantly, rolling into the little town and parking my car outside the white-steepled public library.

"You're jealous," I said to my image in the rearview mirror. "You could have stood there an hour before anybody picked you up."

"Very true," my reflection said back to me. I sighed and got out of the car.

Four hours later I had combed through the back

issues of the two local newspapers, the *Clarion* and the *News*, two Boston papers and *The New York Times*. I also, and for good measure, had skimmed through the relevant issues of *Time* and *Newsweek*. In none was there any mention of the fact that Charlotte Manners was murdered. In each there was an account—much longer, of course, in the local papers—of what was always referred to as "the tragic accident" involving herself and Giles Trelawny (the sole reason for the interest of such national journals as the *Times* and the two newsmagazines), and a brief biography. Charlotte was, apparently, the daughter of a country doctor in New Hampshire. Giles, a captain in the Army Reserve, it was stated, was on leave from his unit, which was about to be sent to Vietnam. More significantly, there was no mention of the autopsy, the fact that Charlotte had died before the crash or that Giles was suspected of killing her by hanging her from the rafter. Of course, it was possible that Nicholas had made up the whole story, but somehow, and for no reason that I could think of, I couldn't make myself believe that.

As for Nicholas reading broadcasts from Hanoi, the local papers made no reference to any rumors about it. But the Boston papers, *The New York Times*, and the two newsmagazines carried stories. There was a photograph that could have been one of the twins, bearded, head down, before a microphone. But it could almost as easily have been any tall, gaunt, dark-haired American. Given the standing the Trelawnys had always enjoyed in American society, one columnist pontificated, such a broadcast, if it had taken place (and the columnist for one believed it had), would indeed have been a propaganda coup for Hanoi.

Then there were the obituaries: of Nicholas first; then, in the papers of a little more than a year ago, of Giles, who had originally been listed as Missing In Action and then reported killed. Both articles mentioned again the rumors about the broadcasts and emphasized the victory this represented in what was conceded to be a propaganda war. Almost, I thought, and if she had been a little more human herself, I would have found myself sorry for the Dowager. Almost, but not quite.

I left the library, did a little shopping, had some coffee and a sandwich, and was about to get into my car when I saw Pete Bradford coming down the street carrying his tool kit. I waited till he came up.

"Hi," I said. "I've been meaning to talk to you."

He looked as wary as a cat. "Yes?" Then he smiled. "More closets you can't open?"

"No," I said carefully, because people were passing and voices could be overheard. "But I stumbled on the contents of that north attic quite by accident last night."

"Yeah? You don't say!" He shifted his large boots. "I gotta be going, Miss Kit. My car's in the garage. I have to catch the bus back to the village."

"I'll take you there." I opened the passenger seat. "Get in."

He looked for a moment as though he were going to bolt.

"Come on, Pete. You know you have some questions to answer."

He hesitated, and again I had the feeling that behind the façade of local handyman was something else. Then he sighed and got into the car.

I waited until we were out of the town until I spoke, then I said, "How long have you been feeding Nicholas?"

"Why don't you ask him, Miss Trelawny?"

"I will. But I know he couldn't have survived without you or Simon or both keeping him supplied."

Pete didn't say anything at first. Then, "Simon doesn't know Capt.—er—Mr. Trelawny is there—or at least if he does he isn't letting on."

"You sound like you were in the service with him."

"Yeah."

"You were awfully young to be in and out of the service."

"I enlisted when I was seventeen."

"Did you like it?"

"It was okay."

It was like pulling teeth. I decided to plunge into the middle. "Why are you helping my cousin Nicholas to hide from the police?"

He took his time answering, and I had the odd impression that he was weighing all his words before he let

110

them out where they could get him in trouble. "Well, he's innocent. As soon as he can find proof of who he is and he can prove that he's innocent, then he'll come out. If he was in jail, he wouldn't be able to do that."

It all sounded so reasonable. But my feeling that I was being fed a line increased, and so did my irritation.

"I don't suppose it has occurred to either of you that, since the house is mine, I'll be held responsible. I see no reason why I should go to jail to protect Nicholas."

"You want to send an innocent man to prison, ma'am?"

If I had been honest, I would have said that I found it hard to believe that any Trelawny was innocent of anything. "No, I don't. But I'm not that sure he's innocent. I don't feel that either of you is telling me the truth, or at least the whole truth. When I was here as a little girl fifteen years ago, I got to feeling like a patsy around the high and mighty Trelawnys. And I'm feeling that way now."

"But you're a Trelawny, miss. Everyone says how much you are."

"Just what do you mean by that? And who is 'everyone'?"

"Well, Granny, for one."

"Mrs. Bradford did not give me what could be called, even allowing for Maine reserve, a warm welcome. So I don't suppose what she said is a compliment."

"Well, you have to understand Granny. She—well, she's had her quarrels with The Family."

"For instance?"

Silence.

"Come on, Pete. It was as obvious as a snake's egg in the middle of the floor that she didn't like me. And since she'd seen me before only when I was a child, I had to assume it was because I was a Trelawny. In fact, the time I saw her in the past, it was when—"

If I had been allowed to finish that sentence and the thought that followed along right behind it, events might have been different. I might have been saved a lot of grief and hardship. But I was not. A loud blast from a car horn assaulted my ears.

"Watch out!" Pete yelled and yanked at the wheel.

The trouble is, I had not been paying attention and

I was not used to country roads. To my urban way of thinking they looked so desolate and neglected that I forgot they weren't. I had strayed into the center of the road just as I was rounding a blind corner with an embankment and a hedge hiding the other side. The car that I almost collided with got past with less than an inch to spare. Startled and frightened, I slowed down. The other car must have turned around and come after me. The next thing I knew there was another blast and it overtook me. Then it stopped just ahead. A man got out who, in the gathering dusk, I recognized as Dr. Seaward. He came back, looking as though he were going to give me a piece of his mind. Meekly I waited.

"Of all the stupid— Oh, it's you, Kit." He so visibly bottled up his fury that I wanted to laugh. But I said as humbly as I could, "I'm sorry, Bill. I was talking and forgot how narrow the road was."

"You could have been killed."

"Yes. I know. I'm terribly sorry."

He stared past me at Pete. "Hello, Pete. Since Miss Trelawny isn't acquainted with our narrow roads up here, how come you didn't prevent her veering over like that?"

"He prevented my running into you, Bill. He yanked the wheel just in time. We both owe him a vote of thanks."

"Well," he said rather lamely, "I'm glad to hear it." He paused. "You two must have been deep in conversation."

"We were—" I started, when I was interrupted.

"Like you said, Doctor"—Pete rode over my voice —"Miss Kit doesn't know the roads up here."

"I've been looking for you," Bill said to Pete. "When are you coming to fix that door of mine? I still can't shut it properly, and it isn't warm enough yet for me to enjoy sitting in a draft."

"I'll be along tomorrow."

"What's the matter with right now, now that I've tracked you down? Kit, you don't mind if I borrow Pete and take him along to my house, do you?"

I was about to say no, of course not, when to my utter astonishment I felt my leg poked. Curiosity as much as anything else made me go along with it. "Bill, do you mind if I take him along with me? I've got a feeling that my broken window is even worse than your door."

What could he say? "Sure. Take him along. Pete, I'll see you tomorrow." And he left the car rather abruptly and went back to his own. Turning his car once again, he went past us without waving.

I started my own car. "All right, Pete. My leg is probably black and blue. What was that about?"

He hesitated for a second, then said, "I've got to see the Capt.—Mr. Nicholas tonight, Miss Kit. I have some food for him."

"I have plenty of food in the house. I could have taken it to him."

"But you wouldn't have known he was needing supplies, would you? And I couldn't have explained it with the doctor standing there."

Plausible enough, I thought. Yet I wondered.

"Is that the real reason, Pete? I have a feeling it isn't. And besides, Nicholas is perfectly capable of letting me know if he wants some food."

"How could he, Miss Kit? With that bad leg he can't get around easy, and if strangers are around he can't be sure that he can move fast enough to get out of their way."

It was true enough. We drove in silence while I mulled over what had been said. I was still strongly possessed by the feeling that what Pete said was as much to conceal as to inform. I was still mulling as we drove up to the house.

"What's going to be your excuse this time?" I said, getting out.

He grinned in the waning light. "Looking for ratholes. Mending the window."

"What window?"

"The one's that's broken, of course."

"I made that up. You know that perfectly well."

"Yes, ma'am. But I think I had better make it true."

And with that he walked off, carrying his large tool kit that I now realized undoubtedly contained food.

"Pete," I called. He turned.

I went up to him. "Tell Nicholas that I want to see him."

"Okay."

With a thousand things to do, it was eeny meeny miny mo as to where to start. But feeling some fresh air would do me good, I collected a hand rake, some powerful weedkiller and a trowel from the storeroom back of the kitchen and made off to the untidy flower and vegetable patches at the back of the house.

An hour later, refreshed and more or less at peace with the world, I returned to the house, absentmindedly going straight to the kitchen. Tess was chopping vegetables into a bowl at the kitchen table. She eyed the bottle and garden tools. "Please don't put that stuff on the table." She sounded irritable and unlike herself.

"All right," I said soothingly. I put the implements on the floor near the door where I could take them out and the weedkiller on the shelf above and to one side of the stove. Simmering on one of the rings was a delicious-smelling concoction in a big black cauldron Tess had resurrected from the storeroom.

"What's that?" I asked, sniffing. "It smells divine."

"Stew." Tess took the vegetables and emptied them into the pot and stirred them with a big spoon. Tied practically under her arms was an apron that would have fit the Jolly Green Giant. All she needed, I thought, was a broomstick and a pointed hat. I said quietly, watching her stir,

> "Eye of newt, and toe of frog,
> Wool of bat, and tongue of dog. . . ."

Rather to my surprise she took it up:

> "Adder's fork, and blind-worm's sting,
> Lizard's leg, and howlet's wing. . . ."

We finished together,

> "For a charm of pow'rful trouble,
> Like a hell-broth boil and bubble"

and ended up laughing. Tess's face was more animated than I had ever seen it.

"How come you know that?" I asked, with a lamentable lack of tact.

She took a sip from the spoon, seemed to think about it, and then said, "You know it, why shouldn't I?"

"Yes, all right, Tess. That wasn't polite of me. But the college dramatic society did *Macbeth* my senior year, and I was Lady Macbeth doubling as the third witch."

Tess stirred her concoction some more. Then she said, "I was in the theater for a while."

"Oh? You don't look old enough to have been in anything for a while."

"I'm twenty-four."

"And where were you in the theater?"

"In school, then in a repertory company. We did a lot of Shakespeare."

"Why did you leave? Didn't you like it?"

"Well . . ."—she put the ladle back in the stew and went over to look at the dough she had been mixing—"things happened."

"You mean Frank happened. Why do you put up with him? He treats you as though he were some kind of sultan and you were his seraglio. The days of the pashas are over. Haven't you heard?"

It was the wrong thing to say, as I should have known. She turned on me. "Frank has tremendous talent. Anyway, why are you always putting him down? I won't listen to you. If you don't want him up here, you shouldn't have let him pay to come. Or me."

"Look, I'm sorry—I shouldn't have. . . ."

The animation was gone. She seemed in the grip of almost hysterical anger, way out of proportion to the cause, or so it appeared to me. "No, you shouldn't! Who gave you the right to criticize Frank? Why should I do anything for you? I'll show you. You can do your own cooking!" And with that, to my utter astonishment, she looked around, saw the weedkiller, picked it up, unscrewed the top and emptied it into the cauldron.

"Hey!" I yelled. "What are you doing?" And I lunged for the bottle.

"I'm fixing it so you can make something else—something you approve of, straight and conventional and

115

true-blue All-American!" And flinging off her apron, she rushed out, colliding at the door with Pete.

"Whoa," he said, neatly fielding her. And then, in quite a different voice, "What's the matter, Tess?"

It looked like the confrontation of the elephant and the mouse. Pete was so large that his hands, holding Tess by the shoulders, seemed to cover them. For a second she stood there. Then she yelled at him, "And I hate you too!" And ran out the door.

I glanced at Pete, expecting to encounter a look of, perhaps, amusement, certainly understanding. And I got my second shock of the hour. Pete's cheeks were red with anger and he was glaring at me.

"Have you been picking on Tess?"

I opened my mouth but that was as far as I got. "Isn't it enough," he fumed, "that she has to put up with that . . . that *jerk,* without your pitching in to her too? I'm surprised at you, Ki—Miss Kit."

I began to lose my own temper. "Don't let any formality stand in the way of your speaking your mind." Turning my back I stared at the stew and at the level of liquid in the bottle still in my hand. "I wonder how much got in?" I said aloud.

"Enough." He came over, took the bottle out of my hand, screwed the top back on and said, "I'm taking this out to the storeroom. This stuff has arsenic in it."

I looked regretfully at the stew. "I suppose that means that the stew here is beyond repair."

"It certainly is." He yanked it off the stove. "Maybe you'll appreciate her cooking next time." Carrying the pot and the bottle, he disappeared in the direction of the storeroom and came back carrying the empty cauldron, and put it back on the stove.

I was still bristling from his last comment. "Is that what you think I was doing? Putting down her cooking? Why don't you stop jumping to conclusions? She went into a rage because I dared to suggest that she was being used and exploited by that toad, Frank."

"Oh." He looked embarrassed. "Gee, Miss Kit. I'm sorry. I've never acted like that before. I don't know what got into me."

"Don't you?" I asked drily. "How old are you?"

"Twenty-six."

"You look younger. That makes it even more surprising that you don't know what got into you. What, by the way, did you do with the stew?"

"Put it in a bucket near the garbage."

"What about putting it down the john?"

Pete hesitated. "These pipes are old. I'd hate to have them back up."

"So would I," I said with great feeling, envisioning the debacle.

"I'll take the stuff out tomorrow and bury it somewhere. I'd do it now, but I have to get back."

"That's okay. Did you put a lid of any kind on it? I don't want Josephine sampling it."

"Any cat I've ever known would know better than that."

"But your cats were not found on Macdougal Street in New York City's Greenwich Village. God knows what Josephine learned to love in that period of her life."

"All right. I'll put something on top of the bucket." He went out again and returned. "I found a metal tray and put it on top. That should discourage her. Er, I'd like to talk to you. Is anybody around?"

I was about to say no, when I hesitated. "The trouble about this house is, you can never say no for sure. Anyway, I drove you here so I'll have to drive you back to the village. Let's go."

We went out and got into the car. In silence we rolled over the turf and cobblestones until we got through the gate and onto the lane leading to the road.

"What do you want to talk to me about?"

"Capt.—Mr. Nicholas says you can come up to see him around midnight."

"Isn't it good I'm not an early go-to-bedder. In the central attic, I suppose."

"No. He thinks that's too risky. He says to knock on the panel leading up to the true attic and he'll come down and get you."

"All right."

"By the way, I broke one of the downstairs windows —one in the sitting room. I made it look like an accident. If Dr. Seaward comes to make sure you were telling the truth, tell him that I said I didn't have a piece of glass large enough to do a good job and was going to bring one from Merton tomorrow."

"Are you really expecting him to come and check up?"

"I didn't say he would. I just said 'if.' "

I drove back to The Fell in a state of depression over Tess, the stew, Nicholas, Pete's suspicions, and Frank, not necessarily in that order. Probably the thought that I would have to be making dinner for four from scratch was the most immediate and accessible of the things bothering me. But behind that was an anger, anger that I was, however unwillingly, a permanent host to Nicholas, who had managed to manipulate me into the position where I could do little but go along with what he wanted. More than anything in the world, I thought, I disliked being obligated against my will. And that was exactly what Nicholas was doing, and knew he was doing and, I suspected (and this was the bitter dreg at the end of the unpleasant drink), was enjoying it.

I said a bad word, got out of the car, and went into the house. It was very quiet. I half expected to see Frank and Tess, packs on backs, coming downstairs to leave for more *simpatico* pastures. I would not have been in the least sorry to see Frank go, but I was genuinely sorry over my fight with Tess (although I could not regret what I had said: maybe, I hoped, it had sown a valuable seed in her mind). But Frank's presence, however talented he might be, was beginning to make me uneasy. Quite why I felt this increasingly, I was not sure. But I did.

However, I saw no one, and stumped off to the kitchen to start making some kind of dinner.

When I got to the door I stopped. Standing in the kitchen, swathed in Tess's apron, cookbook open, slicing mushrooms into a large bowl, was Rod Moscovitch.

I said the first thing that came into my head: "I didn't know you could cook."

"I have been, among other things," he said in a magisterial way, "head chef at three restaurants."

"I thought you were supposed to be an artist."

"That's what I wanted you to think, and anyway, they're not incompatible."

"But you came up because of Pogs."

118

"That's right."

"I wish," I said with feeling, "that everybody up here were solely interested in his, her, or its art. I didn't intend for this to be a hotbed of emotion."

He gave me an odd look, and then started breaking some eggs into the bowl. "In that case you should have settled for a colony of engineers, not artists."

"Don't engineers have any emotions?"

"Yes. But they're all repressed."

"How do you know? And anyway, isn't that a rather sweeping statement?"

"Because I am an engineer—that is, I was, before I became an artist."

"Before or after your career as a chef?"

"I was a part-time chef while I was going to school."

"By the way, I hear that you and Pogs were married."

"That's right." He started mixing things up in the bowl with his hands and then a large wooden spoon.

"And that you walked out on her."

"Correct."

"Then what are you doing here?"

"Trying to undo the fact that I was a damn fool."

"You mean trying to get her back?"

"Yes." He dropped the spoon and stared down at the bowl. "At this point she won't even talk to me."

"Did you treat her badly?"

"I—yes. Very. And finished it all off by walking out on her."

"Why?"

He took a deep breath, picked up the spoon, and went to work on his mixture again. "I married her because she was rich. She was the poor, ugly little rich girl. She was a pushover. She defied the family, eloped with me, got cut off without a penny—and one day I just left. As you can see, I am a man of great character."

"How did you meet her?" I asked curiously. "The very rich don't move in most other circles."

"Oh. Pogs was involved in some of her do-goodism in a settlement house in New York and I was the local carpenter, handyman, and mechanic. I was also going to engineering school at night."

He went over to one of the cupboards and got out a large square pan and poured his concoction into it. "To

119

get off my affairs for a minute, fascinating as they are, do you know that somebody is wandering around the attics at odd hours of the night?"

"Er, no——" I said. And then as I saw his glance come over towards me, I added hastily, "I mean, I think that was me you heard. Josephine got lost and I started worrying about all those rats and went up to look for her."

"I see."

I have never thought of myself as either psychic or sensitive, yet I was picking up something from him and it wasn't making me feel any better.

"What do you mean by 'I see'?"

"It's just that—nothing."

"Rod—you can't leave it like that!"

"Why not?" He carried the bowl over to the sink and started washing it.

"It's not fair."

"Fair to whom?" He put the bowl into the draining rack, dried his hands on a dishtowel and turned around. "I don't think it's fair to arouse suspicions about a fellow guest and then not to be able to back it up with evidence."

I was so relieved at hearing that 'fellow guest' that I felt weak. But I didn't want him to see that so I said hastily, "Frank, I suppose."

"That's what I mean. You don't like Frank, so even though there is no more suspicion—as far as you know —on him than on anyone else, you leap to the conclusion that he's the one having those midnight rambles. Besides——"

"Besides what——?"

But at that moment Pogs walked in. "Tell me what I can do," she said, rather dramatically.

In the best of circumstances Pogs was not a good-looking woman. Today some fancy had moved her to array her angular form in a blue kimono that came to exactly the wrong length—halfway between her bony knees and ankles. Underneath stretched what looked like about a foot and a half of unattractive shin. I looked quickly at Rod to see how this ensemble was affecting him. He was gazing upon Pogs with the look of a man far gone in love.

It *is* blind, I said to myself. Aloud, I commented,

"All right, Pogs, you can help Rod cook dinner. Tess was—not feeling well, and I loathe cooking. Thanks so much." And left before she managed to close her mouth, "Dan Cupid," I muttered, "move over."

Tess did not show up at dinner.

"She's not feeling so good," Frank said.

"I'd better go up and see if there's anything I can do."

"No. I just told you. She wants to be left alone. She's sleeping. She gets this way sometimes."

"Did she tell you what—er—set her off?"

"Nah. She just said she wanted to sack out. I thought we were suppposed to do our thing on our own time up here?"

He had a point. "All right. Tell her that if she wants anything, one of us will get it."

I went up to my room around ten o'clock, yawning rather elaborately. Then I took a long, leisurely bath, washed my hair, dried it, put on a long robe and made my way up to the central attic. I went very slowly, wearing soft slippers that made no noise, and listened every step of the way. By the time I was knocking on the panel beside the door into the north attic, I was quite convinced no one had heard me and no one had followed me.

Nicholas's attic, which was right under the eaves, ran the length of the north wing and, considering the huge vaults overhead, was surprisingly cozy. In it were a low, quite large divan bed, a couple of chests, two armchairs, a table and several hundred books. The tops of six dormers, three on each side, were visible and completely shrouded with black cloth, and the floors were covered with what felt like layers of carpets, rugs, quilts, and blankets. I stared down.

"You must have ransacked every store cupboard in the house. No wonder I had a hard time scrounging up blankets and even had to buy a few," I said indignantly.

"Why not? They're mine!"

This brought my head up with a snap. Not only the words, but the tone was challenging.

"You're really rubbing my face into that, aren't you?"

He grinned. "I just don't want you to get too used to the idea that the house is yours. You might get to liking it."

"I told you the last time I saw you that I'd move myself and my guests out immediately."

"Oh, there's no hurry. One or two things to clear up first."

"Such as murder, treason, desertion, and obstructing justice."

"You've been looking up my character references, I can see."

Against my will I laughed.

"All right, Kit, now that we've got that out of the way, do sit down. Take that chair"—he waved towards a tattered wing chair—"it still has some bottom."

"How on earth did you get these up here?" I asked. He was right to cover the floor, I thought, shivering a little, it was cold up here.

"Here." Before I knew what had happened he had pulled a blanket from off the floor and put it around me. Then he sat down in the other chair, which seemed to fold in.

"I can see what you mean about the bottom," I said.

"Yes. Pete and I got them up and it was a bad choice. Unfortunately, just as the bottom gave out, you arrived, so I couldn't replace it with the one your artist friend uses downstairs."

I was looking at him. Standing, his head was somewhat in the shadows that came down from the vault. Seated, his face was in the light and looked both white and drawn.

"Do you ever get out, get any exercise?"

"Not since you arrived. Before that, sure. That's one good thing about the isolation."

"I'm surprised Simon didn't see you. Pete says he doesn't know you're here."

"I know Pete thinks that. I'm not so sure myself. I have a feeling he does know."

"Would it matter?"

He glanced quickly at me. "It might." The sombre, deepset gray eyes continued to stare at me.

122

"What's the matter? Why are you looking at me like that?"

"You were such a scrawny, scowling kid. I didn't expect you to turn into such a pretty girl."

To my intense irritation, I felt myself blushing. Long study and trial and error had made me stylish and well-groomed. But I had never thought of myself as pretty. I fought against the feeling of gratification.

"Flattery would normally get you almost anywhere."

"But not in this case?"

"No, Cousin Nicholas, not in this case. What are you trying to manipulate me about?"

"Well, you can't blame a man for trying every approach. All right. I'm going to need your help. I'm sending Pete away on an errand. Somebody has to bring me food. I'm afraid that's you."

"Spoken with all the gracious concern for someone else's feelings that I always associate with the Trelawnys. Bravo! You haven't let the vicissitudes of life and imprisonment in any way spoil your natural arrogance, have you?"

"You can always refuse."

"Of course. And it's a delightful choice. Either you starve slowly to death, or you come out of hiding and get caught by one of the various posses after you—as you so kindly pointed out in our last warm, affectionate interchange. And you left out something, Nicholas. I could blackmail you into signing the house over to me, couldn't I?"

"I wanted you to see some of the alternatives yourself. No use doing all your plotting for you."

He was leaning back, his face again in shadow. At that moment something about his lazy, negligent pose kicked off a memory from all those summers before: tea and drinks on the lawn in front of the house. The twins lounging, drinks in hand, identical in their white tennis trousers and shirts, the epitome of indolent aristocracy: Nicholas, his head back, laughing; Giles staring moodily into the sea. The memory brought something else with it—a jab of pain. Because what Nicholas was laughing at was I. There had been a dinner the previous night, involving sticky fruit and finger-bowls, something entirely new to my mother and me.

"You should have seen her," Nicholas was relating laughingly to some visitor. "Poor Kit, she all but stripped for a spit bath."

He was right. But that wasn't what the mocking was about. It was my mother, who had innocently asked the servant behind her if she could have some soap. And there was, for about a quarter of a minute, one of those silences that wither the soul. The dowager, mouth unmoving, but eyes narrowed with laughter, had nodded to the servant, who came back with one of the small cakes of soap put in each guest bathroom. By this time Mother knew she had done something ridiculous, and so she sat there, staring at the little soap, until I grabbed it and plunged into a thorough scrub-off. Nicholas, the master raconteur, was making a brilliant story of it. Even those who knew it was unkind couldn't help laughing, all except Mother and me—and Giles. I had hardly noticed he wasn't laughing until he suddenly got up and said, "But I can top that"—and went off into some story about himself and his twin that made them both look silly. Everyone laughed at that, too, just as heartily—except for Nicholas and his mother.

". . . I said what the hell's the matter?" Nicholas, no longer lazing back in his chair, was staring at me.

"You really were a rotten bastard," I said, with more emotion than I had intended to let show.

"What brought that on? What are you talking about?"

I told him.

"Well, if it gives you any pleasure to think about it, you had all the revenge even you would have wanted after I was captured. Humiliation was one of our captors' favorite weapons."

"I suppose I should protest over that. But I'm not going to. Yes, it does give me satisfaction—at least as far as you are concerned. Not the others, of course."

"My God," he said. "You are bitter."

"It killed my mother."

"Rubbish. Cancer killed your mother. She had it when you visited here. That was why you came. You knew that. The rest is pure self-pity and grudge. Yes. We were cruel. But we paid. Don't you think Mother knew what . . . Giles was doing, making those broad-

124

casts? What do you think that did to her pride? She paid. She paid in full."

"I'm glad," I said, "glad, glad, glad." And with that, burst into tears.

Until I came to Trelawny's Fell I had not cried since my mother died. Within two days I had cried twice. I couldn't prevent it, and I couldn't seem to stop it. It was as though some old, unhealed wound had reopened and were draining. As though the twelve-year-old child still within me were at long last letting go her grief and pain.

And then something very strange happened. I felt a hand on my shoulder. Nicholas had sat down on the arm of my chair and put his arm around me.

"There, there," he said gently. "I'm sorry. I'm really sorry. Sorry for everything."

Astonishingly, unbelievably, I put my arms around him and hid my face in the front of his sweater, while he stroked my head. Then he gently raised my face and kissed me. I jumped up and away. "What's happened to me? What am I doing? How dare you kiss me? I must be out of my mind! Let me go this instant!"

"Who's stopping you? And keep your voice down. Unless, of course, you're aiming to have me discovered without appearing to be responsible for it."

By this time we were facing each other, both on our feet. Nicholas limped towards me, and with the air of a Regency rake accosting a housemaid, chucked me under the chin. "Don't be so virtuous, Kit. What's wrong with a little diversion. I could use it."

His lips were no more than an inch away when I slapped him—or started to. "I'm not about to be your or anybody else's diversion."

He caught my hand and put it behind me and pinned it with the other. I am thin but no will-o'-the-wisp. I have always thought of myself as strong and well able to take care of myself. But I could not move. His other stronger arm around me was like iron. Then he kissed me again and as his lips held mine I became intensely aware of his hard, flat body against my own. And then something happened that I was thoroughly ashamed of. Through strain or fear or fatigue or something, I started to give in. At that second, he pushed me away. "Don't be quite so free with your hands," he said quite gently, but with ice in his voice, "or I'll give you a much more emphatic lesson."

I simply turned and went down the stairs and into the central attic, and as I did so, heard the door slide closed behind me. I was in bed, my mind seething with a welter of emotions, when I realized that there was something about the central attic that bothered me, although I couldn't remember what it was. I knew I should get up and go back and investigate, but I was too angry. The only thing I had to hide was Nicholas. And at this point that didn't seem too important. Fantasies of his being dragged off by the state or military police danced through my head, and I allowed them to play, hoping they would bring all the satisfaction my soul yearned for.

Unfortunately, they didn't. All they produced were nightmares.

6

After a mostly wakeful night I arrived, by dawn, at some conclusions and a decision. The decision was that it was in my own best interests to assist Nicholas in every way I could to establish his rightful identity and thus clear himself. For one thing, living under the same roof with him again—especially since it was his own roof!—had aroused every painful and humiliating memory that I thought I had resolved and buried. When I was with Nicholas, everything I had done or become since I was twelve vanished. Whatever I might appear on the outside, inside I was still the naïve, gauche country mouse that had evoked such withering hilarity. I might—as I had, most of the night—tell myself that this was all neurotic nonsense; that it was I who was replaying all those old tapes again in my head. The fact remained that around Nicholas Trelawny I shriveled, as I had shriveled before his mother and himself and as

I had watched my mother shrivel fifteen years before.

Sometime in the course of the night another unpalatable fact had presented itself to me with blinding simplicity: I had been thinking that it was Nicholas who was my unwelcome guest. I had it backwards: however much he might remain invisible most of the time, Nicholas was my host, and the host, however reluctantly, of all my artists. It was astonishing how much that simple recognition of the true state of affairs took the starch out of me.

What I would like to do was pack up and go, taking my guests with me. And that was exactly what I intended doing as soon as I could manage it. But until Pete got back from his errand—whatever that was— Nicholas had no one but me to bring him food, and much as I detested him, it would not help me in any way either to be accused of trying to help him out of this life so I could take back The Fell, or of trying to blackmail him into deeding it to me. The latter seemed so unlikely I didn't give it much serious thought: lively as it was, my imagination could not achieve a picture of Nicholas allowing himself to be blackmailed.

With plans for my immediate future solved so easily, I should have felt clear in my mind and serene in my soul. What I felt was depressed. "Well," I said to Josephine, "no use lying here and feeling worse by the minute." I sat up, threw back the covers, and stood on the floor. Then I went over to the window. There was a pinkish-gray mist over everything. Then with indescribable majesty, the flaring red disc started to lift itself out of the sea. It was such an astounding sight that I just stood there, shivering in my nightgown. Lines from an English book of verse sifted through my mind:

Light on the Laspur hills was broadening fast,
The blood-red snow-peaks chilled to a dazzling white;
He turn'd, and saw the golden circle at last,
Cut by the eastern height.

Oh glorious Life, Who dwellest in earth and sun,
I have lived, I praise and adore Thee.*

*From "He Fell Among Thieves," by Sir Henry Newbolt.

Not, perhaps, of the first rank of poetry, but apt enough, I thought, and brushed my teeth, put on jeans, a sweater, and sneakers.

It was not until I was down in the kitchen that the problems of taking food up to Nicholas really hit me. Pete had simply carried what everyone thought was his tool kit. That meant that most probably Nicholas had the wherewithal to heat coffee or tea up there with him unless, that is, Pete took a thermos. I went around the huge kitchen, opening every drawer, cupboard and closet. No thermos flask. Did he have a refrigerator? And what, by the way, did he do for a bathroom?

I pondered these interesting questions as I collected juice, milk, cheese, bread, butter and cold chicken. Any ordinary mortal could do with cornflakes, I thought meanly, but Trelawnys weren't ordinary, as they would be the first to tell you. However, to go through the house carrying a tray would be to invite discovery. After some more opening of various hiding places, I found a floppy straw basket and packed it. If anyone wanted to know what I was carrying, I would tell them . . . well, I would make something up.

Perhaps fortunately for my lack of resource, I met no one and got up to the central attic and knocked on the panel. There was the sound of steps on the other side and the panel was pushed aside. Nicholas, who was only partly down the gangway, went on up ahead of me.

"I brought you some breakfast."

"All that?"

"Well, I didn't know what milord would like to have."

"I usually have cornflakes."

I could have hit him with the basket. "You mean just like ordinary folks?"

He stared down at me from his arrogant height. "Do you think if you took a dozen emery boards and an iron file you could get that chip on your shoulder down to manageable proportions?"

I decided nothing was to be gained by returning his nastiness with more of the same, however much I might enjoy it. It would simply waste valuable time that should be devoted to trying to find whatever would establish Nicholas's identity.

"How was I to know what you wanted for breakfast? I just brought everything I could think of."

He grunted and looked over the contents. All he took out was the orange juice and milk.

"Aren't you going to eat anything?"

"No. I'm not hungry. Just thirsty." He poured some orange juice into a glass and then some milk into a cup of coffee.

"I was wondering if you were able to make coffee up here."

"Instant. Or hot water for soup. I have one of these plug-in affairs. But Pete had to run the outlet from below, and the wiring's not that powerful, so it's all I can do."

"I have made a decision," I said.

"Oh. How have you decided to do it?"

"Do what?"

"Dispose of me."

I took a breath. *"Much* as I would like to, that's not the decision I was talking about."

He looked at me over the glass of orange juice. "How disappointing. I was thinking of it as quite a challenge."

I could hear the mockery in his voice and felt the stirrings of anger. Keep it cool, I said to myself. "I have decided I'm going to help you establish your identity so you can get your multitudinous problems out of the way and reestablish yourself as the laird of Trelawny's Fell and chief Poo-Bah of the local establishment."

"How nice of you. I can hardly bear to ask why."

"Because the sooner that's done, the sooner I can get out and wipe you all out of my life."

"Who is 'all'?"

"You and your family."

"But you're my family. Else how would you be here?"

"The moment you can walk downstairs free and clear, I stop being your family."

"But—" He had been standing near the more tattered of the chairs. Quite suddenly he reached out and held on to the back of it. The blackout curtains were down

129

and in the clear morning light his face looked ghastly.

"You're ill," I said.

"Not really. Just not over one or two impairments. I think I'll sit down." And he did. Abruptly. For a minute he sat, his face in his hands, his elbows on his knees. Living miles from a doctor as a child and adolescent I had had fairly thorough first-aid training.

"Do you have a bathroom anywhere available?" I asked.

I thought for a minute he wasn't going to answer. Then he waved a hand to the other end of the long attic, towards the north extension. "Opposite the steps there," he said.

When I got to the end, I saw a repetition of the gangway-type stairs that led from the southern end. Across from where they emerged a bathroom opened off to my right. I got hold of the facecloth in there, squeezed it out in cold water, filled a small pan with more water, and took it back across the attic.

"Here," I said, walking over to Nicholas. I took the cold wet cloth and put it around his head. A shudder went through him. His face burned dry to the touch.

"You have fever!" I exclaimed.

"Yes."

"Do you have any medicine?"

"Over there. In the pocket of my jacket."

Nicholas was wearing the same navy-blue sweater I had seen him in both times before, but there was a tweed jacket over the back of a chair. I went quickly through the side pockets, unearthed a set of keys and a box of what turned out to be pills.

"How many?" I asked, and at that point nearly jumped out of my skin and barely managed not to shriek. Out of the breast pocket of the jacket jumped a plump brown mouse.

"That was a mouse in your pocket," I said.

"Yes. That's Richard. He likes to sleep there."

"You mean you have a pet mouse?"

"I have several. The choice of companionship up here isn't what you'd call varied. But I'm not sure I wouldn't choose the mice anyway. They're nice little fellows."

"Thanks a lot."

"Oh stop taking everything personally and hand me those pills."

He looked so dreadful that I decided not to argue with him. I came over and handed him the box and poured a glass of water from a carafe sitting there.

"What do you have?" I asked.

"The remains of some Asiatic virus. A form of malaria."

The word itself was evocative. Malaria went with jungles and swamps and brilliant green. . . . Suddenly I found myself thinking about the painting in my room. "Did you do that watercolor in my room? The one of the soldier with a boat?"

He wasn't really paying attention. "What? Oh—yes."

"It's good. Really good."

He looked up. "And are you an expert?"

"Enough to know what's real talent and what isn't. In case you've forgotten, that's why I brought all those artists here. It's a subject I know something about."

"What artists? The only one who seems to be doing any work is that spaced-out freak who painted that monstrosity downstairs."

"Well, that shows how much you know about art. I don't particularly like it, but it shows genuine ability."

"I didn't say it didn't. But it's still a monstrosity. You'd better watch out for that man."

"Rubbish. What do you know about really creative people?"

"Now you're the one that's being arrogant. Only the true people can enjoy esthetic appreciation."

"Leave us something," I snapped. "You have all the rest."

He sat back. His face was still tight, as though with pain, but the pills have done something for him because he looked a little better. In this light, I noted, the remarkable Trelawny eyes were more green than gray.

"Tell me," he said conversationally, "what you mean by 'all the rest'? Of what do you feel so deprived? You have education, a good job, and, since status means so much to you, you rub shoulders with the famous and near famous. Or so I gather. Why are you so sorry for yourself? You're not the little match girl. Why do you insist on playing the role? What is it doing for you?"

131

I stared at him, waiting for the fury to hit me so I could fight back. But just as it did, there came into my mind something I heard a lecturer in Jungian psychology say: *we all live our own myths*. Was that my myth? That I was the little match girl?

"Suppose," he went on, "you had never heard of The Fell, had never come here with your mother, would your life have been better or worse? I have a feeling that your visit here, with all the slings and arrows it produced, was the goad that got you where you are. Are you sorry? Would it have been better to live out your life on a Wyoming ranch? And if so, what's to prevent your going back there?" He got up, steadied himself, and moved towards me. "You know, I'm tired of playing chief villain in this drama you've created for yourself. And I would think you'd be intelligent enough to be sick of it, too." And with that, before I could reply, he gave a funny sort of gasp, fell and lay still.

Fortunately for his head and bones, the thick coverings on the floor cushioned his fall. And he had struck nothing on the way down. Even so, having him lying, white and unconscious, on the floor was frightening enough.

"Nicholas," I said, trying to rouse him. "Nicholas!" At that moment he groaned and started muttering. His skin was even hotter to the touch than it had been. Either the pills had not worked at all or they had had a reverse effect.

I had nursed my mother through her last illness, and had taken care of most of the children on the ranch when they had come down with the various diseases of childhood. Illness held no mystery for me. But I knew I had to get Nicholas, all six feet two of him, onto his bed, and thin as he was, he was big-boned and it would be no easy task.

I sat back on my knees for a minute, wondering who I could ask to help me. They all—all the men, that is —paraded before my mind: Frank, Rod and Bill Seaward.

"No," Nicholas muttered, turning his head from side to side. And then more loudly, "No!" It was almost as though he knew what was happening in my mind, and were pleading against it.

I leaned forward. "Sh! Someone might hear you. Quiet!" I hadn't expected to get through to him, but apparently I did, because he stopped immediately. Then said, "Kit?" in a surprised voice. But when I leaned over him again, his eyes, though open, held no recognition.

I thought again of the men in the house who might help me get Nicholas into bed. But looking at him, unshaven, gaunt, and helpless, I couldn't bring myself to get any help. "I'll just have to do it by myself," I muttered. I measured with my eyes the distance to the bed: about ten feet.

"Well," I said. "Here goes."

Fifteen minutes later Nicholas was in bed and I was sitting on the floor, exhausted, and wishing with all my heart that Pete were not away.

Slowly I got up and went over to the bed. I knew I had soon to go downstairs if I didn't want to arouse suspicion. Yet I hated to leave him. To my surprise he opened his eyes and said, "How long was I out?"

"About twenty minutes. Does that happen often?"

He put his hand up to his head. "From time to time. While I'm having a bout I go in and out like a light."

"I don't like to leave you, but—"

"I'm all right," he said.

I hesitated. "Is there anywhere I can get hold of Pete, if you pass out and stay out?"

He had been facing away from me, but he turned and stared.

I stared back and then said, "What's the long look for?"

"I'm trying to figure out if I can really trust you."

Unreasonably, I bristled. "I could have just gone off and left you, you know."

"In view of what you've been saying off and on for the past day or so, or what you tell me you feel, I don't see that my hesitation is so remarkable. However, I don't have that much choice. Hand me my jacket."

I picked the coat off the chair and thrust it at him. His doubt was hardly, as he put it, unreasonable. I knew that, yet I was irritated.

He felt along the lining of the coat and at one point thrust his fingers into what must have been a break in

133

the seam. From this he extracted a piece of paper. "You can get Pete here if you have to," he said in a tired voice. "Go on down now. I'll be all right."

Feeling both huffy and worried I was starting to go down the stairs leading to the central attic, when he spoke again.

"You'd do better to go down the stairs at the other end. It's a longer way around and you may get lost, but you won't be in such danger of running into one of your flock. When you get to the bottom, walk along the hall till you come to the end, then go into the last room on the right. In it there's a clothes closet. But it opens onto stairs leading to the second floor. You shouldn't have any trouble from there on."

"Sometime when you're feeling better," I said with great feeling, "I should like to know why your crazy ancestors built this monster of a house this way. Why all the secret stairs leading out of closets?"

"Your ancestors, too, cousin mine! It's a long story, most of it boring. Many of what you call secret stairs weren't meant to be secret. They were outside staircases that were incorporated into another addition of rooms or some such."

"Including the north attics built like a Chinese maze?"

"Ah! Those were something else. I built those myself with Pete's aid. I'm rather proud of them. Shift a wall here, a door there, and you have an entirely different layout."

"You knew I was getting lost up here that first day."

"Knew it? I created it. I wasn't expecting you, and you almost caught me downstairs in the central attic. I had to get back up without your seeing me. I was right in front of you every step of the way."

"But why didn't I hear you?"

"Because I synchronized all my movements with yours."

"You must have thought it was all very funny."

"I did."

"Ha-ha."

"Well, I always wanted to be an architect, and one of the ways I amused myself in prison camp was by creating the maze. Once I got here it was easy to carry out."

"If you wanted to be an architect, why were you in the Navy?"

Nicholas rolled over on his back. "Family tradition. Before you go into your prepared speech on the subject, you don't have to tell me how empty it all is. I know."

I could almost not bear not to argue with him. Evidently this was all too plain on my face. Nicholas's gray-green eyes, though tired and bloodshot, looked at me with amusement.

"My lips are sealed," I said to him.

"But not for long," he murmured, and closed his eyes.

"I don't know when I'll be back," I said over my shoulder, frustrated at not feeling free to hurl invectives at him.

"That'll teach me."

Surprisingly, I didn't get lost, but it took me fifteen minutes to work my way back to the kitchen where everyone was sitting at the large round table. "Good morning," I said cheerfully.

"Are you all right?" Pogs asked.

"We were looking for you," Rod said.

Tess didn't say anything. She had a soft, dreamy look on her face and gave me a vague smile. Frank was watching me. "Where ya been?" he asked.

"Out. Getting some early morning air," I improvised.

"I didn't see you," he sounded hostile and suspicious.

"Where were you looking?" I poured myself some coffee.

"Front and back."

"Oh, well, that explains it. I was walking in the woods."

"But you'd have to cross some open space to get to them or get back."

I decided to take the offensive. "What are you, anyway, the FBI?"

Rod tipped back his chair. "Yeah, man, what gives? Why the Inquisition?"

Tess said in a little-girl voice, "Frank has a secret life you don't know anything about."

"Shut up," Frank said viciously.

I looked at him. "In my house she'll say what she likes."

"Yeah, that's the question, though, isn't it? Is it your house?"

Fright is such a physical thing. I felt my stomach drop, or that's what it seemed like. "What are you talking about?" I finally asked.

Rod dropped his chair forward. "Yeah. What's that supposed to mean?"

There was no telling where this interesting conversation might have gone if there were not an interruption. There was the sound of a step.

"The door was open so I just came in. Hope it was all right." Standing in the door was Bill Seaward.

I got up. "Of course, Bill. Come in. Er—I don't think you've met my mini-colony. Starting with Tess in the red blouse near you, and going around the table clockwise, there's Rod Moscovitch, Mary Butler-Longman and Frank Morse. Troops, this is Dr. Bill Seaward."

There was a general murmur of greeting and a scraping of chairs, as everybody got up to leave.

"Don't all go on my account," Bill said.

Rod pushed in his chair. "Time to get to work. Nice to meet you."

Frank just walked out. Tess gave the doctor a shy, dreamy smile and followed. Pogs said, "How do you do?" She cocked her head on one side. "Haven't we met?"

"I'm sure not." Bill smiled. "I would have remembered."

"Well I think we have, but it must have been long ago and I can't quite recall where."

"Truly, I think not, Miss Butler-Longman."

"Pogs."

"Er what?"

But Pogs had left, her blue kimono flapping around her blue-jeaned legs.

"What was that she said?" he asked me.

"She meant you to call her Pogs," Rod said. Methodically he was clearing the table.

"Do I have you to thank for breakfast, Rod?" I asked.

"You can thank me for the coffee. But for the bacon

and eggs you didn't eat, you could thank Pogs. What, by the way, happened to her cold chicken? She was looking for it. Apparently she's partial to cold chicken for breakfast."

I could feel the color surging up into my cheeks. "Somebody must have eaten it," I finally said.

"Well, whoever did, did so in the middle of the night, she said. Because it was there just before she went to bed."

It was at that moment I remembered what had bothered me about the central attic when I had left Nicholas the previous night. I had gone up there by guesswork, aided now and again by another flashlight. I had not turned on the lights in the central attic, only too aware of the uncurtained windows and the shafts of light that would pour out of them. But when I slipped through the panel back into the attic, the center light was on. Who had turned it on?

"Oh," I said. With an effort I brought my mind back to the cold chicken. "Somebody must have gotten the hungries in the middle of the night."

"Well I didn't," Rod said, "so that cuts the options down by one."

There was a silence. Then I said as lightly as I could, "Well, neither did I. So that cuts it down by two." Strictly speaking, it was an honest answer, however much of an untruth it was designed to convey. I had not had the hungries in the middle of the night. Nor had I removed the chicken then. Rod stared hard at me. Then he murmured, "See you." And left the kitchen.

"You are under suspicion," Bill said. "Item: one missing cold chicken. Who do you suppose is the culprit?"

I wanted to move off that subject as quickly as possible. "Who knows or cares? My artists have a very slapdash attitude towards life and property, which is one of the things I like about them. I can't see them getting into a Duty, Honor, Country frame of mind over one cold chicken."

"May I?" Bill picked up the coffee pot and pulled a clean cup from the draining rack over towards him.

"Sure. Help yourself."

"Just f-y-i and as an inspired guess, I would be very surprised if that pretty brown-eyed girl—what did you call her? Tess?—were the culprit."

I had a sinking feeling that the conversation was getting into areas that would not make for my happiness. "So should I. But why?"

"Because I would say she's on drugs—at least she was this morning. Did you notice the pupils of her eyes? They were enormous. And ravening hunger in the middle of the night is not one of the symptoms of an addict. Of course, she may have come down off her high and then gotten hungry. But I doubt it. More likely to have taken something to get her to sleep."

He said it calmly, as though he had no idea what a bombshell he dropped.

I said finally, "Are you sure?"

"Reasonably." He drank some more coffee. "Does it tally with what you know of her?"

I sat down. "I don't really know anything about her, other than she is Frank Morse's girl friend, appears to be the antithesis of whatever the Women's Lib. is fighting for, and slavishly does whatever he orders. She said once she'd been in the theater. I think Frank interrupted that. And when," I finished bitterly, "I suggested to her that he was not the best possible thing that happened in her life, she dumped some weed killer into the stew and shot out of the room. Talk about kissing the whip handle! And I would lay you any odds that it was Frank that got her on."

"Very likely. But I doubt if he's an addict himself."

"Well, all the more unforgivable! Wait until I get hold of him!"

"Just a minute before you go off breathing fire and vengeance. All this is supposition. You don't know that he got her on drugs. You don't like him, for which I don't blame you. He's a mean-looking customer. But all he'd have to do is claim that he's trying to get her off drugs. How could you prove otherwise?"

"After giving her a fix or a pill or whatever last night or this morning?"

"Can you prove he did that? Couldn't she have taken it on her own? Maybe he's trying to help her."

"Then why doesn't he put her in a reputable hospital?"

"Who knows? And he doesn't exactly come from that segment of society that goes rushing off to the police out of habit."

It was all true.

"You're letting your prejudices get the better of you. I suggest you get a few facts before you start calling in the authorities."

"And in the meantime, my house is becoming an opium den."

He laughed. "I wouldn't say it was that bad. By the way, my curiosity is tickled. What happened to the stew?"

I looked blank.

"The stuff Tess polluted."

"Oh—that. It's in a bucket in the storeroom waiting to be buried."

"What about throwing it down the toilet?"

"Our plumbing may be too frail and venerable for that. My heart quails at the thought of tampering with what must be several miles of ancient pipe."

"I can see your point. Speaking of the house, I take it that the—er—inheritance is all squared away. No nearer heirs?"

That was the second person in one morning who had asked me that question. I decided to bluff it out. "Isn't that funny? You're the second person who's asked me that today. I wonder why."

He turned his back and took his coffee cup over to the sink. "No particular reason, I guess. But anybody around here finds anything to do with the Trelawny family of absorbing interest."

"Yes, but Frank isn't from around here."

Bill turned around. "Then he must have picked up local vibrations. Now let me ask you a question. Why are you shying so nervously at a perfectly ordinary comment like that? Mr. Trelawny died years ago, and rumors about Nicholas and Giles have been flying back and forth ever since. Despite all the reports, no one around here has ever been sure that both of them died."

I couldn't have been more astounded if he had let off a firecracker. "But the account in the papers—"

"Oh, that. You have to understand rural districts, Kit. In fact, having grown up in one yourself, I'm surprised at your surprise. Don't you know that only the really sophisticated believe everything they read in the papers? There has always been a belief around here that one of the twins—only no one knows which one —survived."

"I see," I finally managed to say. "Well, this is the first I've heard of it."

"You've been working too hard. I'm going into Portland today. I have some business there and I want to drop into the clinic. Why don't you play hooky and come along?"

"I'd love to, Bill. But I can't. There's so much to do here. Each night I go to bed with only half of what I planned to do done."

"You should be enjoying yourself. What if you didn't do any work at all for a day? Would the world come to an end? I bet you have lots of errands you can do while I'm bustling about the clinic."

As a matter of fact, I was sorely tempted. For one thing, my shopping list for various things that could not be bought in the village had grown enormously. I could not put off a visit to some near metropolis forever. For another—and this was the stronger—just suddenly, the whole burden of the house, of hiding Nicholas, of Nicholas's abrasive personality, and the constant warfare between us all seemed to gather itself into a burden that I dearly wanted to be free of for a while. Damn and blast Nicholas! I thought. Let him take care of himself for a while!

Bill walked over and grasped my arms in his hands. "Come along, Kit. Kick up your heels. Let's have some fun. You owe it to yourself."

It was nice to be looked at in that warm, flattering way by an attractive man. In contrast rose in my mind the picture of Nicholas's mocking face and jeering voice that made of his kiss, if not an old-fashioned insult, certainly a joke, a sort of oneupmanship ripoff.

I gave in. "Yes, I will!" I had to let Nicholas know I was going, for both our protections. "Look. Come back for me in an hour. I'll have made up my lists and gotten dressed and done one or two chores."

"That's the girl!" He squeezed my arms, and then, somewhat to my surprise and consternation, bent and kissed me.

I could feel myself blushing like any teen-ager, and pushed away. "Whoa, there!"

"Sorry. I've been wanting to do that. Can't blame a fellow for trying. But I promise to be good—within limits."

It was nice to be wanted and thought attractive. I laughed.

"You'd better get going." For some reason I wanted him to be gone.

"See you in an hour!" He waved and walked out the door.

After I had made my lists and was dressed, I went the long way around to see Nicholas, knowing that the central attic would be occupied by Frank.

When I got there, Nicholas was standing in the middle of the floor, a gaunt, towering figure in his jeans and sweater.

"I thought you were sick," I said, not too graciously.

"Disappointed?"

"No. Suspicious. What are you up to?"

"No good. You can depend on that."

"I do," I said drily. I walked over to where I could see his face in the light. There were black shadows under his eyes and his cheeks looked more hollow than ever. The eyes themselves were overbright. "You're still not well."

"So? Half the work in the world is done by people who don't feel well."

"How spartan. How noble!"

"And how asinine. What was that quack doing here?"

Now I had been of two minds myself about Bill and his kiss. But at this I went up like a geyser. "Who on earth are you to criticize Bill Seaward? At least he does something useful in the world. He heals people. He just doesn't sit around the family estate, gathering tribute."

"No, but he'd like to, given half a chance. Watch out for that sharpie."

"In striking contrast to you and your benevolent intentions towards the world at large."

"I never claimed any benevolent intentions."

"Then why are you so quick to criticize others on that point?"

"And why are you bristling like a hedgehog over Bill Seaward? Don't tell me you've fallen for that fatuous ape?"

All my careful planning about helping Nicholas to establish his innocence went winging away. "And if I have," I shouted—and that was as far as I got.

With one long stride Nicholas was over and before I could get another word out his hand was clamped over my mouth and the other arm was around me, holding me rigid. I could neither move nor make a sound.

"Are you out of your mind?" he whispered savagely. "Or is this your clever way of announcing my presence without appearing to do so. How to turn me over to the police without appearing to take the responsibility. How gutless can you be? If you want me out, go to the nearest police station. They'll do the dirty work. I've always preferred the knife to the kiss as a method of betrayal. But perhaps you don't share my feeling that way."

I tried to bite his hand. I tried to kick his shin. I succeeded in neither.

"Now," Nicholas said more calmly, "I told you once before. If you want to announce my presence, do so. But have the backbone to do it openly." And with that he let me go, almost throwing me from him.

I hadn't meant to shout. I was quite sincere in wanting to help Nicholas since it was the quickest way to get him and his house and family out of my life for good, but I was beyond explaining that or even wanting to.

I was shaking all over, and to my fury, tears were running down my face. "I hate you, Nicholas. I've hated you all my life, you and all your family. I don't understand it, and there's no use my trying, but every time I am in contact with any of you it's some kind of horrible defeat. It's as though you could only exist by rolling over me as you did over everybody else. You not only humiliate people. You use them first. Talk about knives and kisses. Your whole relationship with the outside owrld is one massive exploitation and betrayal. You don't know how to deal any other way."

And I fled out of the attic.

I managed to get my face washed and restored to order before Bill drove up in his elegant foreign car. Nevertheless, I was aware that his eyes were searching my face rather carefully.

"Are you all right?" he asked.

I tried to pass it off lightly. "Is that a medical or a personal question?"

"Both, I guess. You look a little—"

I glanced at him while he cast around for a word. I managed a smile. "Distracted?"

"Yes, distracted. No, something more. Upset?"

"I can't find Josephine. I'm used to her absences, but it's been two days now."

This was not strictly true. She had indeed been absent. But, though I was a little surprised since no matter how far she rambled she usually showed up on my bed at night, I was not dismayed. Josephine had been living a rich, full, vitamin-packed life since she had come to The Fell. Her coat shone, her sides had filled out, and she had given all the signs of total satisfaction. She even looked younger. But I thought it sounded like a good excuse.

"And you suddenly got dismayed by this in the hour since I was here?" Bill asked gently, opening the door and closing it after me as I got into the passenger seat.

I was trying to think of an acceptable reply when he got in his side. "Something else, I think, Kit."

For half a second I was tempted to tell him the truth about Nicholas. My burning sense of being ill used would certainly find a sympathetic audience. And Bill could supply me with information as to how I was to treat some vague Asiatic bug. In fact, if he knew, I could take him up to see Nicholas. But at that point I remembered Nicholas's "quack." He would probably turn ugly.

"Now what was that about?" I glanced up. Bill, who was driving away from the house, had turned his head for a moment and looked at me.

"You know, being around you has its hazards, Bill. Have you ever been tested for ESP?"

He laughed. "No." He eased the car off the cobblestones onto the partly paved road. "But you haven't

143

told me what caused your worry." He glanced down at me. "Tell the doctor, now."

I might have. Bill took his right hand off the wheel and closed it over mine. I liked Bill and I liked the fact that he so obviously liked me. So I don't know why it turned me off.

"I guess it's just that I don't like the idea of drugs being taken in my house. I thought of it while you were gone and felt worse and worse about it, because, I suppose, I don't know what to do."

His hand seemed to slacken. Then he put it back on the wheel. "Well, you can always ask them to leave," he said, but with something less than the total interest he had been showing.

Bill took me to a handsome and expensive lunch in a restaurant that had once been a mill. "Since you have a front-tier view of the ocean all the time, I decided that you should have a rustic backdrop for lunch," he said.

It was a charming place, the dining room jutting out over a stream that babbled and eddied around rocks and in which, now and again, slid speckled trout. The only sound was made by the little brook. We were early, the dining room was almost empty and a sense of peace seemed part of the place itself. I knew this, I felt it, as I knew Bill was putting himself out to be both affectionate and entertaining and I made a concerted effort to let it all flow over and drown out a niggling anxiety I could not get rid of. As though he knew, Bill ambled on about his practice and patients and the village.

I was just congratulating myself that, for once, the Trelawnys were not the main topic of conversation when unwittingly I dragged them in. I had just helped myself to a second hot buttered roll—a specialty of the house, we were told—and I passed the basket back to Bill. He shook his head. "No thanks."

"Don't tell me you're on a diet." It was one of those meaningless comments made mainly because I was feeling embarrassed by my always splendid appetite. "Not that you should be," I added hastily.

Bill's face was so expressionless that I was sure I had trodden on a corn.

"Just cautious," he said lightly. He gave a wry smile. "Something no Trelawny ever had to worry about."

There leapt to my mind again a picture of those graceful, beautiful people. Was there any mockery more barbed than of those blessed of face and form at the expense of those who weren't? How carelessly the twins and their cousins flaunted their well-cared-for bodies, their astonishing good looks.

Bill reached out his hand. "What are you thinking about?"

"About the Trelawnys, who never have to diet. But for all their slenderness they might, like the rich men in the Bible, have a hard time passing through the eye of a needle."

"It's odd you should say that."

"Why? Because I'm thin? My mother wasn't. She came from a long line of Scandinavian farmers, and, like most of the poor, lived off starch. I can remember her sitting there, bulging out of her cotton dress, while the streamlined Trelawnys ran around in slacks and shorts and riding clothes—not an excess ounce visible anywhere. Once, when there was a swimming party on, Mrs. Trelawny offered Mother the loan of a bathing suit, a bikini. I remember thinking how delighted she'd be if Mother accepted and how carefully everyone didn't laugh."

"So you know," Bill said.

"Know what?"

"What she—Mrs. Trelawny—could be like."

"Of course I know. But I thought you had a crush on her."

"I did. Until—"

"Until what?"

He straightened his fork. "Oh, she pulled a similar trick on me to the one she did on your mother. Before I shot up I was short and chunky. The twins were older, of course, but even their cousins who were my age—including the girls—were about a foot taller and athletic. Our *Lumpenproletarian*, Mrs. Trelawny once called me. It caught on right away. I was 'The Lump' for the rest of that summer until my father found me

145

crying one day and made me tell him why. After that it stopped."

"Hurray for your father. I wonder how he stopped it."

"So did I. Whatever it was, it worked, at least it did after one final jibe. Somebody referred once more to me as 'The Lump.' Mrs. Trelawny said 'Oh we mustn't call him that any more. Hurt-feelings department. Such a bore!' "

"I'm sorry."

"Nothing to be sorry about. Water over the dam."

Was it? Was water like that ever over the dam? I thought with anger of Nicholas in the attic and was surprised when the anger seemed laced with anxiety. I pulled my mind back to Bill.

"Why did you go on playing with them? When they were so bitchy?"

"Partly because there was no one else around here— no one of that kind anyway. One or two village kids maybe. . . . Partly because I thought some of their magic would rub off on me."

"Well, some of their snobbery did."

"I guess so."

But I knew what he meant about their magic. I remembered Nicholas's laughing eyes and handsome face looking down at me, his careless kiss to an alien child, and how my heart quivered and plunged. Sometimes then I had the fantasy that he was an archangel, blazing and brilliant. If two wings soaring up behind him had suddenly materialized, I don't think I would have been surprised. But what relation did that towering prince have with the scarred, abrupt, middle-aged man in the attic with his fever and his haunted face? The anxiety pressed a little.

"Hey!" Bill said. "Remember me?"

I smiled. "I do. And let's stop talking about the Trelawnys."

"With pleasure."

"Tell me some more about your practice and your patients."

"Well, let's see. . . . There's old Mrs. Torrey, who calls me ostensibly about her rheumatism, but in reality because she wants me to look at her cat."

"No local vet?"

"Sure. And a good one. But Mrs. Torrey says her Rameses II is a person and needs a person doctor. . . ."

We laughed and I listened some more, refusing to pay attention to a gnawing that was going on somewhere far back in my consciousness. But it was I, again, who, without thinking, dragged the Trelawnys back into the conversation. Bill had just mentioned the Bradfords when I suddenly interrupted him.

"Why does that sour-looking Mrs. Bradford hate the Trelawnys so much?" I made a face. "There I go again. All roads lead to Rome—that is, the Trelawnys. But, since I started, every time I go in there I keep feeling that if she were a European peasant, Mrs. Bradford would make the sign of the evil eye."

Bill looked at me curiously. "I thought you knew, although, come to think of it, I don't know why I thought so. . . ." He paused.

"Knew what?"

"Priscilla, Pete's cousin. She's the daughter of one of the twins."

Of course, I thought. How obvious. Somewhere in my mind I had known it from the moment I saw her. She had all the characteristic Trelawny looks, the light-gray eyes, black hair and a small, feminine version of the Trelawny aquiline beak. I asked sharply, "Which one—Nicholas or Giles?"

"Well, that's the problem. Nobody's quite sure."

Nobody, I thought, except the man in the north attic. He could be sure.

As though answering my thought, Bill said, "You see, it could have been either."

I fought down a sick feeling. *"Either?"*

"Yes. Priscilla's mother, Gillian, was a wild piece. Left home when she was sixteen and went to Boston to work. She encountered one of the twins there and, so goes the story, used to go on drinking sprees with them both. Drugs too, I understand."

The serene peace of that country place was shattered.

"I'm sorry," Bill said, concern in his voice. "I didn't mean to tell you, certainly not here, which I wanted to be a carefree time for you."

"It's all right. But let's go, Bill."

He paid the bill and we left. As we drove I could feel his eyes slide towards me from time to time, but neither of us spoke. It was hard to sort out how I felt, other than in a turmoil. Anger and disgust certainly had a large share, and for a while blotted out all other feelings. But as we neared the city, I was forced to the realization that there were other emotions in the growing discomfort I felt. As we pulled up outside the clinic Bill said, "Look, I'm really sorry I spoiled your day. Let me take you somewhere—a movie, maybe—while I'm in here, to get your mind off that wretched house. Or let me drive you to wherever you want to do your shopping."

"Don't beat yourself, Bill. I'm glad I know. At least it clears up one mystery. If you know what you're dealing with, you can go on from there."

"Yes. That's what I thought," Bill said quickly. "That's why I told you."

It was an odd thing for Bill to say, in view of all he had been saying before. But all I wanted to do was get by myself and sort things out. "I'd rather walk, Bill. It's not far. I'd like the exercise. Besides, I haven't seen the town."

"But what about all you'll have to carry."

"If it's too much, I'll simply leave it there and we can pick it up on the way back. How long will you be in the clinic?"

"A couple of hours at least. Maybe three. Will you be all right?"

"Sure. I'll meet you back here at your car then."

"Promise?"

"I promise."

We both got out. Bill put his hand on my shoulder. "If you want to lessen my guilt, take that look off your face. You're not responsible for the crazy acts of your family."

"No. I know. Okay." I smiled at him. "I'm fine. See you." And I walked off towards the big department store where I had to find all kinds of linen. After about five minutes I looked back to see Bill's coat disappearing inside the clinic. I knew, somehow, he would be watching me as I walked away, and I wanted to be sure he had gone into the clinic. I went on another few minutes, looked back and made sure the coast was clear, then took a right turn. Facing me was a small park. I went there and sat down on a bench.

I thought that all I needed was to be alone and able to think, free from distractions, for everything to fall into place. But I was wrong. The anger and disgust were still strong as I pictured the two drunken young men sharing an equally drunk—or perhaps drugged?—girl. I had lived in several countries and mixed with people who were proud of their liberated status from the shibboleths of the past. But as the Jesuits are often quoted as saying, "Give me a child until he is seven. . . ." And until I was much older than seven I lived a sheltered life among often rowdy but morally conventional and strict people. I suppose it was that moment that I identified at least one of the emotions that was giving me so much trouble—bitter disillusionment. And that surprised me more than anything. I felt I was second to none in my disapproval of everything the Trelawnys stood for. . . . Yet I must still have taken them at their own evaluation: their superiority to the rest of us ordinary mortals. Why else should I feel such crushing disappointment at their shabby habits?

But I looked at that unpleasant aspect of my own psyche, and accepted it for all that it portended, because it explained a frightening lot of my own actions. I was still the little match girl trying to fill the image of the all-conquering Trelawnys. And when in my heart of hearts I couldn't believe myself in that role, I took refuge for my wounded ego by thumbing my nose at them.

"You're almost as bad as they are," I said aloud to the pigeons strutting around my bench hoping for a handout.

I recalled then the scene when I had been in the Bradfords' store fifteen years earlier. Nicholas, drunk, leaning over the counter. Mrs. Bradford's face gray with rage and frustration. Giles hauling him out.

"Yuch!" I said, and got to my feet, thinking I would start on my shopping tour. But something held my feet.

To this day I am not sure whether or not I believe in ESP or, if I do, whether it was indeed telepathy that was trying to get something through to me or, more likely, that my unconscious memory was jabbing at the boundaries of my conscious mind with the message of something being wrong. Whatever it was, I found myself walking rapidly away from the park back towards the main road on which the clinic was located. When I got there, I stared down at the clinic and at Bill's car, parked among others in the adjacent lot. I also stared at a telephone booth not twenty feet from me. But if I called, I would have to explain to somebody about Nicholas's presence and how to get up to the attic. I was weighing this when a car with "Taxi" painted on it cruised towards me. I didn't stop to think. I just stepped out in the road and hailed it.

"I want to go up near Perkins. Can you take me there?"

"Perkins? That's more than thirty miles."

"I know. Can you take me there?"

"Sure. But it'll cost you fifteen bucks there and for the return journey empty."

"All right." I got in. Somehow all doubt was past. I knew I had to get back immediately.

I said to the driver. "Drive past that parking lot there. I want to leave a message with one of those cars."

The driver gave me an odd look in the rearview mirror. "Okay."

I could, of course, leave my message inside the clinic, but I very strongly did not want to run into any possibility of encountering Bill Seaward. Opening my bag I took out a spiral notebook and scribbled a few words. *Sorry. Telephoned home and found I have to return right away. Am taking a taxi. Thanks for a nice day anyway. Kit.* Then I folded and refolded it.

"Here, miss?"

"Yes. Wait for me." I got out and ran over to Bill's car and pushed the note under the windshield wiper.

"Okay," the driver said, when I got back into the car. "Where near Perkins?"

"Trelawny's Fell," I said. "Do you know it?"

"Doesn't everybody?" The man gave me another strange look in his mirror. "You a Trelawny, miss?"

"Yes."

"Lots of funny things going on up there, I hear."

"Oh? Like what?"

"All them artist types."

I relaxed. Anti-bohemianism seemed mild compared to what I was afraid he might say. But my relaxation was short-lived.

"And then there's all those stories about which one of the Trelawny boys is dead, and which one is MIA"—he encountered my startled gaze—"missing in action."

"I know what MIA means. I thought he was reported killed?"

"Yeah? Well, I never heard that."

"Tell me about those rumors."

But they didn't turn out to be much more than I had heard before. Half listening to him, I watched the empty country roll past. Here it was hilly and wooded and somehow, on this return journey, almost desolate. Perhaps it was the absence of farms or any other signs of habitation, but The Fell had never seemed so isolated The disquieting thought slid into my mind—suppose I needed help? Where would I get it?

I shook my head. Why would I need help? But it was curious. Having taken the step to go back to The Fell, I thought my anxiety would be alleviated. But the nearer we drew to home, the worse it got.

Why? I kept asking myself. So I started toting up items in my head: There was the light on in the central attic when I had emerged the other evening. Rod mentioned hearing footsteps. If he had, perhaps others had also—and weren't fooled by my story about looking for Josephine. Someone had knocked the flashlight out of my hand. Who?

What did all this add up to? It was obvious: Someone other than myself knew Nicholas was up there.

So?

But I couldn't push my deductions any further. Something jammed there.

By the time the taxi rolled over the cobblestones to draw up before the rear door I all but flung the money at the driver and got out. But I didn't dare to hurry after that, not knowing how many eyes might be watching. Forcing myself to the normal pace, I strolled through the rear door and up the stairs. On the second floor I stood there, listening. There did not seem to be anybody about. Turning, I went quickly along the hall and through the connecting door to the north wing. Running to the other end and through yet another door, I turned at right angles, went up a flight of stairs to the third floor, into the room containing the closet stairs and up those into the attic.

I didn't see Nicholas at first. The covers on the bed were in wild disorder, as though there had been a fight. Then I saw him. He was lying on the floor, drawn up, one arm flung out, clutching the quilt on the floor. His face was so white that for the space of two heartbeats I thought he was dead.

7

If I had been a few minutes later it would have been too late, because Nicholas would have been unconscious and I might not have found out in time what had poisoned him. As it was I saw his eyes half closed, half glazed over.

"Nicholas!" I ran over. "What is it? What's the matter?"

He managed to say, "You should know. You left it." He gave a gasp and made a convulsive movement. Then he said, "Stew. Over there."

I looked around. The bowl, spilled over, was behind one of the armchairs. Spread over the quilt on the floor was the stew in which Tess had dumped the weedkiller and Pete had exiled to the storeroom. Only somebody had brought it back, and as I bent nearer, I could smell from it a strong winey aroma. Whoever had brought it up here had covered the poison by drowning it in wine. But who? And why had Nicholas tasted it? But these questions would have to wait. I turned back to Nicholas. "Tess threw the weedkiller into it. That's arsenic, isn't it?"

"You—" a spasm quivered through him. Then he said, "Salt—over there."

I looked around and saw the saltcellar lying on the floor. Of course, I thought, the oldest remedy in the world.

"Help me up," he gasped.

He had managed to sit up and one hand was grasping the arm of one of the chairs. I went over and got his other arm around my shoulder. Even in that confused moment I was aware of my own reluctant admiration for the steel will in the man struggling to his feet, a will that punished and overcame his shuddering body.

"Now," he gasped. "Let's go."

When we arrived at his bathroom I quickly made up the calculatedly revolting mixture of warm water and salt and handed it to him. Then I loitered outside in case he fell. It was, for him, an exhausting and wracking twenty minutes, but successful. When it was over, cleansed now of the poison, he staggered over to the bed and lay on it. I covered him up, found a couple of heating pads in one of the many linen closets and put them at his feet and midriff, and bathed his face and forehead with a cold wet cloth. He said, just before he drifted off to sleep, "Thanks."

I sat there as the afternoon waned and thought . . . and thought. Nothing made sense. The unasked questions marched through my mind and I didn't know answers to any of them:

Who knocked the flashlight out of my hand?

Who had turned on the light in the central attic last night?

Who had brought up the food for Nicholas to eat?

And (most astonishing of all) why on earth had he eaten it?

This last was so incredible that I found myself on my feet walking around, as though in motion some answer would present itself. Nicholas mutteerd and turned. I bent down, took off my shoes, and started walking again, my feet cushioned by the quilts, blankets, rugs, and carpets that lay two inches thick on the floor. I have always thought better while moving, which was why, I suppose, I was walking round and around, staring out of the tops of the dormer windows onto the sea, into the woods in back. At that point I encountered the overturned bowl again, with the stew strewn out on the quilt. I wanted very much to know what was in that concoction, so I carefully picked up the thin blanket and the bowl and paced them at the end of the attic, where I would see them before I went down. Then, behind another chair I came across a tray. Scotch-taped to the tray was a typewritten note: "Here's your lunch. Hope you enjoy *boeuf bourguignon.*" And underneath was scrawled my inititals in a handwriting that even I would have sworn was my own if I had not known I had never written that note.

I was standing, staring at it when I heard Nicholas's voice behind me. "Don't destroy whatever prints are on it."

I turned. Nicholas was awake, looking considerably better, and sitting on the side of the bed.

I indicated the note. "You thought this was from me?"

"Of course."

"Who brought up the tray?"

"I don't know. I was in the bathroom and when I came out, it was over there, at the head of the stairs. I assumed you'd pushed it there before you left."

"But you didn't eat it right away."

"No, only a short time before you arrived."

"It's lucky you waited that long. You might be dead by now if you hadn't been able to reach the salt by yourself. Why *did* you wait that long?"

"I wasn't hungry," he said briefly.

I stared back at him. "But when you did eat it and realized it was poisoned, you must have thought I was trying to kill you."

"As much as anything can be said to have crossed my mind when that stuff—whatever was in it—started to work, you can say that that thought did present itself."

"It wasn't me, truly."

"No. Your heroic and messy efforts on my behalf convinced me of that. Did I say thanks?"

"Yes. Before you went to sleep."

He leaned back against the wall and closed his eyes. "Nicholas," I said, "I've been trying to think.

154

There've been other odd things." And I told him about the flashlight and the light in the attic. "Somebody knows you're here, and is not only trying to get rid of you. . . ."

"But is trying to make it look as though you were the culprit."

"Yes."

"But who? And why? What does whoever he, she or it hope to get out of it?"

"*Cui bono?*"

"Yes."

After a minute he said, "You'd be surprised, or maybe you wouldn't be, at some of the lengths people have gone to to hang onto The Fell."

"You mean Trelawnys."

He raised his head and opened his eyes. "Yes. Trelawnys. Our family. Yours and mine." He smiled faintly when he saw my face. "Is the idea really all that horrifying to you?"

And then suddenly I remembered what in the crisis of the past few hours I had forgotten: Bill's story about how either of the twins could be the father of Mrs. Bradford's granddaughter.

"Now what?" Nicholas said, watching my face.

"Nothing. It doesn't matter."

"I think it does. Tell me." Even as I resented it, I responded to the authoritative note in his voice.

"Bill Seaward told me that either you or Giles could be the father of Mrs. Bradford's granddaughter—the pretty one who helps out behind the counter there and who looks like a Trelawny. Somehow the picture of the two of you in a romp *à trois* with the girl's mother has a little of the same effect on me that the salt and water did on you."

Nicholas stared at me but didn't say anything for a minute. Then, "speaking of *cui bono,* I wonder what Bill got out of telling you that story?"

"What do you mean?"

"In view of the fact that in everybody's sight—and however much you may dislike the idea—you are a member of the family, it was an odd bit of gossip to unload on you."

155

For some reason I got angry. "Probing Bill Seaward's motives I find, somehow, less crucial than discovering whether or not what he said was true."

"Would you believe me if I simply said, 'No, it is not true'?"

The late-afternoon sun was pouring through opposite windows and a small skylight onto Nicholas's face as he sat half propped up against the wall. I found myself wondering which Trelawny ancestors had brought with them from Ulster or western Scotland those strange gray-green eyes. From no other—

I held my breath while everything stood still. Then I heard myself say, "You're *not* Nicholas." It wasn't even a question.

He pulled himself up and stood there for a moment. Then he said, "No. I wondered how long it would take you to realize that."

"Your eyes are wrong for Nicholas. His were always that silvery-gray in all lights. Yours change. They're sometimes blue-gray and sometimes greenish."

"Yes. But I don't think such subtle differences of eye coloring will have much weight with the authorities."

My mind was going around in circles. "But you told me the authorities thought you *were* Giles and that your problem was to convince them you were Nicholas."

"That was because you assumed I was Nicholas and it was easier to let you think that."

"Why?"

He wiped his hand across his forehead again. "I think I'll sit down again." He did so, and wrapped the quilt from the bed around him. "Would you believe anything I told you?"

"No," I said.

"Then considering the way I feel at the moment, I won't put myself out to convince you."

He leaned back against the wall and closed his eyes. Then he made an odd whistling noise. Before I had time to wonder what he was doing, the brown mouse whom I recognized as Richard appeared from behind a piece of furniture, ran across the floor and up the quilt to around his neck. There, to my astonishment he sat up and began cleaning his whiskers. But my surprises were not at an end. From behind the same piece of furniture ventured a white mouse, who also ran up the quilt but stayed in Giles's lap, where it sniffed delicately over his hand. The hand stirred. One long finger gently stroked the white mouse's head. Richard ran down to join the massage. Their high squeaks were the only sound in the attic.

I had not made a single move. I had been too rooted in astonishment. But then, curiosity winning out, I started towards the bed. The mice scattered and tore towards their hiding place behind the chest and the armchair. Unfortunately, there must have been some remnants of the poisoned stew there, because they paused, sniffing delicately. Giles suddenly sat up. "Don't let them touch that!" he said sharply and started to throw off the quilt. I went over and picked up the small quilt on the floor that had received some of the stew.

"I'll put it with the other," I said. "I want to have it analyzed to see what was in it."

"You said it yourself—arsenic." Then he added, "Why did you move? You chased them away."

"What is the white mouse called?" I asked.

"Emily."

Suddenly I started to laugh.

"What's so funny?"

"We're talking about your tame mice. Over there is evidence that somebody tried to poison you. Whoever it was wanted to implicate me. You're hunted by the authorities, and besides all that, you're not who you said you were. And we sit here discussing your mice!"

He smiled a little, pulling the quilt back over him. "It's not quite as crazy as you think, discussing mice while the bastille is falling around us. I learned that while I was a prisoner. When things pile up and there seems no way out, if you think about them—the situation you're in—too long, you go under. So you can create a whole hierarchy of other things to think about. Mice are as good as any, in fact more attractive than some of the other phenomena of natural history I made pets of back in the Mekong Delta."

I looked at him, knowing I would have to come to terms with what he had told me. "How do you feel now?"

"Hungry."

"All right. I'll get you something."

"You notice, I trust you, even though it seemed to be your note that came with the stew. In view of that, how about your giving me some trust? We have to begin somewhere, Kit."

I stood staring at him, some part of me holding back from crossing that final barrier.

"If you want to be existential about it," he said, shifting his back, "call it a leap of faith. If you can't make that, then I think you should call the police. I'm not sure that I want to fight you inside along with everybody else outside."

Quite suddenly I made my decision. "All right. I'll trust you."

He looked up with his faint, uneven smile. "Is that from the head, the heart, or *faute de mieux?*"

"I don't know."

"All right. It'll do. Now get me something to eat— nothing very complicated. We can't talk until I get something inside me, and there are things I have to tell you. By the way, what did you say in your note to your boyfriend?"

"That I'd called home and found I had to get back."

"Idiot!"

"Thanks. What else should I have said?"

"Never tell a gratuitous lie if you don't have to. You could simply have said you had forgotten something. Now you will have to verify that call, because believe me, he'll come back wanting to know who and what."

"You're suspicious of him."

"Aren't you? After all, it was in your absence as arranged by him that all this took place."

"It could have been someone else, knowing I was going to be gone for the day. In fact, it was obviously whoever brought up the tray."

"Who?"

"Frank Morse, for one."

"Yes. I thought you'd say that. He leaps to the mind."

158

"Well, you're the one who said he was dangerous—or implied it."

"Yes. I know. But I've begun to think that too many things point to him. He's too neat. Too obvious."

"Neat he isn't."

Giles grinned. "Don't be so literal. And please get me some viands before I pass out and before Seaward arrives."

I picked up the basket I had brought the breakfast in and the soiled blanket and quilt on the way down, and then wondered what I was going to do with them and how I was going to "verify" that phone call I had been stupid enough to claim (Giles was right about that, I was forced to admit). And while I was on to that, who had brought the tray up?

I went first to my room and took a suitcase out of the closet. I folded the blanket and quilt into that and locked it and put it with the other suitcases piled up on the shelf. Then I picked up the basket and went down to the kitchen. For the moment luck was with me; there was no one there. Hastily I put some bread, a container of milk, powdered broth and a couple of cans of boned chicken in the basket, plus a can opener. And then the door opened and in walked Pogs.

"Oh, hello. I thought you were having a day off in Portland."

"I was. But I came back." I watched Pogs fill the kettle and put it on the stove. "Pogs," I said suddenly. "Will you do something for me?"

"Sure. What?"

"Bill—Dr. Seaward—is liable to come surging back any time within the next hour or so, maybe sooner. If you see him, would you tell him I phoned home and you asked me to come back. Maybe a pipe or something had burst."

Pogs gave me a long look. "Like that, is it? Well, okay."

"It may sound strange to you," I started.

"Nothing sounds strange to me any more. If you're trying to avoid Bill Seaward or any other man you have my sympathy."

I saw and was grateful for the fact that Pogs seemed

159

to have gotten hold of the entirely wrong reason for my unreasonable acts, but I was perfectly willing, in fact eager, to have her put it down to a lover's quarrel. But how was I going to get my packed basket out of the kitchen without her knowing it?

But she settled the matter for me by pouring herself some instant coffee and leaving the room with it. "It's okay if I take this upstairs?" she said at the door.

"Of course!" I tried not to sound too enthusiastic.

"And I can keep an eye on the drive from my window. When Dr. Seaward comes, I'll go down and tell him about the pipe. If he asks for you, are you available?"

"No. I'm going upstairs to take a nap."

An understanding smile lit up Pogs's face. "Capish," she said in a conspiratorial way.

I felt far worse about getting her sympathy under false premises than if she had exuded suspicion. Could Pogs have taken the tray up to the attic? My emotions rejected it while my mind conceded that she could have, as much as anyone else. When she had gone, I picked up the basket and made my way via the long route to the north attic.

"I don't know where to say the trouble started," Giles said, finishing his second chicken sandwich. "Maybe when we were born—Nicholas and I, I mean. The psychologists would undoubtedly have a rare old time with all the complexes and neuroses involved, but the objective fact, known by just about everybody, was that Nicholas was Mother's favorite by quite a margin. To do her justice, she made no secret of it. She also was completely happy to admit that I was Father's. The trouble is, Father died when we were eight."

He got up and started walking around.

"You better sit down," I said. "Pogs is right below."

He didn't seem to hear me, but he sat down. "I was in prison in Nicholas's place before I realized that practically everything I have ever done was somehow to make up for my not being Nicholas. I didn't know why but it was something about which I felt tremendous guilt. We weren't anywhere near as alike as people thought. We didn't even look that much alike. Every now and then some sharp-eyed person would point this out, but Mother always somehow turned the point. By the time she'd finished pointing out what she called the 'little differences,' the listener would emerge with a sense of how identical we were. I told you about thinking about things in prison. Well, I would allow myself only a certain amount of time in which I would think about what could be called 'real problems.' More than that and they became roads to depression that could lead to suicide. But when I did let myself think, I went back over my life and certain facts started standing out. One of them was Mother's insistence on how twinlike Nicholas and I were. When I was younger I rebelled against this. I wanted to go to a different boarding school from Nick and, later, to a different college. But I was made always to feel that even to suggest such a thing ran against the tradition of the family. We were famous for our twins. Mother went on the theory that if you have it you flaunt it; we should therefore flaunt our twinship.

"When I put it like that, it's an exaggeration. But that's what it amounted to. So we went to the same school, the same college and even went for a couple of years over to Cambridge in England. That was another tradition—by school and/or university and often marriage keeping up the transatlantic ties.

"It was when we got back that I made my first serious attempt at independence. I said I wanted to study architecture. Mother couldn't stop me—both Nick and I had private money left by Father. But I found myself agreeing to go into the Army first—to get my military service behind me. Nick had gone into the Navy as a flyer. We had both taken flying when we were at college, Nick reveled in it. I could do it—I could even fly jets as well as Nick—but I wasn't that crazy about it. Mother, of course, wanted me to go into the Navy with Nick. But, having lost the battle about architecture—somehow I found myself feeling guilty again, as though I had let down the family and Nick and the whole goddam tradition—I balked at dutifully following him into the Navy. I agreed, instead, as a sort of compromise, to go into the Army."

He paused. "It's hard to explain about Mother, and the power she had."

"Not to me it isn't."

"No. I had forgotten that. But you saw just the one side, the cruel manipulative side. She could be as charming as she could be cruel. And she could use both—my God! how she could. I think, although I never put it into words myself, that I felt I was helping her, as well as making up to her for something, when I did as she asked."

"Making up for what?"

"I don't know." He paused. "But there was something. I don't think it was just the clever games that she played."

"What do you think it could be?"

"I don't know. But I think that was what she meant me to find out when she sent me that message."

"What message?"

"I got a message just before I got back here—"

I looked up. "By Western Union?"

"Yes," he said, "I know. I'm leaving out a big chunk in the middle. I'll go back later. Anyway, I got this message, never mind how, but messages can be gotten through, that there was something in this house that would straighten things out for me. By that time Nicholas was dead. He died, not of enemy fire or of wounds in prison camp, but of an overdose of heroin. The broadcasts that were supposed to have been made by him were pieced-together tapes taken at various times while they had him. It was such a clumsy job that even the troops and the sailors to whom the broadcast was beamed could tell that it was phony. And of course, in line with his usual pattern, he had given my name instead of his own. He'd done it before, dozens of times, at school, in college, in England."

"Why on earth did you put up with it?"

He made a gesture. "Now, standing here, after all that has happened, it seems as crazy to me as it must to you. I can only tell you that I was brought up to believe it was my responsibility. That there had always been this genetic kink in the family. But the other bad eggs had not been the heirs; that Nicholas was and must be protected or the great name of Trelawny would suffer. You've got to understand that the Trelawnys always had this English view of the importance of the eldest son. All the trusts were set so that the eldest would inherit almost everything, as though the Trelawnys had, singlehandedly, brought the law of primogeniture to the North American continent. And I bought it. So when Nick sometimes used my name to weasel out of a bad situation, I went along. And it was a good put-on. The establishment—school, college, and so on—was always running around trying to decide who did what, while we sat back and laughed and let 'em work it out. Another thing—I never actually suffered from any of Nick's forays into using my name. Fines were paid by the family and the general attitude on everybody's part was that the twins had pulled off another joke. Mother was always particularly grateful to me. She made me feel that she and I were partners in keeping Nick out of trouble. Maybe that's part of the reason I did it. Maybe . . . I don't know."

"But *why*? Simply because she loved him best?"

"That's what I always thought."

"It doesn't seem enough."

"It is, if you knew how Mother doted on him, but I think you're right, that there is more to it."

"What did that message you got say?"

"Simply that the evidence that would put everything right was back here in this house. There was more to the message—involving something I'd sent. But it was too garbled."

"How did you get that much?"

"It doesn't matter. Those ways are still being used to reach some of the American soldiers captured or missing in action."

"All right. But there are so many questions—I don't know where to begin. You say Nicholas is supposed to have died in prison with six witnesses. Did he?"

"Yes. After we'd been switched. The North Vietnamese did that."

"What do you mean? Why?"

"Nicholas got into drugs in Boston, not too long after he'd gone into the Navy. Not the hard stuff at first, but pills, speed, LSD. He was careful. He'd only play around when he was on leave or passes. I didn't know this until we were both in Asia. We usually tried to get leaves together—that is, he got leave and I tried to get

163

one at the same time, still in my role as loyal, steady brother out to protect the heir of the family. It sounds —and was—so repellingly pious, so completely anachronistic. Yet I knew something was wrong with him although I didn't know what. For all that we were kept together, we weren't that close. For one thing, we had different groups of friends. Anyway, this time in Saigon, I finally got leave. Nick had been on his for a week before I joined him, and I had a hard time running him down. He wasn't at the hotel he was supposed to be at. But I had the usual streak of luck involving people confusing us. The desk clerk certainly didn't stop to take an extra look at either my face or my uniform. We both wore khakis, though of course he had the Navy insignia while I was wearing the Army. Anyway, I asked for Nick's key and went up to his room. I waited there for a couple of days but Nick didn't show up. With anybody else I wouldn't have thought too much about it. But by that time I was worried about the changes in him. If I had gone to the authorities, which is what I should have done, that would have been blowing the whistle on him. I was at my wits' end when I had what seemed a stroke of luck. The phone in the bedroom rang and the person who called obviously thought I was Nick. It was a buddy of Nick's just beginning leave himself, and I didn't enlighten him as to his mistake. I just let him talk on and I learned quite a lot, none of it reassuring. He casually dropped a few names and addresses. Even so, it took me a while to find Nick, and before I did, the rest of his leave was canceled. He got a telegram—which was delivered to me, of course—telling him to get the hell back to his carrier. There was some big push on. I found Nick that night and he was in very bad shape. By this time it was the hard stuff."

"Where was he?"

"Oh, in a house somewhere with a couple of girls. Quite a luxurious house. There were one or two of our guys there and a couple of what I thought to be South Vietnamese officers. As it turned out they were extremely skilled North Vietnamese agents. The whole thing was a setup to get Nicholas Trelawny. Somebody —an Englishman, I think—said that the U.S. lost the

Vietnam War not in the paddyfields but on television and in the newspapers. And I think he was right. It was a propaganda war, and their propaganda was aimed at vulnerable listeners back in the States. To get a Nicholas Trelawny V or VI or whatever to spout their speeches over TV or radio or at a press conference, would be like getting a Cabot or a Roosevelt or a Kennedy. Still, there was no excuse for my stupidity. I played straight into their hands—and into Mother's. The old knee-jerk reflex was there. Nicholas, the heir, must be protected. People must not know. No price was too great to shield the name, blah, blah, blah.

"Somehow I got Nick out of there, but the next question was what to do with him. I knew that if I took him to where he ought to be—a military hospital—it would be dishonorable discharge, disgrace, public scandal—the works. After all, I had spent the best years of my life making sure that didn't happen; I couldn't be expected now to do the obvious and only sane thing. The family name came first. Nicholas was the family. Ergo, he must be preserved. But time was running out. Nick was due back at his ship within a few hours. Without stopping to probe my own motives, I wrote Mother what had happened. After all, if Nick needed it (I told myself), she had friends in the American Embassy in Saigon, the State Department, the Senate, the Pentagon—any high place you could name. And she could, if necessary, pull powerful wires. After that I made some inquiries and put Nicholas, under another name, in what I thought was a medically irreproachable sanitarium outside Saigon.

"Under my own name, I contacted my C.O., spun him a yarn about Mother being ill, and got extended compassionate leave. After all, I had been assured that Nick would be all right in a few weeks, that his addiction was recent, and so on and so forth. Then I did what I had always been programmed to do—took Nick's place. There was no great problem there. As I said before, I could fly jets. I'd gone up with Nick many times and been at the controls. Of course it was against the rules—but what were rules?"

"Why didn't you simply get sick leave for Nicholas?"

"They would have found out."

"Couldn't you have depended on all those lofty contacts to cover up?"

"The lofty contacts might have worked. But don't forget the press and the growing disillusionment with the war."

"Weren't you afraid you'd be found out by the other officers?"

"No, not really. We'd done the switch so often that I knew all the tricks. Cruise along, don't offer anything. Laugh when the others laughed, pretend I'd been there all along. You'd be amazed how unobservant people are—particularly men with a lot on their minds. It was a big carrier. Nick hadn't been there long enough to make close friends. There were a lot of men. I got away with it for the short while I was on the ship. I went on one airstrike against a railway line and got back. I was scared out of my clothes, practically—I never did have Nicholas's blind, daredevil courage. But the second time was different. We went right up into North Vietnam, and were flying low to try and get a munitions factory. The antiaircraft was like lightning all around. I had turned and was heading back when I got it. I bailed out and found a reception committee on the ground."

"Did you say you were Nicholas?"

"Of course. Name, rank and serial number and I gave Nicholas's name."

"Were you tortured?"

"Some. Not as badly as a lot because I bailed out a long way from Hanoi and it took my captors a while to get me up to where the main prisons were. They were fearfully pleased with themselves and wanted to show me off. So they put me in a cage and took me around for a while."

Giles stopped.

"That must have been . . . awful."

"It was. It was there I learned about the strategic and tactical uses of humiliation. Killing the enemy isn't enough—not by a long shot. A dead soldier, even if he's an enemy soldier, has some dignity. The whole point of that war was to reduce the American, the white man, the Westerner—and I was all three—to the ape. Strip him of any rag of dignity, so that he could be

166

spat on and laughed at, in front of as large an audience as possible—or even better, be on his knees pleading."

Giles swallowed and went on. "By sheer good luck —these weren't the trained sadists they had in the POW camps, and they were supposed to be bringing me in, not having fun and games on their own—I managed, just managed, to keep from pleading. But one day they evidently got orders from Hanoi and they stopped playing around and got me up there. By this time I wasn't in great shape. In fact I could hardly walk and my mouth was so swollen I couldn't even talk. I heard via the grapevine that my escorts got their heads handed to them for shillyshallying. The big boys in Hanoi had plans for me, and those plans didn't include my being a zombie or corpse. Anyway, the next thing I knew I was in a hospital, being given the best they could supply. It took a while to recover, and I didn't look forward to good health. I knew they were fattening me up for something, and I didn't know whether I could take it.

"Afterwards, I saw they had, from their own point of view, made a mistake. They should have just disposed of me immediately and brought Nicholas into the prison as himself. But again, they wanted the satisfactions of total, visible conversion. So they took me out of the hospital when I still looked like hell and was barely ambulatory and put me in the prison with the others. They interrogated me, and I daily expected the worst. It was unpleasant, but the worst never happened. Then one fine day, when I looked a lot better, I went for interrogation in the usual way. But instead of questioning me they put me in a car and drove me across Hanoi and into the country outside to a kind of makeshift wooden house and I was locked into a room by myself.

"I don't know what they actually planned to do with me. You see—they hadn't planned on me, on my taking Nick's place. When they heard Nicholas had bailed out and been captured you can imagine their confusion because they knew they had the real Nicholas tucked away in Hanoi—by this time they had got him out of that sanitarium I had put him in and flown him up north. Then, when they figured out that the man pretending to be Nicholas was actually Giles, they adjusted their game plan. I think for a while there they were going on the theory that if one Trelawny was good, two would be even better. But something—maybe the shape I was in or the way I acted—made them return to their original plan. Nick was to be their star exhibit. So they put him into the cell I had been in. Poor Nick! He did his best! But by now he was totally hooked and all they had to do was to threaten withdrawal. He made a few broadcasts and managed to botch them as much as possible."

"But he used your name."

"Yes, he did. Or tried to. But that's not what they wanted. They wanted Nicholas himself. It was Nick who was the golden boy, the one who was always in the papers. Most of all there was that big article about him —'One of Our Airmen,' or something like that—that was printed and reprinted. And then the interview on television. For both sides he was some kind of symbol."

"When all this was happening, where were you? Didn't any of those articles or interviews mention you?"

"Oh, sure—this generation's Trelawny twins, that kind of thing. A mention, that's about what it was, plus, maybe, a picture. But by the time of the article I had gone into Intelligence and was being as invisible as possible."

We were silent for a while. Then I asked, "You know, if Nicholas was their prize showpiece, I'm surprised they allowed him to die of an overdose. What do you think happened?"

"I don't know for sure. Maybe no one will ever know. But what I think happened was that he managed finally to fool them. He overplayed how much he needed and in that way got them to overdose him."

"You mean he committed suicide?"

"Yes."

"That's a bit romantic, isn't it? Was there anything in Nick's life to make you think he'd play such a Sidney Carton role?"

"In his last recording he suddenly stopped in the middle of some obviously prepared speech about the iniquity of the U.S. venture in Vietnam and said in another voice, 'Giles, I'll meet you back at The Fell under the rafter.' And then he went right on as though he hadn't said that at all."

"Isn't it odd they didn't cut it out?"

"I don't think they saw what it meant, and anyway it added some genuine local color to their captive."

I thought for a while. "Why didn't any of this get in the papers?"

"What do you mean? It was in the papers."

"Not that he died of an overdose."

"Who knew? Who could be sure?"

"Those things get around. Anyway, you knew."

"I told you. I was in Intelligence. What I've just told you came through our usual contacts."

"And what about you? When Nick died, why didn't they shove you in his place?"

"By that time I had, believe it or not, escaped. For a while I thought that it had been set up by them to justify shooting me and kept waiting for that bullet to zing through my back. But when did they ever need justification for knocking off an American?"

"When did you learn that Nick was dead?"

"After I had got back into South Vietnam and after I had discovered that while my C.O. had put it out that I was missing in action, if I did return I would be faced with a charge of desertion and, in view of Nick's saying he was Giles, of broadcasting on behalf of the enemy— that is, of treason."

"Couldn't you have told him the truth?"

"If it had been my original C.O.—the one who had given me the compassionate leave—maybe. I think I would have tried. But he had been recalled to the Pentagon and another guy sent out. I couldn't risk it."

"So you are officially missing in action? I'd heard that you'd been reported killed."

"That's right. My dogtags were found."

"And Nick is officially dead."

"Yes."

"So if you turn up as Giles, you'll be arrested for doing those broadcasts and for murdering Charlotte. What if you turn up as Nicholas?"

"The same. You see when the men got back from Hanoi and the military authorities started putting things together, they came to the interesting conclusion that they didn't know which twin had done what. That's why, when Mother's message eventually came through to me, I managed to get back here by myself, to see if I could find whatever she was talking about and unravel the mess."

"How long have you been here?"

"About six months."

"Maybe if you had had some medical treatment in that time you'd be in better condition now."

"Undoubtedly. But I'd rather be in poor shape and free than given the latest science has to offer behind bars."

I thought for a while. The mice suddenly reappeared and shot halfway across the floor. There Richard stopped and sniffed the air. Emily got as far as Giles's quilt and hid behind it. "Where did you get your four-footed friends?"

"You don't have to *get* mice. They live here."

"Even the white one?"

"No. Pete rescued her from death down the toilet by his grandmother."

"I can't see that grim female tolerating mice."

"Well, apparently the granddaughter, Priscilla, had ordered it. She's animal-mad and had seen an ad in a catalogue and ordered herself a mouse. When Emily arrived, Mrs. Bradford raised hell and was heading for the bathroom with Priscilla behind crying and pleading when Pete arrived. Pete's fond of Priscilla and he likes animals too, so he removed Emily just in time and brought her here."

I asked abruptly, "Could Priscilla be your daughter?"

"No. She could not. Her mother was Nick's fancy."

I remembered that day in the store fifteen years before. "Why did Nick kill Charlotte?"

"I don't know. He was on and off speed at the time. I sometimes think—"

"What?"

"I don't know."

"What you don't know about everything connected with your being here could fill a police blotter."

"How true!"

"Did you love Charlotte?"

"I thought I did. But when I was in prison I had plenty of time to think about that one, too. Was I really in love with her, or was this one of my bids for independence from Nick, Mother, and the whole Trelawny thing?"

I looked up at him quickly. "I didn't know you felt that way about it."

He gave me a satirical look. "Any enemy of the Trelawnys is a friend of yours—even a Trelawny. Is that it?"

"I suppose so. Is it so exaggerated—in view of my first encounter?"

"No, not really. And you're not the only one. We have that effect on people. I'm not sure whether it isn't worse now. Or was. . . ." His voice trailed off. He got up. Emily flew across the floor and up onto the straight chair on which his jacket was hanging. Then she got herself into his breast pocket, turned around, and settled in with her head out. My mind was momentarily diverted. "Have you ever thought of having a mouse circus? Like a flea circus?"

"It would be a pleasant way to make a living." He was moving around in his stockinged feet.

"What do you mean, 'worse now'?"

"I'm not sure. But there were times when Mother seemed to get her chief delight in humiliating people. It wasn't just you. Charlotte got it too. So did Bill Seaward and his father, old Dr. Seaward. Bill was a little younger than Nicholas and me. But there weren't that many kids around and we played together a lot. You think she put you down! By comparison with the way she acted towards Bill, she was courtesy itself. Until he grew up he was short and pudgy. She'd take constant digs at him, always in public."

" 'The Lump'," I said. "Bill told me about it."

"That's right."

"Did you call him that, too?"

"I'm afraid so. Do you remember, when you were a kid visiting here, you told me we were not kind? Well, you were right: we were not kind, and that included me.

Curiously, no one had ever said that to me before. But I knew it was true. I was a grown man and you were barely twelve, but you made me—ashamed."

"Bill said it stopped."

"That's right. I never knew what happened, but it did. After that, Mother acted as though he weren't there, and she picked on somebody else. That's how I got interested in Charlotte. Her father was a friend of old Dr. Seaward's and she was visiting them. They came over for tea or swimming or whatever and Mother started in on her. One day I found myself telling her to lay off."

"And you got interested then?"

"No. She was only about fifteen at that time. But after that she looked upon me as a cross between Galahad and Che Guevara and I guess I found it pleasant."

"Then how come she switched to Nicholas?"

"Because Nick put himself out to charm her, and when he wanted to do that I haven't seen the human being, man, woman or child, who could hold out. You certainly didn't. Even though he wasn't that nice to you."

I thought back and again saw myself walking obediently, hungrily, into the aura of charm that Nicholas cast around him like a glittering net. And, like Giles, I felt ashamed. "Why are some people like that? People who are absolutely evil, and yet the world comes to eat out of their hands?"

"I don't know. But I had time to give it plenty of thought. And I decided that one of the problems is that the blame isn't entirely theirs. They are the seducers; but there are also the seduced, who allow themselves to be seduced. Why? The seduced must be getting something out of it as well."

And for a remembering second I knew he was right. Because what I felt when Nicholas smiled and put his hand out to touch me came back to me, and I saw it now as a sort of credulous greed. "He made me think—"

Giles smiled at me faintly. "That you were something extraordinary, had to be, to attract anyone as remarkable as he?"

"Yes. Something like that."

"So that when he turned the cutting edge of all that light against you, you were totally vulnerable."

"Yes. How stupid I was!"

"No use to kick yourself. Most people are just that stupid."

"Did he use it on you?"

"Oh yes. Why else do you think I covered for him so often? Both he and Mother did. As I was sitting there in one of my jungle prisons with scorpions and God knows what else crawling over me, I thought a lot about that. I knew then that what I had done for Nick wasn't because I was noble or self-sacrificing or altruistic—whatever that is. It was because I thought I was buying some special kind of love. I guess maybe I thought Mother would love me more, as she did Nicholas. I deserved what I got."

"I'm sorry, Giles. And I'm sorry for my snottiness. You had it so much worse."

"I told you," he said harshly. "I asked for it."

I looked at his face and decided to change the subject. "Speaking of drugs, Bill Seaward says Tess is on them. She was the one who threw the weed stuff into the stew. When she next turned up, it was when Bill was there. After she left he said her pupils were huge."

"Well, he should know. His father was hooked."

"Bill's father?"

"That's right. His father. He had some kind of back trouble that was pretty painful and the stuff was there at hand—morphine. You know, until the drug culture burst on the country, doctors were among the most frequent users."

"How strange. Didn't people object?"

"I don't suppose they realized what was happening. I knew because Nick told me."

"Who told him?"

"Mother. But I don't know how she knew. Nick confided this to me when we were halfway across the world and I couldn't ask her."

Questions were tumbling over one another in my mind and behind them, not quite conscious yet, were doubts and gaps that hadn't resolved themselves into questions. But one thrust itself to the forefront.

"Giles, what was the real reason you let me think you were Nicholas, since the truth was that no matter which twin you were, you were in trouble?"

He turned. "Do you remember, as you first saw me, you said, 'Nicholas'? I remembered your childhood's hero-worship of Nicholas. I thought you'd be more liable to give Nick the benefit of the doubt."

He stopped abruptly. Faintly there came the sound of a car engine. He went over to the east dormer and looked out. "Here's your Lochinvar, breathing anxiety and suspicion."

"Why do you dislike him? Particularly after what you told me. You seemed sympathetic to him."

"Because, even though I felt sorry for him when Mother sharpened her blade on him, he was a dislikable kid. Toadying to us one minute, bullying some of the village kids next."

I remembered what Bill had said. "He told me he thought some of the magic might rub off on him. As for bullying, maybe he passed along what your mother gave him."

"Maybe," Giles said.

"Or maybe if his father was off in Cloud-cuckoo-land a large part of the time he had reason to be obnoxious."

"Yes. I see all that now. But there's something about him beyond all that that bothers me. He's a little too nice. A little too phony."

He said it in an offhand way, but I heard again—or thought I did—the old arrogance and Trelawny insensitivity to the problems of growing up around his family. So I opened my mouth and put my foot in it.

"Jealousy?" I asked blandly.

Giles looked over at me. "You're a nice girl, Kit. But aren't you overestimating your fatal charm?"

It could have been his mother or his brother. Was there, after all, that much difference between them, despite all he said? I got up.

"I guess I asked for that."

"Yes. I think you did. However, granting, for the sake of argument, your charm, why don't you go down and use some of it on your lover?"

I started towards the stairs. "He's not my lover."

174

"Not at the moment."

"Is that a suggestion?"

"Why not? You could divert his interest from me."

"And of course helping you must remain my ruling preoccupation."

He looked down the attic at me. "You know, Kit, you should watch yourself. For a moment there I almost thought it was Mother. If you turn me in, you'd make an admirable successor to her."

I knew he was baiting me. I didn't know why. "How nice of you, Giles. It would be quite an achievement to rival the late dowager in arrogance and manipulation."

And with the dubious satisfaction of having got in the last word—however rude—I went downstairs. I heard him laugh as I reached the closet door and just managed not to slam it.

8

I found Pogs waiting outside my room. "He—Bill—*insists* on seeing you. He says there's an unexpected emergency and he needs your help. I told him you were taking a nap, but it was all I could do to stop him coming up himself."

"Oh. All right. By the way, Pogs, what did you cite as the crisis that brought me home?"

"I said one of the washers in the upstairs bathroom —the one I use—had broken and the water was gushing out all over everything and I couldn't stop it. And that you had tried to explain how to find the valve to close the pipe further down. But I'm stupid about things like that and couldn't locate it and so you came home."

"Did it satisfy him?"

"No. He asked why I didn't ask one of the men. It was easy to say that Frank didn't know. But somehow when I said that Rod didn't know, I could feel skepticism coming from him like a fog."

"Why didn't you say Rod was out?"

"I didn't think soon enough." She sounded aggrieved.

"I'm not good at this conspiracy business. Especially since I was working blind."

"I'm sorry, Pogs. You did marvelously and I shouldn't have laid the whole thing on you."

"It's all right," she said, more in her old apologetic tone. "I'll forgive you if you do something for me."

"Name it."

"Lend me that watercolor in your room, the one with the boat and the houses up on stilts and the soldier. I'm illustrating a kid's book about Southeast Asia and that's exactly what I'm looking for."

I don't know why my heart gave a jump when she mentioned that painting. Why should it set off an alarm? "Sure," I said. "It's by one of the twins—Nicholas, I think. When did you notice it?"

I tried to make the question sound as casual as I could.

"Just now. I went in to arouse you from the nap you were supposed to be having and which, for all I knew, you might be having. When you didn't answer my knock I stuck my head in. I saw the picture and went in and looked at it. It's a marvelous watercolor."

"Yes. It's very good." And then she added casually, "But I'd be surprised if it was Nicholas. I bet it was Giles."

"What do you mean, Pogs?" I said sharply. She recoiled so visibly from my tone that I forced myself to say more calmly, "I'm sorry. I just didn't know that you knew them."

"Oh sure. Of course, I was much younger then. But I knew that Giles was the one who had the interest in art. He wanted to go to art or architecture school or something, but the old witch wouldn't let him."

I said carefully, "I only met her once myself. I mean I stayed here a week when I was a child. She seemed to me—arrogant."

"That's putting it mildly. Mother had known her at school in England."

"Was your mother English?"

"No. But Grandfather was at the Embassy in London and Mother went to boarding school near Oxford."

"What did she say about the dowager—Mrs. Trelawny?"

Pogs gave me a funny look. "Mother said she was the social climber of all time."

My eyes must have all but started out of my head because Pogs said in a kindly way, "Yes, I know it's hard to believe. But you see, I gather that there are Trelawnys and Trelawnys over there and some have rather come down in the world. Mrs. Trelawny's family had. Mother only found out by accident. She got it from Daddy, who, being on the Embassy staff, was aware that an American citizen was getting married in England. I don't know all the details."

"Could you find them out?" I couldn't keep the eagerness out of my voice.

"Well, it's a bit difficult. You see I'm not speaking to my family."

"Oh Pogs. It's *important*."

She looked at me owlishly for a minute and then sighed. "All right. I'll write."

Without thinking I reached over and hugged her. Pogs turned bright pink. "Same to you," she muttered, looking pleased.

I went downstairs. "Bill," I said, before he could say anything. "I'm terribly sorry about leaving you that way. But you do understand."

"I guess so. Although I find it hard to think that that guy, what's his name, Rod something or other, wouldn't know how to find a plumbing valve. He looks like a type who could install an entire bathroom."

"Yes. I know," I lied glibly. "It's amazing. I asked him to help with some handywork around the house once and he was entirely agreeable and willing, but totally thumbs." I hurried away from the dangerous topic. "Pogs said there was an emergency. What is it?"

"I stopped by the Bradfords' on the way here. My answering service said one of the neighbors had called —both Mrs. Bradford and Pete are away—and that the girl, Priscilla, had become quite ill. I went by and she's all right now. But she did come down with some kind of food poisoning. I don't like to leave her there alone, and for some reason, any friends she might stay with are either full up or away, and I was wondering if I could bring her here. I know it's awkward, given the circumstances, and of course I never would have asked if any of the old family were around. But I know it doesn't matter to you, and it's nearer than taking her into the city to the hospital. All she needs is a place where she can rest and somebody can bring her hot soup."

I thought rather grimly that there seemed to be a rash of food poisoning and looked at Bill's face carefully. All I could see there was worry and concern.

"Of course," he said, "if you'd really rather not. . . ."

"By all means. Bring her here. Do you need any help?"

"Yes, as a matter of fact. The neighbor that called me was on her way to visit her daughter. The child is in bed, and while I can perfectly well pick her up and carry her down if she can't make it by herself, she might like you to help her dress or something."

"Okay. Let's go."

We drove there via Bill's office, where he wanted to pick up some medicine. His office formed the left side of his house, an attractive classic New England house —white clapboard, four windows above, two below and a garage attached. It was just outside the village and about a quarter of a mile from the sea.

"Come on in," Bill said, smiling a little shyly. "I had to come here anyway, but I was glad of the excuse to show you the house."

"It's lovely," I said with perfect sincerity. "Much more my idea of a home than that rambling monstrosity I'm living in right now."

We got out and started walking up the path to the house. Behind it the evening sea was a dusky lavender. "Yes. I suppose The Fell is a monstrosity. But it's so much a part of the history around here, and the family is too, that it's hard to think of it as just a house—it's an institution."

"Well, that's exactly what the family would like everyone to think. That the house and the Trelawnys are a national institution and therefore not quite like other homes or people. It was that attitude coming through loud and clear when I was here before that irritated me so much."

Bill didn't say anything.

After a minute I said, "Sorry if I sounded like I was

practicing to be the modern Patrick Henry. But there are times when all my old resentment comes up and spits in my face."

Bill unlocked a door at the side of the house. "Why now, particularly?"

The moment he asked, I knew the answer: because of Giles's abrasiveness of which, that morning, I had had such a taste. Bill was watching my face. At that moment, he opened the door and putting out his hand, took mine. "Why, Kit?"

I felt his hand around mine and it was very nice. It was more than nice to have a man concerned about my feelings and not be afraid to show it. It was delightful to feel that I had in Bill a protector, and not a combatant from whom I could expect either arrogance or insensitivity. I squeezed his hand. "I guess, looking at this house, Bill. It's a *home,* not a showpiece for family ego." Again, I had the odd feeling that he was disappointed.

"I had sort of hoped it was more than that."

I tried to draw my hand away. "What do you mean?" I sounded to myself just like some Victorian heroine.

"Well, I was hoping it might be because of some feeling between us."

"Why would that stir up resentments against the Trelawnys?"

"Oh, being in love can key sensitivity to a high pitch. All feelings become more intense, like all colors."

I didn't know what to say. My own feelings towards Bill were confused; I didn't want to hurt his feelings; I was grateful to him for his kindness and affection. Yet there was something that didn't ring true.

"I don't want to rush you, Kit, but think about it."

"It?"

"Us. Getting married. There now, I've asked you."

So help me it was in my mouth to say, "But this is so sudden." I wondered if all my years of reading Victorian novels was beginning to come up in a rush of clichés. "We haven't known each other that long, Bill, nor seen each other that much."

"I know. It's just hard to keep in mind that somebody else's feelings don't go apace with my own. I was pretty sure the first time I saw you." He bent quickly and kissed me. "As I said, think about it. Now let me get that medicine. You can go into the waiting room there on the right and get absorbed in my medical magazines. I'm going upstairs a moment."

All waiting rooms tend to be the same, whether in New York's Park Avenue or in a Maine Cape Cod house. They can be large or small, glossy or shabby, but there are the same easy chairs, anonymous pictures, thumbed magazines, muted lamps. They were, I thought, rightly called waiting rooms; these rooms were where one awaited the verdict: *It's all right, he passed you by this time* or *I'm sorry, but time is running out, he's waiting for you.* And who was *he?* Death, of course, the great enemy.

I shivered and continued to stand in the middle of the room. The chairs looked comfortable enough, and I had come in with the intention of sitting down in one. Yet I went on standing there. After what felt like a rather long time but was probably just a minute or so, I was aware of a sense of discomfort. Where it came from I didn't know. Nor could I think what was causing it. There was absolutely nothing in that room that was in any way extraordinary, except the feeling that was growing within me.

Instead of sitting down, I went over and opened the door opposite to the one I came in by. It gave onto what was obviously Bill's private office. Unlike the waiting room it was highly individual. There was a modern desk in the middle, but over to one side against a wall was an old rolltop affair. The chairs were leather and old. Several metal file cabinets covered most of one wall. On the other walls were photographs. I knew perfectly well I had no business in that office. But my curiosity has always been rampant, so I walked up to one wall and started looking at the photographs.

There were quite a few of them; more than half of people I didn't know and whose identity I could not guess. But there was no doubt at all about a large picture of The Fell taken facing the rear. There was the huge Greek E, the center part thrust forward with its porch and columns, the two extensions at either end, also projecting towards the camera and in between on each side the long wings with the steep roofs and the dormer windows. But I could see even more easily than when looking at the house itself how much those wings consisted of bits and pieces added at different times. In the north wing, for example, there were two separate portions of roof. The part close to the center house dropped down by several feet. Halfway along, the roof was higher again, not as high as over the main building but higher than the low one in between. The windows, also, of the two portions, were not perfect matches. I moved on to the next photographs. There was the dowager Mrs. Trelawny, a candid shot, one hand up, holding back the dark waving hair from being blown over her face. How much the twins looked like her, I thought at first, and then, as I looked, I realized that while the face could almost have been that of Nicholas, it was by no means as similar to Giles's. I moved to the next photograph. It was a color group shot of children. First to leap to the eye were, naturally, the twins. Both in sweaters and jeans, both black-haired but other than that, and considering how identical they were always described as being, amazingly different. One was considerably taller than the other, but which? I peered more closely. It was not a large photograph, and there were a lot of children in it, but when I got closer there was no mistaking which was which—Nicholas's pale eyes looked at me from out a boyish version of his mother's face. He had the same delicate bone structure, the finely chiseled nose. Standing next to him and at least two inches taller was Giles, his eyes a greenish-blue, his bones more prominent, his cheekbones sticking out in the thin face like flying buttresses, his hands, crossed over his arms, like huge paws, promise of the big man to come, while Nicholas's, hanging at his side, were more finely shaped. The other children were strangers to me, I thought, and then my eyes stopped. That little girl looked familiar. I paused, but no name came. I went on. Next to her stood a plump boy, the trousers wrinkling above his heavy thighs, the sun on his blond hair. I don't know how long it took me to realize it was Bill. What was it Giles—and Bill himself —had said? Until he grew up he was chunky. This boy, with clothes plainly too small for him, was about on the edge of adolescence.

"Admiring my art gallery?" Bill's voice said behind me.

I jumped as though he had caught me at the open safe and turned. "Sorry, Bill. Curiosity killed the cat and should have killed me long ago. The door was there beckoning me, so I opened it and came in."

"You were certainly bending your attention to the group photograph. I take it you recognized yours truly. I must have been the most unattractive kid in the New England area." I wondered how much bitterness his light tone covered.

"Those are horrible years, aren't they?" My eyes went back to the picture. "And the awful part is, you never entirely lose the cowering child inside you. In the midst of some of life's best moments it's in there, thumbing its nose and yelling 'Yah, yah, fool you!' "

He didn't say anything, so I turned and was startled by the still, set look on his face. "I'm sorry," I said. "I didn't mean to stir up old pains."

His face changed. The mouth relaxed, his eyes lost that almost shiny look, and reflected the warmth I was used to seeing. "I look upon those years from about eleven to about fourteen as my purgatory paid in advance. You probably don't know what I'm talking about."

"Oh yes I do. My time at The Fell was only a week. But the effects remained with me for the rest of my life." I glanced again at the pictures. "In view of the bad time she gave you, I wonder why you have Mrs. Trelawny's photograph here."

"Oh, she's part of my past. We New Englanders are very high on past."

"Even a painful past?"

He smiled. "Especially a painful past. We think it's character-building."

"Yes—but what kind of character?"

"That's heresy."

I laughed. "All right. By the way, who's the girl next to you?"

"Charlotte. Charlotte Manners."

"You mean Giles's fiancée."

"Yes. He met her when she was staying with us. Her father and mine were cousins."

If I had any doubts about how sick Priscilla was they were allayed the moment I went upstairs in the little house and saw her. She was lying awake, propped high on pillows, her face pinched and gray. Her lovely Trelawny hair, black and thick and waving, lay damply around her face. When I walked in she tried to sit up. "Miss Trelawny," she said, sounding a little dismayed.

I went over. "Bill told me you'd been sick. I'm sorry, and he and I both want you to come and stay at The Fell until your mother or your cousin gets back. It's not right for you to be here alone, but I think you'll be less lonely if you're there with us rather than in some hospital."

"But Granny——" she started, and then paused.

Bill came into the room. "Don't you worry about Granny. I'll fix things with her. Here, take a swallow of this." He pulled a bottle out of his pocket and poured a small amount into the big cap. "Toss this off."

Obediently she tilted her head back and swallowed it.

"Ugh!" she said, making a face.

"That means it's good for you."

"Why is everything that tastes nasty good for you?"

"It's a law of life. You can talk it over with Kit later. Now I want you to trust me to know what's best. You do, honey, don't you?"

It was amazing and more than a little touching the way Priscilla's face blazed with something approaching worship as Bill moved closer to the bed. He reached down his hand and she eagerly grabbed it, hanging onto it with both her own. "If you think it will be all right, then I'm sure it will be," she said.

I looked at Bill's face expecting to see—what? Kindly amusement? Fatherly affection? Older-brother protectiveness? None of those. It was as though he'd shut her out. He said briskly, "Now Miss Trelawny is going to help you dress. If you can't make it by yourself, I'll carry you downstairs. But I don't want you here alone. Do as I say. There's a good girl."

"All right, Bill."

I felt like shouting at him, Don't just stand there being Dr. Welby and giving orders. This child adores you. Give her back something.

The huge gray eyes, pale in that little face, kept on his.

"You're not angry, Bill, are you?"

"I won't be if you get yourself up and dressed so we can take you to The Fell."

"Grandmother would hate it so," she faltered.

"But I think she would want me to do what is best for you."

"Whatever you say, Bill." And obediently she sat up and started to throw back the covers.

"That's my girl. I knew you'd do the right thing." He smiled and left the room.

The pale face flooded with color. Her eyes shone. A moment ago she had looked like a drowned kitten. Now she was showing the promise of genuine Trelawny beauty. I had seen that face looking out of two out of three portraits at The Fell. Vaguely I remembered reading in a book on genetics that in some families the characteristic looks were so strong that though the original strain was reduced with every generation through new blood, yet the same features cropped up again and again. Look at the English royal family, I thought, taking a suitcase out of the wardrobe. How many generations had it been? And yet those heavy Hanoverian looks reappeared in every batch of children. The Bourbons were another lot. The portraits of Marie Antoinette and Philip II of Spain both showed the long jaw, heavy chin and lower lip that descendants of the Bourbons today still sported. And, like the Hanoverians and the Bourbons, the Trelawnys were given to intermarriage.

While I was brooding over these thoughts I was putting things Priscilla had handed to me into the suitcase. She had pulled on a pair of jeans and a sweater and was lacing on sneakers. She looked up at me. "You're frowning," she said shyly. "Is anything the matter?"

"Am I? Sorry. Nothing at all. I was just thinking about genetics."

"Oh. Is it a subject you're interested in?"

"I suppose you could say that. Have you got everything?" I didn't want her asking me why I was interested in such a difficult and controversial area of science.

She stood up. "Yes," she started to say, then her face went suddenly white and she swayed. "Whoa!" I said, and grabbed her. "Bill!" I called. "Can you come up?"

In two seconds Bill was in the room. He took one look and said, "Go on down, Kit. You can take her bag, can't you?" Then he picked her up. "I'll follow you."

It was quite a procession that entered The Fell. By the time we arrived there it was night.

"Where do you want me to put her?" Bill asked.

"I'll show you the way."

"I can walk," Priscilla said, but without much conviction. Her color was even worse than it had been.

"Not a chance, young lady! You don't want to deprive me of my opportunity to show off, do you?"

I glanced at his face. This time I caught the look of tenderness before his withdrawn look settled over it. What an odd man, I thought, almost as though he were fighting against his own feeling for the child.

On the way up the stairs we met Rod and Pogs.

"This is Priscilla Bradford," I introduced her. "She had a bout with food poisoning and is going to recuperate with us."

"Hi," Rod said. "Anything I can do?"

"Nothing, thanks," Bill said.

Pogs hopped from foot to foot. "Can I help?"

"Not this time. Thanks anyway." I led the way down the hall to the room next to me, went in and turned on the light. Bill stopped in the doorway. "Isn't this room a bit cold for Priscilla?" He looked down at the head drooping on his shoulder. "I think you'd rather have that room down the hall facing the land side, wouldn't you?"

"Yes, I guess so."

I had a strong suspicion that until Bill had mentioned it, Priscilla wouldn't have cared one way or the other. Still, there was no reason why she shouldn't face back rather than front, and possibly Bill was right. There was certainly less wind on the land side. And heaven knew there were enough rooms! I didn't add that taking care of Priscilla would be easier for me if she were next door than almost at the other end of the central building. I turned off the lights and we proceeded down the hall.

"This better?" I asked, switching on the light.

Bill came in carrying Priscilla. "Much better." He went over to the bed and put her down, pulling the folded quilt at the foot up over her. "Kit'll take care of you. Now I want you to get a good night's sleep, so take one of these about half an hour before you turn off the light." And he put a small box of pills on the night table.

He came over to me. "I can't thank you enough. But then, knowing your kindness, it was to be expected."

"I don't know what kindness you're talking about, but thanks. Is there anything else Priscilla should take?"

"No. Just the sleeping pill."

"What about that stuff you were giving her earlier?"

"That was just to settle her stomach." He smiled at Priscilla. "How's your stomach now?"

She gave her shy smile. "Much better."

"I'll stop by in the morning." He turned towards me. "Why don't you walk me down the hall?"

I looked at Priscilla. "Back in a moment."

As we got past the door Bill took my arm. "Give her some hot broth, if you have it, and maybe some soda crackers. Nothing more ambitious than that."

All this was so close to what had happened to Giles upstairs that it was all I could do not to ask Bill to go up and have a look at him. I thought Giles's suspicions preposterous and, for all his admission and repudiation of the family hauteur, a remnant of it within himself. But even so, if that was the way Giles felt, I couldn't bring myself to betray him.

"A penny for your thoughts, Kit."

I smiled. "That would be an inflationary price. What happens if Mrs. Bradford returns suddenly? Given the way she feels about The Fell and the Trelawnys, she'll be livid. I don't want to be had up for kidnapping."

"I'll take all responsibility." He smiled lightly. "I told you, didn't I, that people around here don't really believe both twins are dead. Well, the latest rumor, which I picked up at the hospital today, was that one of the twins was back and hiding here in one of the famous attics."

"Famous?"

"Oh, yes. Even before you got lost there were legends about those attics. More than one Trelawny who had gone gently, or not so gently, around the bend was kept up in those attics. At least one, odd Miss Deborah Trelawny, circa 1870, is said never to have come down but been buried in the wall."

"I don't believe that," I said indignantly.

He grinned. "No, nor do I. But apparently they did smuggle her body out at night and bury it."

"But *why?* Everybody has dotty relatives."

He looked at me for a minute, the smile fading. "You know, even though you got flicked by it, I don't think you really appreciate the extent of Trelawny pride. The family came first, long, long before the individual member."

"Well, what about all those black sheep, my great-grandfather included? They couldn't exactly hide those."

"That was different. They'd never admit to it, of course. But there was a certain *panache* in having a thoroughgoing rip for a son or brother or twin. After all, I don't think being lawful meant that much to them. It was being above the law that mattered."

A shiver ran through me because I knew he was right. The law was for ordinary people. Trelawnys were never ordinary.

"But to get back to that rumor I was telling you about. It's a fairly active piece of gossip. Either Giles or Nicholas is up in these attics. Only they don't know which one."

For some reason, I was really afraid, which was odd, considering that only a few minutes past as well as earlier that day I had seriously thought of telling Bill about Giles. I decided to bluff it through, "Well, if the rumor is that rife, you'd think the police would hear it."

"I'm sure they have."

He said it calmly, his eyes on my face. I suffered that sensation that is generally described as the stomach dropping and hoped, devoutly, that no hint of it appeared on my face. "Will they come and investigate?" I asked.

"Oh yes," Bill said, starting down the stairs. "In their own time. And in their own way."

"Meaning?"

"Meaning nothing in particular. But because the constable in blue hasn't come knocking on the door, demanding to be shown over The Fell, doesn't mean that you, and this house, and everyone in it, is going unobserved."

"Bill! You're making me nervous!"

"Good! That's what I wanted to do. I want you to be on the alert. Then you won't be caught unawares."

"By whom?"

"By anyone hiding in your attics."

My bluff had been called with a vengeance. I could do nothing but go on. "Do *you* think there's someone up there?"

He didn't answer for a minute. "I don't know. I think it's possible. I'll go further than that. I even think it's likely. Which leads me to my next question. Would you like me to move my things over here for the next few nights?"

I was touched as well as alarmed. "No, Bill. It's sweet of you to offer, but there are plenty of people here."

"None of whom seems to be of much use. But I'm not sure that my presence would do any good. All it would do would be to postpone the inevitable."

"What inevitable?"

"Discovery," Bill said, but I was sure that was not what he meant. "Listen, Kit. Keep an eye on yourself and on Priscilla. I'll be by in the morning."

He started to come back up the step, and I knew he meant to kiss me. Without thinking, I backed. "Good night, Bill. I'll be all right. Thanks, though, for the offer."

He stood there for a second. The hall light was behind him and I couldn't see his face. But there was a rigidity about his body that made me wonder what I would have seen there if I could.

Then he turned. "Good night, Kit."

I went back to see Priscilla. She had undressed and got into the bed and was lying back against the pillows, her eyes half closed. "Would you like some soup?" I asked.

She shook her head. "No, thanks. I'm not hungry at all. In fact," she put her hand over her stomach, "I'm not feeling too sharp there at all."

"Even though you told Bill you felt better?"

"It comes and goes."

It was easy to believe her. Her face again had that pinched look I had noticed there before.

"Is there any medicine I could give you? I have some of the usual stomach soothers. But Bill took the stuff he gave you before with him."

"I know. I'm just as glad though. I'm sure he was right. It did calm my stomach, at first. But I started feeling terrible after that again, and sort of down."

I went over to the bed and looked at her. If she were my daughter or sister, I thought, I'd get a doctor so fast. . . . But Bill, who was a doctor, had said she was on the mend.

"Look," I said. "If you don't feel all right, I'm going to call Bill and have him take you into Portland to the hospital."

"No, please. I'm fine. Bill wouldn't leave me unless I were okay. Truly. He's been just super to me all my life."

When she talked her light eyes lit up. Ringed by black lashes, they were startling and beautiful. She looked more herself. I smiled. All right. But any more pinched looks and I call.

"I feel much better now."

"All right. Don't forget the pill you're supposed to take. I'll get you some water." I went into the adjacent bathroom and returned with a glass.

Priscilla swallowed her pill but said, "I always worry about taking a pill. You know my mother—" She stopped.

"Yes? Your mother?"

She looked up at me rather timidly. "Perhaps you know, anyway. Granny said I was born addicted and should never take any pills."

Grandmother, I thought, had all the more lovable characteristics of the Trelawnys. She was fully worthy of being one. Obviously, her New England pride, galled by what had happened to her daughter, was taking it out on her granddaughter.

"That wasn't your fault," I said as gently as I could, wondering if the child knew who her father was. If so, I could at least offer whatever consolations cousinship could afford. But she might not know.

"No, but Granny says it's in the blood."

Nice Granny. Just like Red Riding Hood's, complete with teeth and wolf ears. "What does your Cousin Pete say about it?"

"He says not to pay any attention. That when I'm bigger, he'll send me to college so I can get away."

I smiled at that. I could just see that large and competent young man supplying some practical solution. "You must be looking forward to it."

"Well—"

"No?"

Her hand played with the quilt. "Not everybody has to go to college. It takes so long. I mean, I'd be twenty-two before I was finished."

"I know it's irritating for an adult to say this, but that's not so old."

The magnificent eyes looked up at me. "It's eight years. That's a long time to wait for—" She stopped abruptly.

I have been that young myself. "For waiting for somebody you love?"

The color then came, suffusing her face. She nodded.

"Who is it?" I don't know what I was thinking of— some boy at the high school with her, I suppose. I certainly was not prepared for her to say, in a rush, as though she simply could not keep it in, "Dr. S—Bill."

I said very carefully, so as not to sound shocked or —God forbid—mocking, "There's a rather large age gap between you, isn't there?"

"I don't think age makes any difference, do you?"

"Well, maybe not all that much. Still, twenty or so years is a lot." I remembered that he had said—or was it Giles who had said?—that Bill was a little younger than the twins. "I'd guess Bill to be about thirty-five."

"He's thirty-four." Priscilla said it as though she considered she had scored a point.

"All right. But I still think if Pete wants to send you to college you might go, just to get away, if only for a year or so. If you and Bill are really in love with each other, another year won't make any difference."

"Why do you care, Miss Trelawny?" She was looking at me with something not far from hostility. Adolescents are as sensitive as anyone else—more so, often enough. Perhaps she had sensed something in Bill's attitude towards me, and in view of what she said she wouldn't like it. Yet—I remembered the look I had caught on Bill's face. Outrageous as it might seem in view of her youth, it was Priscilla he cared for. He might have tried to hide his feeling for her, but he didn't succeed one hundred percent of the time. In that case, what was he doing proposing to me?

"I don't, really, Priscilla. I mean, it's not up to me to tell you what to do. You must be the judge of that. I guess I just thought that it would be fun for you to be on your own for a year or so. At least I've liked it."

The slightly hostile look went. She smiled. "I'm sorry. I thought just for a minute or two when we were at home, that Bill—well, liked you a lot. I guess I was jealous."

Poor baby, I thought. She was headed for a painful time. At that age wounds go deep. I didn't know what, if any, games Bill had been playing with her. If it hadn't been for that one look of tenderness, I would have said none. I would have put Priscilla's yearnings down to adolescent hero-worship built on nothing more than kindness (a rarity in her life, I was sure) and a nice smile. But there was that look. And there was that proposal to me.

"Whatever your true heart's desire is, Priscilla, I hope you get it." It sounded nice and was, on analysis, quite safe.

"Thank you, Miss Trelawny. I'm sorry if I was rude."

How isolated this child had been, I thought. Didn't she know that many of her contemporaries felt—and acted as though they felt—as though civility, let alone good manners, were selling out to the establishment?

"You weren't." I bent and kissed her. "Pleasant dreams! If you want me in the night give a shout. I'm just down the hall."

She smiled and snuggled down.

I went to the door. "Do you want me to turn out the light?"

"Yes, please. The pill must be working—I'm quite sleepy."

I snapped out the light and closed the door.

I stood there in the hall, wondering what I should do next. Something told me that I ought to let Giles know that Priscilla was here and the fact that, according to Bill, the countryside was alive with rumors about his— or Nicholas's—presence in the attic.

On the other hand, my stomach told me that I hadn't had anything to eat since that extremely early lunch.

I decided to have a sandwich first and then go up and report to Giles. It had been a long day and I needed sustenance.

But my day was not over yet. I was eating a sandwich and drinking some hot soup when the rear main doorbell rang. Muttering to myself, I got up and made the long way through the reception rooms and the halls. At the door, I hesitated. Living in New York had made me reluctant to open any door without finding out who was on the other side. As far as I knew, the rest of my colony was upstairs doing its various things. The draining dishes in the kitchen had attested to the fact that they had all eaten. Or they might have piled into either Pog's or Rod's car and gone to sample some welcome urban blight in the way of a movie or discothèque.

"Who is it?" I yelled, and then remembered to switch on the light outside the front door.

The doors at The Fell were thick. The voice on the other side was faint. But I did hear, "Cousin Kit. Open up."

Jeremy, I thought. Naturally. I unlocked the door and swung it open. Jeremy was there all right, holding onto a tall man in a parka and hood who seemed to be swaying slightly. Jeremy said, "Come on, Cousin Kit. Open up. I can't hold him up forever. He's too big."

"Who is he?"

The tall man raised his head. But even before he did I knew. I looked into the light-gray eyes that were blazing with mischief and something else. "Hello, Cousin Kit. Home is the sailor, home from the sea, and the prodigal home from the husks."

I stood there like a dummy and he laughed, a laugh that sent quivers of remembered pain up my skin.

"Come now, don't you have a welcome kiss for your Cousin Nicholas?"

9

I stood paralyzed as Nicholas pushed his way through the door and swayed and lurched down the hall into the sitting room with Jeremy and me trailing behind. There he sat down in the big winged chair opposite the portrait of Nicholas I. "Salut!" he said, lifting an imaginary glass. "Greetings, from the last Nicholas to the first."

A million questions were bursting in my mind like a Catherine wheel. Finally I said, "I thought you were dead."

"So did a lot of people. But the reports of my demise were grossly exaggerated." There was a satanic glint in his eye and I found myself thinking, he's not normal.

"Where did you find him?" I asked Jeremy.

"I didn't," Jeremy said gloomily. Never had I seen his usually complacent face look so irritated. "He found me."

"What do you mean?"

"He means this, cousin dear," and Nicholas took a pistol out of his pocket and waved it around. Then he gave his diabolical grin and turned back to the portrait.

"You mean he held that on you all the way up here?" I asked Jeremy.

"Forced his way into your apartment and said he had nothing to lose so if I didn't drive him up here he could blow my head off and be none the worse. I must say, Cousin Kit," he went on with an air of decided injury, "Aunt Ingrid certainly got herself mixed up with some queer people when she married into your father's family."

Somehow the implication that Mother, Jeremys' Aunt Ingrid, had married unfortunately when she latched onto a Trelawny, was, combined with everything else, too much for me. I felt hysterical laughter coming on and bottled it in. "I wish the dowager had been alive to hear you say that."

Nicholas, who had seemed too drunk or stoned to follow much, was obviously quite able to tune into our conversation. "If Mother had been alive, none of this would have happened. Grand old girl, Mother."

"None of what?" I asked sharply.

He made a wide sweep with his hands. "Everything."

"Pot or booze?" I asked Jeremy, who usually was knowledgeable about such things.

"I'm not sure. Maybe neither. But something."

I went over to Nicholas. "I—everybody thought you were dead—dead in a Hanoi prison."

"More fools they."

"It's been more than seven years."

"How well I know."

"Where have you been?"

"Going to and fro in the earth and up and down in it."

I had not been brought up in a Bible-reading, fundamentalist family for nothing. "How apt," I said.

Nicholas grinned.

"All right. Why have you come back?"

Suddenly he looked sane and every inch a Trelawny. "To take over my estate."

"Your estate has been hanging all these years. Why haven't you come before now?"

The cunning, slightly lunatic look came back. "First I have to find Giles."

"And where do you think he is?"

"Here, of course. Where else?"

"Nonsense," I put as much conviction as I could into it. "He's not here."

"Oh yes he is. I told him I'd meet him under the rafter back at The Fell."

That was when I shivered. Until that moment I had had the feeling it was all some crazy kind of a joke. Those were the words Giles had repeated to me as said by Nicholas in the middle of one of his broadcasts.

Nicholas was watching me. "So you know about that, Cousin Kit." And he got up. As he came towards me I thought, how could they have ever been considered alike? Having been with Giles so much, the difference screamed at me. Nicholas, not quite as tall, not as heavy-boned, was more lithe. The same eyes that upstairs looked out of Priscilla's face were looking at me now: lake-gray, ringed with black, tilted a little at the corners. It was hard even to realize that he was a man of forty-two. He looked ten years younger, or at least he had until he was only two or three feet from you.

"He's here, isn't he, Cousin Kit?"

"No, Nicholas. He isn't."

"You're lying. I know you're lying." He had put the pistol back in his pocket, but his hands crept up towards me.

"Who the hell are you?"

We all swung around. Frank Morse was standing there, his usual offensive self, hands jammed in the pockets of his filthy leather jacket.

Nicholas turned and seemed to grow. "I'm Nicholas Trelawny. What are you doing in my house?"

"I thought it was *her* house." Frank took one hand out of his pocket and started picking his teeth. "What's going on?"

"I should tell you," I said, "that my cousin Nicholas here has a pistol in his pocket."

"Yeah? So?"

But I hadn't been able to deflect Nicholas from his main interest. He turned back. "Where's Giles, Cousin Kit? Don't tell me he isn't here, because I know he is."

"Sorry, Nicholas. You're wrong." I could not, at that moment, have answered any kind of a question as to why I was so determined that Nicholas should not know of Giles's whereabouts. Was I protecting him? If so, why?

"Am I?"

Nicholas was continuing his almost languid progress in my direction. Before what I saw in his face I could not keep from backing. That he was certifiably insane I believed. Anybody looking at him, at that hatred and malice, would have known. I tried to play for time.

"Why do you hate him so much, Nicholas? He's your brother, your twin."

"Because . . . because." He stopped for a moment. Then one hand waved in the direction of the library. "Did you read any of these books on twins, Cousin Kit?"

"No. I meant to. But I haven't had a chance." I knew I was playing for time. His eyes had dulled a bit. Perhaps, if he were drugged, it—the drug—would continue on whatever cycle it was on, and he would pass out. Perhaps something—although I didn't know what —would intervene.

"You should have. You really should have. You might have found something that would interest you very much indeed." He started to laugh, that same mocking laughter that I remembered so well, and at that moment he started towards me again.

"Nicholas—!" I tried to back again, but I had reached the wall. He laughed again as he reached me.

The long fingers were around my neck. There were voices, both Frank's and Jeremy's. And then I heard another voice. "Take your hands away from her throat, Trelawny. I have you covered and I wouldn't hesitate to kill you."

Nicholas dropped his hands and spun around. Bill Seaward was standing in the doorway, a pistol in his hand. "Now come away from her. Kit, come over here."

I moved. So did Nicholas, like lightning. There was a melee at the door. I saw a hand upraised and then Nicholas was lying on the floor, knocked cold.

Bill got his bag from the hall. "I'm going to give him a shot that will put him out for a while," he said grimly. "Then I'll call the police."

A few seconds earlier a policeman would have been one of the most welcome sights I could imagine. Now —what if a policeman insisted on searching the attics?

"Not tonight, Bill. I don't think I can take any more right now."

"You mean you don't mind leaving this maniac at large?"

"You said you'd put him out."

Bill stared at me. "Perhaps you're right. Okay." He opened his bag. "This should keep him quiet for at least another eight hours, and then I'll give him a sedative."

I shivered. "He's insane, isn't he, Bill?"

"Completely. The whole family's tainted and should be wiped out or put behind bars."

"All of us?"

"Sorry, Kit. I didn't mean you."

Jeremy spoke up with a wealth of grievance in his voice. "If Cousin Kit is *not* nuts, it's entirely due to her mother's side of the family. *My* side. Can I have something to eat, Kit? I haven't had a bite since that madman came into the apartment waving a gun."

"How do you suppose he knew where to find you, or who you were?" I wondered.

"Who knows? But I want you to know it's not what I'm used to." He went off towards the kitchen.

"Crazy, man. Crazy," Frank muttered. Bill turned towards him. "Help me get him on the sofa there," he said.

With Bill at his head and Frank at his feet they hauled him onto the sofa. "Thanks," Bill said.

"Bill," I said, feeling like I was confronting a jungle of unanswered questions. "How did you know Nicholas was here?"

"I passed their car when I was leaving. Not that many cars come up this road, and I recognized your cousin. I wasn't sure about the man sitting beside him. But I guess something on an unconscious level must have come through. I went on home to pick up some things—I had decided I was going to come back here anyway—and came back as fast as I could."

"That was sweet of you," I said, wondering what was bothering me about that statement.

"Your safety means a lot to me."

It was kind and thoughtful. I was grateful for the protective impulse that had brought him back. I was also uncomfortable, although I did not know why. What I did know beyond any doubt was that I had to get upstairs to warn Giles. A sense of his danger was coming over me strongly.

"What is it, Kit?"

"Nothing. It's been a long day. And I still can't believe half of it. I'm going to bed."

He came towards me. "You're all right, aren't you?"

Without thinking and without plan, I backed. "Yes, Bill. I am. Just tired." That, at least, wasn't a lie. "Let me show you to your room. You can have the room you turned down for Priscilla, the one next to mine."

I hadn't realized the implications of that until he said, "Can I construe that into anything flattering?"

"No. I'm afraid not. It was purely practical. I'm just not sure that any other bed is made up."

He made a face. "I think I'll stay down here. There's an even bigger sofa in the library. In fact, I seem to remember it makes into a bed. I'd prefer to stay nearer to my patient." He nodded his head towards Nicholas.

"Will he be all right?"

"Oh, sure. If he wakes, in spite of that shot, I'll hear him. What I gave him should be enough to put him out for hours, but if he's been on drugs it might not be anything at all for him." He turned and looked at me. "My father was a drug addict, you know. Morphine, acquired in the course of taking something for an injured back."

"Oh—?" Just in time I saw I could not have known that. "How terrible," I finished rather weakly.

"You didn't know?"

"No. How could I?"

"Yet you sounded there as though you were going to say something indicating you did."

"Bill—don't watch every word. I'm too tired to know what I'm saying—let alone what anyone else is saying." I went firmly to the door. "Hasta mañana."

He smiled. "Good night."

I went first into Priscilla's room, poking my head in to see if she were asleep. The moon had risen, but was still on the other side of the house. Nevertheless, some of its light was filtering through the open windows into the room. The dark hair spilled over the pillow. I stood there for a moment. Everything seemed to be in good order, so I left, pulling the door closed behind me as gently as I could. Then I went back to my own room.

As once before, I filled an hour with taking a bath, washing and drying my hair, turning down my bed and doing some laundry. I also took some time out to worry about Josephine. Had she discovered Richard and Emily? No use worrying about them either. With more immediate problems confronting me, two mice, however tame and engaging, had a rather low priority. Or should have.

I put the new flashlight I had bought into my robe. Then I took the long way up to the attic, going through the second floor to the north wing and through that till it joined the far extension. I went up the stairs to the third floor, into the bedroom closet and up the stairs.

It was dark in Giles's attic. Even if I had known where to switch on the light I wouldn't have dared to, not knowing whether Giles had drawn the curtains. The blankets and quilts underfoot muted any sound I might have made. Unfortunately, they also muted any sound anyone else might have made.

"Giles," I whispered. "Giles."

There was no reply. Gingerly, and with my hand half over it, I switched on my flashlight.

"Giles," I whispered, and then wondered why I was whispering. We had spoken before in quiet but ordinary voices. I advanced down the attic, shining my light here and there. I became aware that I was afraid, but I didn't know what I was afraid of, beyond the fact that it had to do with Giles, as though he were in danger. The bed was neatly made. I flashed the light around and in every corner. There was nowhere he could hide. And he was not there.

Stupidly, unbelievingly, I stood there, trying to grasp the fact that Giles, who had been a prisoner in his own attic for months, had left. Where on earth could he be? My sense of his danger was now extreme. Or was it my own danger?

My eye was caught by the top portion of a drop leaf chest. It looked as though the catch had not fully closed and the flap might fall at any moment. Without thinking, compulsively neat, I went over and pulled it out, preparatory to slamming it shut. Instead, I stood staring at what was inside. I am neither an engineer nor an electronics expert. But what I saw looked typically like a two-way radio. It was while I was staring at it that I heard a click. It came from across the attic where I had entered. Leaving the flap open so I would not make a noise I ran over and down the little staircase leading into the bedroom closet on the floor below and turned the handle of the door leading into the room. It was locked from the other side.

I don't know how long I stood there, staring down through the dark at where my hand was on the handle. The implications were obvious: someone not only knew about the attic but knew I was there and locked me in. Worst of all, it could be—most likely was—Giles. Then I remembered the entrance to the attic at the other end. I went back up the stairs and raced along the attic and down the gangway at the other side. Thank heaven, I thought, that door was open. I stepped through into the big central attic.

It was lit, but only with a small lamp, so that the great vaulted roof was in shadow. I saw immediately that the easel had been moved and was trying to guess the implications of that when, out of the corner of my eye, I saw something hanging from the center beam. It moved then, swinging, its face turned in my direction. It was Priscilla. I cried out and heard my own voice just before the whole world seemed to break over my head and I blacked out.

I woke up aware of a terrible headache and gingerly put my hand up to discover a lump at the back of my head. For the first few seconds I thought I was in my own bed, and lay there wondering why I should have such an aching head and such a swelling. Then I became aware that instead of the usual darkness of my room when I woke in the middle of the night, there was a light on, and above me, instead of a ceiling, there was a steeply sloping roof and beams cutting across it. Beams. With that word memory came flooding back. I sat up. Nausea came over me in a wave.

"Oh," I said, holding my head. At that I heard a noise and saw, bent over something on the floor, a man's back. My heart went flying up. Giles, I thought. Then he turned and rose and it was Bill Seaward.

"Priscilla?" I said.

"Dead, I'm afraid."

"Oh no! No! Who killed her?"

"Nicholas. He's a killer. A maniac. He'd kill anyone to get The Fell back in his hands. Surely you know that." He came over to me.

"But why would Priscilla threaten his ownership of The Fell. He owns it anyway."

Bill frowned. "She's his daughter."

"Yes, I know. But that doesn't make sense."

Bill stood staring down at me, frowning. Then, incredibly, he said, "You and I will be married."

A chill like icy water went over me.

"You'll marry me and we'll live here. We'll be owners of The Fell. Then there'll be no Trelawnys left. We'll have paid them back."

"Paid who back, Bill? What are you talking about?"

"Priscilla is dead. Nicholas and Giles will be too, soon. We'll kill them together."

He had taken hold of my hands and was holding them tightly with his own. I stared down at them and wondered how I could get loose and get help.

"Bill," I said, as steadily as I could. "That's not sane. Killing people is no solution to anything. Please let me go."

"Why?"

The trouble was, his face was in shadow. If I had thought Nicholas mad, then in Bill there was a madness far more dangerous, because it masqueraded as sanity. "Let me go downstairs and call the police to come and get Nicholas," I said, hoping it would work.

"Oh no, Kit. Not until you tell me where I can find Giles. It's no use just getting one. We have to get both."

"How should I know where Giles is?"

"Because you've been hiding him. You and Pete." He moved then and such light as there was fell on his face. His eyes had that odd, shiny look they had had before.

"What makes you think that?" I was, again, playing for time, hoping that someone would come up—anyone. But Bill's questioning about Giles was reassuring. It meant that he had not yet found him, because if he had, Giles, like Priscilla, might very well be dead.

"I don't think it. I know it. Pete let something fall

to Priscilla. And Priscilla told me. You must have seen how she feels about me. She tells me everything. Before you came—But that was a while ago."

"What happened before I came?"

"Nothing. Only I had made up my mind to marry Priscilla as soon as she was old enough. It was easy to make her love me. After all, she never had any father. She was hungry to be loved by a man. Hungrier than you, my dear. But you will marry me and I will take the name."

"What name?" I knew the answer but I asked it anyway. At the back of the question-and-answer charade I was trying frantically to think of a way I could distract his attention and make for the stairs. With all his talk of marrying me, I wasn't by any means sure I'd get out of the attic alive.

He frowned, as though I had asked a silly question. "Trelawny, of course."

"But why do you want to take the name of Trelawny?"

"It's the only name that matters. If you're a Trelawny, you have everything. If you're not, you have nothing." He paused. "You *are* nothing. You should know that. It happened to you. She did it to you, too."

"Yes, Bill. It happened to me. But it's not that important. You can't base your whole life on some petty humiliation when you were a child."

Another voice said, "That's good to hear, Cousin Kit. I thought there for a while you had done just that."

Bill turned. I stared at the door as his words slowly penetrated. Nicholas, his graceful body lounging against the door, was holding a pistol. "Now, Bill, what's this about Priscilla?"

"She's dead," Bill said, his eyes on the pistol.

Without lowering the pistol or taking his attention away from Bill, Nicholas went over to the girl and bent down. He put his other hand on her wrist and over her face. "Quite so," he said. "Why did you kill her?"

"Because I decided it would be easier and quicker to marry Kit instead."

"But why did you intend to marry Priscilla before?"

"Because I had found out that you had married her mother. She's legitimate. She's your heir—after Giles."

"But you say Giles is not dead."

"But he will be. You will kill him or he will kill you."

"And you were going to arrange that. How?"

"Like this!" And before I knew what was happening Bill had yanked me off the couch and in front of him. As he did so he fired, and Nicholas fell to the floor.

"Now," Bill said. "You and I are going to find Giles."

"You must know you'll never pull this off."

"Oh yes I will. I've planned it down to the last detail. I've been thinking about it ever since I came back here. The only thing that surprises me is that Nicholas is still alive. I thought he was dead. I thought I had made sure of that by getting him onto drugs."

I was still in front of him. His arm was still pinning me to him. The pistol, still in his hand, was pressed against my stomach. I was not in a mood for conversation. Yet I thought that in keeping him talking lay my only safety. "You got him onto drugs? How?"

"It's not that hard if you have the right contacts, and I did. I got them through Father, so I could keep him supplied."

"But why would you want to keep your father addicted?"

"If Father had ever managed to shake the habit, I was afraid he might try to destroy his records and then discover that I had removed them and start asking awkward questions."

"What records?"

"He had something on the Trelawnys. I knew that. He told me. But he never told me what it was. Now let's go downstairs and look for Giles."

But at that moment Priscilla groaned.

Bill swore under his breath. "I thought she was dead, or nearly so." I felt his arm loosen and pushed it aside with all my strength.

"Come back here," he yelled at me.

I thought I would never make it to the door before that bullet hit me and when I heard the sound of the shot I waited for the pain. But nothing happened. Slowly I turned. Bill, his hand on his arm, staggered, bumped against the easel, and then fell.

Nicholas was sitting up, the pistol in his hand. "Are you all right, darling?" he said to me, in Giles's voice.

"I think I'm going mad," I said.

Giles got up. "I wouldn't blame you. But you didn't discover I was Giles just this second."

"No. When you first came in just now and picked up on my statement about basing a whole life on a childhood humiliation, I knew it was you. Nicholas wouldn't know about that."

"Nice work," a voice said from the doorway. There, pistol in hand, stood Frank. "Let's see how the doctor is."

And before my unbelieving eyes Frank walked over to Bill. "He'll live," he said, and then, "Just for safety's sake." He took a pair of handcuffs out of his back pocket and slapped them on Bill's wrists.

"Priscilla," I said.

He went over. After a minute he said, "Her neck's bruised and she's been doped. But she'll be okay, too."

"You're a *policeman*."

"Surprise, surprise," he jeered in quite his usual manner. "I'm going down to call for an ambulance. Keep an eye on him."

Giles went over to Bill and looked at his shoulder. "You're just grazed."

Bill started to get to his feet. Giles helped him up and over to the divan. "Better sit down. You lost some blood."

Bill stared up at him. "You're not Nicholas," he said slowly.

"No. I'm Giles."

"But I thought—"

"Yes. That was what I wanted you to think."

"But why?" I asked.

"You tricked me," Bill said slowly. "I was sure it was Giles hiding up here. I had it all planned. I could have gotten away with it."

"Gotten away with what? Killing Priscilla?"

Bill nodded wearily. "That's one of the things that Father had on the Trelawnys: that Nicholas had actually married Priscilla's mother, so that she would inherit The Fell after the twins. There was something else Father knew, older than that, that he used on Mrs. Trelawny when she was bullying me. But I never found out what it was."

"If you had," Giles said, "you would not have had to try and kill Priscilla."

I wondered what he meant, but was preoccupied with Priscilla. "But thinking Priscilla would inherit, you made her love you so that you could marry her and have The Fell?"

I thought about Priscilla's adolescent adoration, the trust in her face. "Well, if you aspired to Trelawny heights, let me assure you, you made it. They were a cruel family"—I looked at Giles, who was watching me —"with one exception. And you"—I looked back at Bill—"did the scummiest trick of all, making that lonely child fall in love with you."

"I didn't get away with it," he said after a minute. "I fell in love with her. It was crazy that I should fall in love with a child. But I did. She was like that woman"—he glanced at Giles—"your mother might have been, once." He went on. "I didn't have any mother myself. I adored her until—"

I could see it: the motherless, isolated boy, with a drug addict for a father, identifying everything that was desirable and beautiful with the woman who turned around and humiliated him.

Giles said, "I knew if you thought I was Nicholas it might shake you. You might break and make a mistake."

"Yes. I used to put myself to sleep imagining what I would do to Nicholas, he was so much a part of your mother's merry ways. Well, one of my consolations will be to think of you trying to prove you're Giles and that you didn't do any of the things—broadcasts, killing Charlotte—that Nicholas is supposed to have done. You're going to have a fine old time. Before they let you out somebody may do the neighborhood a favor and burn the place down."

"It won't be that hard," Giles said. "I finally found the message Mother was trying to get to me. It was—"

The door burst open. Pogs, in jeans, sweater, blue kimono, and bare feet said, "Kit, I'm terribly, terribly sorry, and it's truly not my fault, but the picture you lent me has disappeared. Honestly, it wasn't me. . . ." Her voice wound down. She stared at all of us and finally at Bill, sitting handcuffed, the blood seeping down his sleeve. "I *thought* I heard a noise. Somebody's shot Dr. Seaward!"

"Pogs—" I started.

"Hello, Giles," she said. "I've been thinking you were here."

"Oh?" Giles said. "That's interesting. How?"

"I'm psychic," Pogs explained with simple pride.

"I'm not sure the U.S. Government, to say nothing of the local constabulary, is going to accept that, if they're looking around for proof of my being here."

"Well, I don't know why not. It was because he knew I was psychic that Uncle Jasper wanted me to come up here. He said something funny was going on. And he was right."

I stared at her. "Uncle Jasper? You surely don't mean that stuffed Brahmin, Mr. Edgerton?"

Pogs stifled a giggle. "He *is* like a stuffed Brahmin. At least that's what everyone thinks. He's also a leading member of the local society for psychic research."

"That should teach you," Giles said to me, "never to jump to conclusions."

I shook my head. "Frank Morse a cop; Mr. Edgerton into psychic research. The world has slipped its axis."

At that point the police arrived with two ambulance bearers and a doctor. The police took Bill Seaward away. At the door he glanced back at Priscilla. Then he said to me, "I want to go before she wakes up. She was out—I gave her a shot while she was asleep, so it wouldn't hurt. She won't remember anything about . . . about."

"Was that why you didn't want her next to me and gave her the sleeping pill?"

"Of course."

"All right. But—" I sorted among the jumble of unanswered questions. "Was it you who slipped Giles the stew and wrote that note forging my initials?"

He nodded. "Yes. I didn't leave quite as soon as you

thought. I got it set up while you were in the attic and got it up there after you left."

"He could have seen you. It was sheer luck he was in the bathroom."

"Oh, that was just gravy. I would have left the tray at the bottom of the staircase, making plenty of noise so he could hear me, but leaving before he came out."

"But my initials that you forged, where had you seen them?"

"Grocery lists at the Bradford store. You send them by Pete and he puts them on a nail in a wallboard."

"And the shot you gave Giles? The one that was supposed to put him out for eight hours?"

"Sugar water. Since he was to have been held responsible for killing Priscilla, I had to have him up and around."

"Why did you cut Priscilla down—if you wanted to kill her?"

"Because you almost caught me redhanded. You came in two seconds after I'd got her up there, and I couldn't be sure you hadn't seen me." He looked over at Priscilla again. "She'll have to know, I suppose. Will you tell her I'm sorry?"

The police doctor stood up. "There's not too much wrong with her. I can take her to the hospital, but she'd do just as well here."

"I'll go down with her," I said.

We got her into bed. There was a bruised look about her neck and in places the skin was rubbed raw. "Are you sure she's all right?" I said to the doctor.

At that moment she muttered and turned. "Bill?" she said. The gray eyes opened.

I leaned over her. "Priscilla, go to sleep. Everything's going to be all right. I promise."

She sighed and stretched, closed her eyes and snuggled back into the pillow.

"I hope I can keep that promise," I said.

The young doctor smiled. "You probably can. She's young." He gave her then a very male and unmedical look. "With those eyes she's going to be a smasher. I hope I'm still around and available when she's grown up."

Later, Giles and I were in the sitting room.

"Giles," I said, "I don't understand any of this. Is Nicholas still alive?"

"No. He died in prison camp as I told you."

"Then why—"

"As I said, I had to shake Bill up. He was pretty sure I was here and had been for quite some time and had a neat plan whereby I would be caught trying to kill Priscilla and would be shot by him but in apparent self-defense. Then he would marry you."

"Was it really what your mother did to him?"

"I think that added to it considerably, and there was more to it than I told you before. The trouble is, he didn't have any mother and his father was out of it, as far as he was concerned, large part of the time. How did you put it? In Cloud-cuckoo-land. Anyway, he was over all the time and evidently built up a whole fantasy that Mother was really his mother and he was really a Trelawny. I can see why. His home was bleak. He didn't have anybody to talk to. So poor Bill had this fantasy, which at first was just that, but then became reality. I don't really know what happened. I wasn't there, I only got it second hand from Nicholas and Mother. But one day for some reason, he started acting out the fantasy—embracing Mother or something, calling her 'Mother.' "

"He didn't mention that at all when he gave me his version."

"Well—" Giles looked down at his hands, "Maybe he blocked it out. Anyway, I guess you know the effect that would have on her. Absurd and anachronistic as it sounds, Mother felt about the Trelawnys and The Fell the way Louis XIV felt about the monarchy."

"Pogs said that . . . that her branch of the family in England had come down in the world." Giles looked up at me and something registered as I went on. "She —Pogs—said your mother and her mother went to school together and that Mrs. Trelawny even then was a social climber."

"Quite true. That was the origin of it, or at least— what is the origin?—it was the link further back in the chain of cause and effect. Mother was brought up by a family that had come down in the world. Two generations earlier they had gone to the right schools, come out in society, all that jazz. Then after World War I things got tough. The next generation didn't make the right schools, and in the England of that day that dropped them below the main social barrier. It was something they couldn't forget. Mother was very clever and eaten up with ambition to get back into the ranks of the upper class. She got a scholarship to that school Pogs's mother went to. I think she thought that from there—with the friends she'd made there and her looks—she could marry as high as she wanted. But things didn't quite turn out that way, and when Father went over to go to Oxford and he was the American equivalent of what she wanted, she married him. The family and all it represented became a mania with her. So when Bill suddenly, and without anybody realizing what was going on in him, announced himself as part of the family, I suppose he threatened the one thing that mattered to her, particularly in view of the queer circumstances of our birth."

Giles stood up. "God—it's good to get out of that attic. I thought I'd go mad." His face suddenly showed up in the light, his eyes above the dark-blue sweater the strange gray-green I had noticed before.

I sat bolt upright. "Giles—your eyes. It was those that made me think you were Nicholas. They're different now. They're a different shade."

He looked at me and grinned. "Contacts." Then he put his hand in a pocket just under his belt and brought out a little package wrapped in tissue paper. "See?"

I got up and went over. I had seen clear contact lenses plenty of times and knew that actors, playing roles were eye color was important, would wear lenses changing the color of their irises. I looked down at the tiny pale-gray discs.

"Like Columbus's egg, it's simple when you know how," Giles said.

"But in every other way as well you were like Nicholas. You looked smaller, slighter."

"I've had long experience in making people think that."

I went back to my chair, "Go on." I sat down and

curled my feet under me. Giles picked up an afghan that was lying on the sofa against the wall and put it over me.

"What were the queer circumstances of your birth you were talking about?"

Giles was bending over me. "In a minute. I love you. Did you know that?"

I reached up and touched his face. "I wasn't sure. I'm glad. Do you know that I love you?"

"Yes." He kissed me again. "When you tried so hard not to admit I was here, even to Nicholas when you thought I was Nicholas. I knew then, and I'd like you to know I found it very hard not to abandon my role and be myself." He started pulling me to him. Fire seemed to run along my limbs. I put my arms around his neck. Then, as the door opened, I dropped them and Giles stood up.

"Oh, sorry," a blue kimono whisked back out of the door.

Giles bent down again.

I put my hand on his shoulder. "Finish answering my questions, Giles, or. . . ."

He didn't move. "Or?"

I felt a little breathless. "I may not get to them."

He laughed and stood up, "All right. Where was I?"

"Queer circumstances."

He went over to the wing chair and stood, leaning on the back, looking at the portrait of his mother. "Mother wasn't sure at first she wanted to marry Father. I got that from Cousin Hermione. She turned him down the first time. Father went off mad, took himself to London and while there, in a fit of pique, married a kid working in a nightclub. I wouldn't be surprised if it weren't some kind of deliberate slap in the face to Mother, who had tried to pull rank on him as the English Trelawny as opposed to the Colonial variety. Anyway, it—the marriage—was a disaster from the first and Father got himself divorced. Apparently Mother was shaken up by this and not as sure that she would marry into *Debrett's* as she had been. So when she and Father ran into each other again, she said, this time, 'yes.' They were married, and a year later, back here, Nicholas and I were well on the way.

"Shortly before we were due to put in our appearance, Father got a letter from a lawyer in London. It seems he rather carelessly got married a bit too soon. His divorce was not final. Ergo, his remarriage was not valid. Father's first thought was that he was being blackmailed, but apparently his ex-wife, who had also gotten remarried, had discovered what had happened and was merely informing him through her lawyer.

"Anyway, you can imagine the effect it must have had on him with what he hoped was his heir on the way. He told Mother, and the shock was so great that it proceeded to precipitate—er—our arrival. Moving heaven and earth and pulling all the wires he could without letting on what it was for, Father got a clergyman to agree to come to the house and perform another marriage ceremony. Of course, the ideal thing would have been to go there, but by this time Mother was in bed going through all the preliminaries of a long and difficult birth. The clergyman and Dr. Seaward arrived within a few moments of each other. But before the parson could do his thing, Nicholas was born—illegitimately.

"It was then around eleven o'clock at night. Dr. Seaward knew, of course, that another birth was imminent, but nothing was happening. So he came downstairs and told Father to let him know when Mother started labor pains again. He had been up most of the night before, as we learned later, and he wanted to catch some rest before the next arrival. So he went through there into the library and lay on the sofa. Then the minister arrived. Telling him nothing except that his wife had been ill, and bundling Nicholas into another room with one of the servants, Father took him up and the marriage ceremony was performed. Father then thanked him, paid him, and got him off the premises as quickly as possible. I've often thought that whole scene would make a marvelous comedy. . . .

"Anyway, I arrived three hours later, at two a.m.—technically the next day, and, of course, legitimately. Father, who had put the clergyman under some ministerial seal of secrecy, assumed that Dr. Seaward knew nothing about the marriage ceremony. As it turned out, he was wrong. The doctor did know but decided that it was none of his business—then. But what he did do, without anyone's knowing, was to take a small sample of blood from both Nicholas and me when we were born. Maybe because of the Trelawnys, maybe because he would have been interested in the subject anyway, the old doctor's hobby was twins. He'd even written a book on them."

"Of course!" I suddenly remembered. "I saw it in your library catalogue."

"That's right. I don't think when he took those samples of blood he thought anything other than that it was more research for his files."

Giles walked around the chair and sat down. "But it turned out to be more than that. Because of bustling Nicholas out and bringing him back much later, the two of us got mixed. It's not as rare as you might believe. That's happened several times with twins. And there's sometimes hell to pay—as in this case, where inheritance was concerned. Anyway, Mother, who knew the first twin was illegitimate, poured all her devotion onto Nicholas, born, as she thought, after the marriage. And the fact that he turned out to be more like her just added to her feeling for him. In the meantime we were all growing up and Bill was part of the scene.

"Then he made his fatal mistake of acting out his belief that he was part of the family—and Mother was unbelievably brutal to him. It wasn't just that she ridiculed him for being chunky and fat. You know what her voice could sound like. She cut him to ribbons half a dozen times a day.

"Then suddenly one day he went berserk. Flew at her, screaming. I think she was frightened. He had to be taken home."

"He said his father found him crying."

"No, he really went to pieces. The next day Dr. Seaward came. He told Mother that if she ever mistreated Bill again, by word or deed, he would not only make public that one of us was illegitimate, but that the legitimate one was not Nicholas but me—and that he had the blood tests to prove it. Contrary to what everyone thought, we were fraternal, not identical, twins. Our blood types were different, and he had the blood tests to show which of us was which right back to the beginning, because he had taken various samples from time to time for one reason or another and had early on discovered the mixup.

"Mother wouldn't believe it, at first. She insisted we were identical twins. But the doctor showed her the records—the results of routine tests proved we weren't.

"I think that was when Mother changed towards me. She couldn't forgive me for being the legitimate one. Hence her constant dwelling on how alike Nicholas and I were—she wanted the whole world to consider us identical, not fraternal twins. I guess she figured the more we were considered identical, the less chance of discovery."

"Fraternal twins aren't really twins at all, are they? I mean they are like any other siblings, and can have different blood types and so on."

"Yes, whereas identical are just that—identical: skin, cells, the whole body chemistry. Needless to say she didn't tell Nicholas or me, and went on with the fiction of how identical we were, and how Trelawnys were always producing twins. As I told you, I had my moments of rebellion, but usually got argued out of them. She managed to make it clear—without actually saying so—that by going along with her I would win her affection. That, I suppose, is my rationalization. If I went along with her, it was my fault."

"When did you find out about all this?"

"Last night. I kept thinking about her message— that the information I needed was with something I had sent her and I kept trying to figure out what it was. I had just about given up when I remembered the watercolor I had done on a leave over there and sent her before I took Nicholas's place. Then, when I went to your room to look at it, it wasn't there. After that I combed every room and found it in Pogs's. You remember when she came in and said it was missing? I took it back upstairs and took the frame off. Sure enough, Scotch-taped to the back was this." And Giles pulled a thick package of folded sheets from his pocket. "Everything went for her when Nicholas died. She knew, of course, I was in Intelligence and while I was officially Missing In Action and quite probably dead, she sent a message through a friend in the Pentagon in case I should show up.

"This is one of the saddest documents I ever hope to read. She wrote it just before she died. And in a way, although she does nothing but set down the narrative, it's a sort of apology."

He took a breath. "Anyway, it will help to establish what I did and didn't do. Pilots, right before they take off, have blood taken from them for various purposes of medical research concerned with the relationship between stress and blood conditions such as cholesterol and so on. Nicholas, of course, had his taken dozens of times, and so did I, when I was flying in his place."

"Won't you get punished for taking his place?"

"Reprimanded, certainly. But my blood will match the blood taken from me before the air strikes I went on, and one of the tapes, complete with date, was recorded by poor, stoned Nick while I was still on the carrier."

"And Charlotte?"

"Blood samples were taken then, too. Nick had artistically banged himself up in the supposed accident."

"So you can clear yourself!"

"Yes."

"Why did Nicholas murder Charlotte?"

"He told me that, one of the last times I saw him. Mother more or less ordered him to. I didn't believe him. As a matter of fact, I nearly killed him—or would have, if he hadn't been so sick—when he unloaded that bit of information. But it seems he was right. Mother was opposed to Nicholas and Charlotte marrying. This made Charlotte mad. She had snooped in Dr. Seaward's files when she was staying there and playing secretary to him, and had found out about us and threatened Mother with exposure. She should have known better. Mother told Nicholas to get rid of her."

"But she didn't mind you marrying Charlotte?"

"Oh, no. Charlotte was good enough for me. But not for Nicholas."

"By the way, how come all the papers called it an

accident? There wasn't a word about the autopsy."

"The examiner was Dr. Seaward. You know what she had on him—drugs. God knows what kind of pressure she put on the police chief. But nobody wanted a scandal. It just never got out."

I said suddenly. "Your mother was proud and the Bible says pride goes before a fall."

"No," Giles corrected, "what the Bible says is, *'Pride goeth before destruction, and an haughty spirit before a fall.'* "

I thought about it. "Yes, that's even better. Because what your mother had was a haughty spirit." I looked up at Giles. "It must have been very hard for you, loving her, knowing she loved Nicholas more."

"I think it's one of the things that—until now—made it difficult for me to show affection. I guess I was afraid to. It never worked with Mother, and in some way, in the depths of me, I knew it was wrong. Even with Charlotte—" He made a face. "I daresay my inadequacy in that area made it easier for Charlotte to switch to Nicholas."

"Until now," I repeated.

He took my hand and kissed it and held it against his cheek. "Until now," he said.

Awhile later I asked, "Is Frank really a policeman?"

"Oh, yes. And a very good actor."

"He certainly threw himself into the part. Did you know he was a cop?"

"I suspected it."

"Well, you didn't sound as though you did when you told me that his painting showed him to be a dangerous man and I was to watch out."

"That painting is the product of a talented but very disordered mind. It seems Frank borrowed it. Its real creator is right now in a private sanitarium."

"Yes, but a lot of people in New York thought he was a painter."

"Who saw him actually painting? He produced canvases and said they were his. That was his cover."

"Then why did he come up here?"

"Because he was the ideal cop to send up here. He's a federal cop, you know, and rumors about my being here had filtered down to Washington."

"What about Tess? Was she on drugs?"

"If by drugs you mean heroin, no. If you mean was she a pill-popper, yes. Hence her going to pieces all of a sudden. Frank really is fond of her and he was trying to get her off. He should have waited and had it done more professionally. But apparently it's working. I hope she stays off."

"And Jeremy? You obviously didn't go all the way down to New York to get him. You didn't have time."

"No. When you left for Portland I got in touch with Pete by that two-way radio and told him to call Jeremy and tell him to get up here. I thought you needed to have some other relative keeping an eye on you and I felt fairly sure—or at least Pete told me— that underneath that galloping opportunism Jeremy's very fond of you. Pete got back in touch saying Jeremy had reacted immediately—gotten himself onto the air shuttle to Boston where he intended to hire a car to drive here. Pete wired him some money to the airline counter, I think. Then, when everything started breaking loose, I got out of the house and stopped his car and talked him into putting on an act with me. Not only is he fond of you, he feels that our family, the Trelawnys, didn't sufficiently appreciate his side of the family and he was out to prove their merit."

"Well I'll be damned! I guess I've never appreciated him enough."

"You needn't bend too far the other way. His last suggestion as we were coming up the drive was that after seeing the rooms full of treasures at The Fell he should open up a with-it antique shop."

"That sounds just like him. What about Pete? Where does he come into all this?"

"He was assigned by my former boss at the Pentagon to keep an eye on me. He may not look it, but he's still an active member of the military."

"That sounds like the right hand of the military didn't know what the left was doing."

"That happens more often than you'd care to believe. My own boss's faith in me was personal and unofficial."

"Was it Frank who knocked the flashlight out of my hand?"

"Almost certainly. He couldn't afford to have you turn it on and blow his cover."

"But he never discovered actually how to get into your attic?"

"No. But I'm not sure he wouldn't have if things had gone on much longer."

Something that had been in the back of my mind bothering me suddenly surfaced. "I know now why I felt uncomfortable when Bill walked in on us in this room while you were playing Nicholas. He said he'd seen you in the car and that he'd recognized Jeremy. I knew something was funny, because he'd never seen Jeremy."

"It was me—I—he recognized. But he couldn't be sure, and he didn't want to pretend to knowledge he didn't have."

Giles came up to my chair again. "Come here," he said, and pulled me up. "All questions answered? All doubts resolved?"

"Yes to the latter. No to the former. I'll probably be thinking of questions for the next ten years."

"Just so long as we'll be around one another to ask them. In case you're not too quick on the uptake, this is a proposal. Now say 'yes' and take me out of my suspense. I've been wounded in the service of my country, food-poisoned, knocked down, and all but killed, and I feel I deserve to be pampered."

"Yes," I said. "I think you do." I put my arms around his neck and proceeded with the pampering immediately.

After a short and very pleasant interlude, I said, "Giles, what are you going to do with this palace?"

"We."

"All right. What are we going to do with it? I'm not one for acres of light housework and dusting."

"I think I'd like to turn it into a school for various types of orphans, including some Indonesian kids." He looked down at me. "Planning that was one of the things that kept me going when I was in that goddamn bamboo cage and later in prison."

"A school it shall be. On the whole, I think it will be less harrowing than an artists' colony."

"If you believe that, you don't know boarding

schools. But it will be fun for you to find out." He saw my expression. "Don't worry. I'll be around to protect you. In fact— Well, well. Look who's here!"

I turned. Tail up, her fur glistening and about one hundred percent heavier than when she arrived, Josephine came into the sitting room, her loud voice muttering and chirping. Then she rubbed against my leg and, standing on her hind legs, sharpened her claws on my robe. But for once I didn't mind. "Ye gods. She must have eaten a dozen mice. I hope Emily and Richard are all right."

"They are."

I looked at him suspiciously. "How do you know?"

"Because they're in my inside breast pocket."

"I might have squashed them!"

"Oh, I don't think so. They would have let you know if you had. You'd have heard them." He stooped down. Josephine stood on her hind legs, her front paws on his knee, sniffing suspiciously in the direction of his pocket. Giles felt her belly.

"Congratulations, Josephine." He stood up. "You too, Kit. You're about to be a grandmother or something."

"That's impossible. She's too old."

"You forgot to tell Josephine, to say nothing of your friendly neighborhood tom."

I bent down. Purring so loudly that she rattled, she rubbed her head against my hand. "Well, Empress," I said. "Mazel tov."

"It's like one of those old-fashioned musical comedies," Giles commented. "Everybody ends up happy, pregnant and married."

I stood up. "But not necessarily in that order."

"Order," he said, kissing me. "Isn't everything."

ABOUT THE AUTHOR

ISABELLE HOLLAND, born in Basel, Switzerland, attended the University of Liverpool and Tulane University. She has combined a career in book publishing with writing. Her novels include *Cecily, Amanda's Choice* and *The Man without a Face. Trelawny,* her second in the field of Gothic suspense, follows her recent novel, *Kilgaren.*